YOSHIO DAGGETT

ISBN: 979-8-9866011-2-0

DEDICATION

To Mom, Dad, and Thomas, thanks for being here every step of the way. I could never have done it without you guys, and couldn't ask for a better group of people to be my partners in crime on this journey of mine.

To Emily, Ethan, Heidi, Noah, Rayah, Rylee, Sophie, and many many more, thanks for being such great friends, and putting up with my endless book rants.

To my aunts, uncles, grandparents, cousins, and family friends, thank you for your endless support, it means the world to me.

And of course, to all of my wonderful readers, thanks for enjoying my work, none of this could be possible without you.

To all of you

who love a thrilling adventure,

buckle up. I hope

you enjoy.

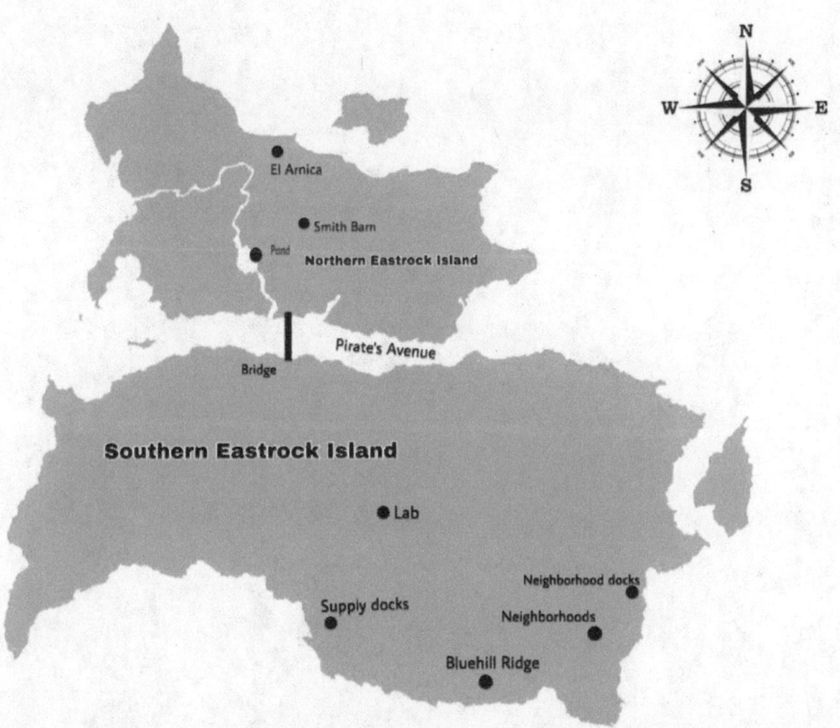

N
W
E
S
El Arnica
Smith Barn
Pond
Northern Eastrock Island
Pirate's Avenue
Bridge
Southern Eastrock Island
Lab
Neighborhood docks
Supply docks
Neighborhoods
Bluehill Ridge

PROLOGUE

I lie on the ground, waiting for death. Well... sort of.

The frigid breeze brushes against my cold body. It softly swipes at my clothes, sliding across my cheekbones. I crack my eyes open just enough so that I can see. At first, I take in nothing but darkness. My eyes take a moment to adjust, but soon I register the soft grass I lay on and the silhouettes of two other bodies beside me.

Of course, I knew they were there. I'd never actually gone to sleep, but by their relaxed breathing floating through the air, it sounds like they finally have.

Silently, I wipe the grogginess from my eyes. Pressing my palms against the damp earth beneath me, I slowly stand. Now, I look down at the two unconscious forms. Elizabeth had been in the middle, and Griffin on the far left.

I've never had any *genuine* friends in my life before, so the strong bond I feel for them now is a sensation I relish. Sure, we only met a couple of days ago, but I've never trusted any two people so strongly.

It's a shame really, because I know deep down that I'm about to lose it all. That my end is inevitable, inescapable. The only thing I can do now is carry out the unthinkable act I plan to do before my days here on earth come to a grim conclusion.

I sniff, wiping at my nose, and wrap the clothes I'd been given tightly around me. In addition to the cold, I've begun to experience waves of nausea running through my body.

"Stay focused" I whisper to myself.

Yes. Yes, I think I can remember my plan. My mind doesn't want to cooperate, two rogue horses attached to a chariot that I've lost the skill to operate.

The phone... The phone, I need the phone to know where I'm going. I stoop down and withdraw it from Elizabeth's sweatshirt pocket. The screen glows a faint light, illuminating my face in the dark. The battery is extremely low now, so I tuck it away into my own pocket.

This is all I need.

I back away from my friends, trying to stomach the fact that I'm guaranteed never to see them again. They'd hate me for this, leaving them in the dead of night, but what choice do I have? The least they can do is allow me this one last act. After all, it is for them.

They'd still stop me.

But they are asleep, a peacefulness across their grimy faces that I haven't seen since I met them. Somehow, it makes me like them even more.

"Goodbye" I whisper, my silent words carried away by the cold wind.

And, one foot in front of the other, I carry my sick and exhausted body away into the thick of the forest. Stars twinkle down at me, the moonlight filtering through the branches above.

I walk, my eyes darting back and forth. I have to be careful. Those... *things* might be stalking me, watching without eyes as I make my way through the woods. I shiver, and it's not just because of the cold.

But I keep walking, stomaching my fear, and continuing on. I come to the road, and follow it for another few minutes, listening to the dead silence that has replaced the hooting owls and chirping crickets.

I'm here. At the place where the road turns to the left, and zigzags its way down the hill that I now stand atop. Far below, illuminated by the moon, I see the town lined against the coast. The power must be out, so the streets and cheerful buildings are shrouded in darkness.

This is where I must go. This is where my final act is to be.

Yet, I have to force my feet forward step by step, because I know what happened there. It's almost as if the horror-stricken screams echo up the mountain, ghosts of what had really gone down in the bloodstained streets of the town.

And then my ears *do* pick up something, and I'm pretty sure I'm not imagining it.

The inhuman shrieks and chattering of strange creatures waft through the icy-cold air, reaching me as I make my way down to the very streets in which they roam.

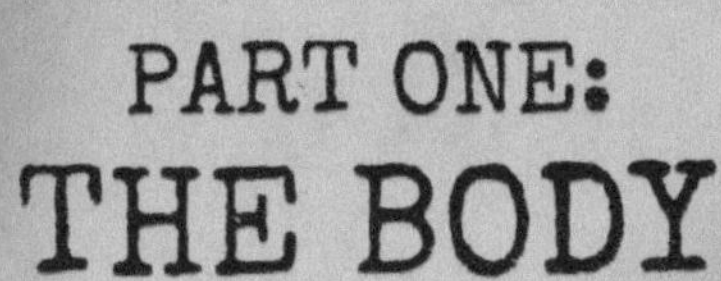

PART ONE:
THE BODY

CHAPTER ONE
TEN DAYS EARLIER

The empty streets and shuttered windows give the town an abandoned feeling.

A cool breeze presses against my face, despite it being summer. It never gets hot here, always staying at a nice crisp or cold temperature. If I didn't know any better, it could almost be winter.

The constant sound of crashing waves floats through the air, all the way to where I am, on Main Street.

The bell in the bell-tower swings slightly on its hinges, the clapper occasionally hitting the side of the metal formation and producing muted ringing, struggling to be heard over the constant breeze and lapping waves against the shore. Here on Eastrock Island, the loud surf and lazy fog is a constant. We're off the coast of Oregon, and the cold Pacific Ocean surrounding us pretty much determines our weather.

It's Sunday, so most people are either relaxing in their warm homes or at church. I myself came out to the town for a nice stroll near the ocean, and this is where I ended up.

The stoplight swings ever so slightly on the wire strung between two buildings. The light keeps turning different colors every now and then, despite the lack of vehicles on the road.

I pass the bakery, the butcher house, the church, which is giving off a warm glow, and even the large supermarket (probably the only big store in Bluehill Ridge, our town), which is still open today.

The stone sidewalk is cracked beneath my shoes, and small weeds struggle to poke through and reach the little sunlight available. Today, however, they might have a little luck. The brilliant sun is poking through the clouds and mist, lighting the town up as it does so rarely.

I can see the ocean ahead sparkling in the dazzling sunlight. Everything seems to take on a vibrant shade.

The unexpected appearance of the sun adds a little cheerfulness into my step as I make my way to the crashing shore. The warmth feels good against my cheeks as I reach the small dirt path veering off from the sidewalk.

The dust rises from behind my footsteps, but settles back down quick enough as to not become a problem. I pass the thick foliage lining the coasts of Eastrock Island, and finally emerge onto the cold sandy beach. I can hear seagulls calling out to one another over the waves.

I sit down on a damp rock near the shore and slip off my backpack. Unzipping the top, I peer into its depths, which still holds a few stray pencils from the school year that just ended.

Reaching my arm in, I grasp a small, smooth, rounded container and pull it out. I flip the top open and pull out wireless earbuds, which I proceed to connect to my smartphone.

When I have the earbuds popped in and music going, I begin jogging down the sand, my bare feet digging into the moist, soft earth.

The sun comes and goes over the next few hours as I run, but it's brighter in general today. I wonder what the rest of my friends are doing.

I don't actually have any *"genuine friends"* here in Bluehill Ridge, but there's a group of other kids at my high school that let me hang with them sometimes, so they're the closest to it.

Despite my attempts at being likable, funny, and whatever other 'appealing' trait a person could have, I can't seem to find anybody who likes me for... well, me. I'm somewhat good at science though, particularly Biology, so they keep me around for homework help and such. It's pretty much the only reason I'm allowed to *'sit with them at lunch'* or *'be a part of their study group'*. Oh, what a person will do for social acceptance. I don't even know why I hang around them anyways.

But it's finally summer, and though I may not have anybody to hang out with except my little sister, I don't have to worry about all the social pressure as much anymore.

The freshness in the air sweeps across my face as I take a rest on another rock maybe ten feet above the shoreline.

Panting, I reach into my backpack and fish a water bottle out. I guzzle the rest of the liquid down in one swig, before leaning back against the rock, which is still warm from sitting in the sunlight all day. The sun is sinking lower over the ocean and the clouds and mist have closed against the sky once again, blanketing the town in fog.

● ● ●

The door is locked, so I fumble around in my pocket for the house key I always keep on me. The door swings open freely once I've unlocked it, and I step in, closing it behind me.

I slip my shoes off and wander the house, looking for things to do. For a second, I wonder where my younger sister Calla is, but I then remember she went over to one of her friends' houses for the day.

Since my mother is at work, and my father is off the island this week I am the only one at home. I exhale an exhausted sigh and collapse onto the small cozy sofa in the living room. Grabbing the remote, I turn the television on and prop my feet up on the footrest.

After a long evening of binging TV, I look out the window to see it's pitch-black outside. Calla gets back around nine. When I hear the knock on the door, I leap up and switch the television off.

I run to the entrance and unlock it, allowing Calla to enter the house. When I swing the door open, she walks in tracking wet mud all over the bright red rug draped over the floor.

"Calla!" I exclaim, "You're getting everything muddy!"

She slouches, flinging her pink glitter backpack off her shoulder, adding a layer of sparkly powder to the muddy rug.

Finally, she slips her filthy shoes off and into the designated area. She holds her backpack out to me without a word, and, after a roll of my eyes, I take it from her and hang it on a hook beside the chipped mirror we have in the mudroom.

"Calla," I say in my best scolding voice. "You tracked in mud everywhere!"

She responds with her usual eye roll. "Maddie and I were playing in puddles!"

"What puddles?" I ask, because it hasn't rained recently, and it's not scheduled to for another couple of days.

"We had a kiddie pool in Maddie's backyard!" Calla informs me, wiping her hands on her skirt. "When we dumped it out, it made a huge puddle!"

I sigh, ordering her to a shower. She grumbles a bit, but reluctantly walks down the hall and into the bathroom, tracking mud down all the wooden floor behind her. I shake my head, already starting to walk towards the kitchen to get the cleaning supplies.

● ● ●

The next morning, I wake to find the house smelling of fresh flipped pancakes and eggs. I rise out of bed and change into my clothes for the day; a pair of blue jeans and white t-shirt with my school's logo printed across the front. ***BLUEHILL RIDGE HIGH*** it reads in big letters.

"Hey Mom!" I say, walking down the staircase and into the kitchen, "Smells really good!

"Yup! Breakfast; want some?" She asks, sliding two heaping bowls of steaming food onto the kitchen counter.

"Yes please!" I say, sliding the stool out and sitting down. I rub my eyes trying to get rid of the tiredness, despite it being almost noon. "Where's Calla?"

"She went over to Maddie's house." My mother says as she opens the refrigerator and retrieves the ketchup sitting on the door.

"Oh," I say, serving myself a heaping plate of food. "So, what're you doing today?"

"It's Monday," My mother says, smiling. "Work. Yay."

I smile.

"Just you wait, when you're older you won't think it's funny."

"I don't think it's funny." I say, taking a forkful of eggs and sighing in satisfaction. "And-" I attempt to chew my food, "If you're going to work, why are you still here? It's almost noon!"

"Some big group is renting the restaurant for a party today. Don't have to be there 'till twelve."

"Oh," I say, attacking my pancakes, "I didn't know you could do that."

"You can at the diner. It's right on the beach, so it's a fun party. Food and the beach right in the same spot, you know?"

My mother owns a small diner right on the coast of the island, and it's been a family business for a while. I go in to help out every now and then, but I'm mostly free for the summer. My father normally partners with my mom in owning the place, but he had to go to the mainland for a meeting that has something to do with his second job as a consultant.

"Cool." I say, and continue working on my food.

My mom laughs. "I might need your help this Thursday, there's going to be a graduation party there for a college class."

"Sure, what time?"

"Seven or so."

"Yeah, I can help."

"Great!" My mother says, picking up her plate and putting it into the sink. She walks to the front door and slips her shoes on over her socks. "See you at eight, okay?"

"Okay! Bye!" I reply, turning back to my food.

She ruffles my hair and grabs her purse before walking out the front door and closing it behind her. I sigh and scrape the last bits of food off my plate.

• • •

The day is more of the same misty skies and cold wisps of air that skirt across the town. Everything on Main Street seems too quiet, which is funny because it's normally only loud during the tourist season, which is coming up in a few weeks.

The shop windows are dark, and there are signs that read "CLOSED" pressed against the glass, which catches my attention because it's Monday and the stores are supposed to be open.

I'm about to knock on one of the storefront doors, when a loud, irritated voice catches me off guard. It's a woman's.

"Yes Dave, give me a minute, I'm about to get in the car right now. Tell the rest of the shopkeepers I'm on my way."

I hear the clicking of shoes on concrete, but still can't see the speaker.

"No, of course I'm not telling anyone," The woman argues loudly. I now realize she must be talking to someone on the phone. "something like this can't reach the rest of the town, God knows what kind of problems that would cause."

The loud start of a car catches me off guard. I turn around to see a small silver Nissan pulling out from behind one of the stores and turning onto the desolate road.

Once in position, the car darts out to my right and races down the asphalt.

For a moment, I stand there and watch the car grow farther and farther away. It's going fast, faster than anybody here on the island normally drives. What's going on?

I'm silent as I think, running the words the woman had said through my brain. "Something like this can't reach the rest of the town." She had told whoever *Dave* is. I can't help but be curious, interesting things never happen in this town and when they do I want to be in the know.

A thought begins creeping into the back of my mind. Why not? After all, it sounds like this has to do with everyone in town. Why shouldn't I want to know? It's not like I have anything better to do for the rest of the day. A little investigating won't hurt, right?

Making my decision, I begin jogging down the road, following in the silver car's path. There's really only one place down this road, one place the car is likely going.

I run for maybe five or so minutes, before reaching the destination. Panting, I finally round one last turn and realize I've arrived at the docks. Where I'd expected to be. Sure enough, the silver car is parked in the parking lot. The large wooden structure juts out into the open ocean, waiting for the boats to drift in. This is where the whole island gets it's supplies. Food, wood, tools, you name it.

What seems like half the island's cars are stopped in the large parking lot of the docks. It's weird to see that many cars in one place when it's not tourist season. How many people are here and why?

I have a sneaking suspicion this isn't exactly for me to witness because it has a surreptitious feel to it, but I quickly dart out to the other side of the road, the one facing the ocean. It's a little bit of a climb, but I quickly scramble down onto the sandy beach. The wet sand squishes beneath my shoes, and I'm guessing the tide is about to come in.

I see a large group of people, only adults, standing at the base of the raised docks. Quietly, I scamper over to and under the long wooden platform, the sand muting my footfalls. It isn't until I'm right beneath their feet that I stop and tap into their conversation, listening intently.

I don't know why I'm doing it. Yes, I'm curious, but I'm normally not this nosy. Why am I so intrigued by this turn in events? Is it the sense of secrecy? Or maybe it's just that nothing ever happens on the island, and I want to know what it is when something does, which *definitely* makes me nosy. Am I? I hope not.

"-So then what?" A man above me says, and I can see he's wearing black tennis shoes with white grips on the bottoms. "We just sit here and live off of... what?"

"All I'm saying." A woman to the left says condescendingly, and by her voice I can guess she's older. Maybe Tammie the butcher? "People don't just shut up and do what they're told in situations like this. There will always be those that just don't cooperate."

"Hey, listen, we don't know for sure-" A man's squeaky voice protests, but another man cuts him off in a deep, gravelly voice.

"Then try to explain why all seven shipment boats that were scheduled to arrive this morning haven't shown up."

What? The shipment boats haven't arrived? This island relies completely on those shipments. Without them, what would happen? Maybe they were late? Or maybe something went wrong back on the mainland?

"So many reasons!" The first man says loudly, obviously flabbergasted.

"All I'm saying is that we don't know what's happening, that's all." The old woman says, her voice strict and firm.

"Yes, yes, I know." The man who had protested says, "It's just that, there are so many other logical reasons for why they haven't arrived. What if the dock back on mainland is disabled somehow?"

"All seven boats are coming from different locations." The man with the gravelly voice huffs.

"Maybe they encountered some sort of storm, or something." The man protesting says. I can tell that he is obviously trying to avoid whatever fate the others are predicting will happen.

"Then they would go around to the other side of the island, they know how important those supplies are to us. Plus, we are so close to the coast, we'd see the storm if it was big enough to delay the shipments."

"We're far enough to not be able to see the mainland." The man says, and I'm guessing he points to the ocean for a second, because everyone is silent.

"That's because of the mist, Rob." The old woman says finally. "At any rate, this talking isn't changing the fact that the shipments haven't gotten here."

"So, what are we going to do? Tell the mayor?"

"We'll tell the mayor, but keep it from the public for now. The boats will probably get here tomorrow."

"Okay."

"So, everyone here agrees to keep the news from everyone in town?"

There are grunts of agreement and presumably nods.

"Okay then, let's get off of these bloody docks before I pitch myself into the ocean, shall we?"

The men and women walk off of the dock, making the wood creak with every step. I wait under the pier until I am certain every car has driven away and I'm alone. I clamber up the rocks lining the end of the beach, and reach the top.

The parking lot is empty, and I step onto the sidewalk that stretches to the wooden dock where the people I'd been eavesdropping on were just standing.

I make my way there, and when I arrive, I gaze out into the open expanse of blue ocean. There is no hint of the mainland or the boats, and for once, I am sure it's not the fog blocking my view.

If those people are right, if those boats really aren't coming, if we're really on our own...

Well, it won't be pretty.

What did I just witness?

Is it true? Are we really alone now? Cut off from the rest of the world? The mere thought unsettles me.

But, of course, I'm overreacting. The man is probably right, and the boats were just delayed for some unknown reason. Maybe they'll pull into the docks tomorrow morning with all the supplies we need. Plus, even if they don't,` we have boats of our own, and we have our own supplies here on the island, however little it may be. We could probably last a few weeks on our own anyway.

In the end, I come to the conclusion that there's nothing to worry about. Still, I plan on bringing it up to my mother this evening at dinner.

Until then, though, I'm on my own with nothing but my thoughts to keep me company. I turn the problem over and over in my head as I walk back to Main Street. When I finally arrive there, I find the shops are once again open and awaiting customers. The people at the docks must have been the shop owners awaiting their much-needed supplies.

Curious, I step into Tammie the Butcher's shop, because I had recognized her voice at the docks.

"Hello, darling." Tammie says, smiling down at me in her own special stern way. "What brings you here today?"

"Just looking." I say with a smile and step towards the counter. I decide to attempt squeezing some information out of her if I can. "So, what kind of meat do you have?"

I have been in the butcher's shop before, and Tammie knows that. She gives me an odd look.

"Just the usual. Pigs, Chickens and such."

"Where do they come from? Do we raise them or do they come from the mainland?"

"We get them from the mainland, but every now and then we slaughter them here on our own" She says informatively, "They always seem to taste fresher that way of course, but it's much more time consuming."

"How do they transport the animals?" I ask a little too obviously, "By boat or..."

Tammie thinks over my question for a second, then seems to put two and two together. She gives me a harsh look.

"Out boy, out! Keep your head down and mind your own business!"

"This is my business! It's all of our-"

"Talking back, now, are we? Out, and let the grownups take care of things!" She says and ushers me out of the door. There's a jangle of a bell as the door swings shut tightly behind me. Well, I hadn't exactly been discreet.

All the other shops are now open once again, as if nothing had ever happened, and maybe nothing has. All I can do is wait for tomorrow and see for myself, but until then, I can spend the rest of my day at the beach, as I always do.

I turn down the street and make my way to the narrow dusty path veering from the road that weaves down to the sandy beach.

• • •

That night, I lie in my bed staring at the blank ceiling. We'd had dinner in dining room rather than the kitchen counter, and Calla was sitting right across from me, so I couldn't bring up the absence of the supply ships. Once dinner was over, I couldn't bring myself to say it for some reason.

I'll make it a point to visit the docks tomorrow afternoon, just to be sure the supply boats have arrived. First though, I must go to the diner my parents own to work for the morning, as I'd promised my mom I would. With curiosity burning bright in my chest, it's hard to fall asleep. Eventually though, I manage, and I am plunged into the sea of dreams and void.

When I awake the next morning, it is not the sunlight streaming through my bedroom window, nor the birds singing in the trees that rouses me. My mother stands in the doorway, knocking loudly on the wood.

"Finally," She sighs and gestures for me to get out of bed. "Luke, we need to go now."

I groan. "What time is it?"

"Six thirty." She says, walking out the door, "We need to be there by seven. Get dressed and come down to eat."

I unwillingly comply, dragging myself out of bed and sluggishly get dressed in a clean pair of jeans and a random t-shirt I find in my dresser, before making my way down the stairs and into the kitchen. My mom takes one look at my outfit and knits her eyebrows.

"Change your shirt, your pants would be fine but you need to get a pair without any holes."

I look down to examine my outfit. Jeans with several rips in the knees, and a black t-shirt with the Nike logo printed onto the fabric.

"But mom, everyone has ripped jeans." I protest, but I really don't care. I just don't want to go back up to my room to change. Call me lazy, but climbing a bunch of stairs when I can barely stay awake isn't exactly what I want to do.

"Well, wear them another time. Not at work."

"Mom, it's not my work."

"You're sixteen, you should have a good summer job." My mom says with a sniff.

"I do have a job, mom."

"Then why aren't you there?" She asks, fully aware of why I'm home instead.

"Because," I say, and look down. "I took this week off."

"And why did you do that?"

"To enjoy my summer." My socks are suddenly very intriguing.

My mother gives me a loving but firm look. "No one will want to hire you if you're unreliable." She says in a stern voice.

"I know mom."

She ruffles my hair and sighs "C'mon then Luke, we're leaving now. Go change."

I do so, slipping into a polo shirt and pulling on intact jeans before sprinting down the stairs and jumping into the car. Calla is sitting in the back, propped up by her booster seat.

"I don't need this anymore!" She protests.

Our mother adjusts the mirror and smiles at Calla in the reflection. "Just a little while longer and you won't have to use it."

"I don't wanna!"

My mother flips the key to the car and the engine roars to life. The car is a small sad thing, a little rusted by the salt in the air, but it works and you really don't need cars to get very far here on Eastrock Island.

We pull out of the driveway and onto the cracked pavement that leads down to Main Street, driving through and out of the small little neighborhood, toward the coast.

When we finally get close, and I can see the blue expanse of the ocean, my mother slows down into the town. As we arrive, I see the other shop owners flipping their store signs to read closed, and driving away towards the docks. This makes me want to just jump out of the car and check if the supply ships have gotten here, but I have to help my mother first.

"Are you supposed to get your supplies today?" I ask my mother tentatively. She shakes her head and tells me that she already had the shipment she needed the week before.

The car engine flips off as we pull into the parking lot. I open the door and my mom tosses me the store keys as she walks back to open the door for Calla.

I hop up onto the concrete sidewalk and slip the key into the keyhole of the small restaurant; "Bluehill Diner"

The door unlocks and slides open with the jingle of a bell. The restaurant is dark, so I grasp around until I find the light switch. When I flip it on, the restaurant floods with blinding incandescence.

I squint for a second, momentarily stunned by the sudden brightness. Soon though, my eyes adjust and I quickly pull all of the chairs off of the tables and scoot them into their proper places.

My mother walks in, Calla holding her hand.

"Calla, you can go into the back and play on my phone, okay?" My mother tells her, handing over the smartphone. Calla snatches it away and gives me a smirk before going behind the counter and disappearing into the depths of the kitchen.

I roll my eyes and finish sliding the last chair beneath the table. My mother walks over to the counter and powers the computer on. She types the password in, unlocking the device.

I make my way to the kitchen and step behind the counter.

"The rest of the workers should be here in a few minutes, so be ready." My mother says, pointing at the kitchen.

"What am I doing today?"

"You can take the orders and clear the tables." My mother says, and I respond with a sigh because that's what I always do.

I spend the remainder of my morning taking orders and clearing messy tables after the customers. I'd like to work in the kitchens, but my mother would never allow me.

"You're more helpful doing what you do." She would always say.

When I finally finish, my mother says I can get going, but if I want, I can stay and help more. I tell her I need to do something and ask if I can borrow her car.

"Sorry," I apologize, and I really mean it, but checking the docks is much more important. "Can I borrow the car? I promise I'll bring it back by the time the diner closes!"

She agrees, thankfully foregoing the whole discussion of "getting a license instead of sticking with your permit" because it isn't exactly legal for me to drive alone. The island here is so small though, that they don't have a big DMV and I don't want to have to go all the way back to the mainland. She strongly disapproves of my breaking the rules, but the sheriff doesn't really care. Everything is so close together here it doesn't really matter. My mother nods, and then says something I hadn't expected.

"Take Calla with you, you can go to the beach or something."

"But mom," I say, glancing at the kitchen.

"Take her, please."

I sigh. "Fine. Calla! C'mon!"

Calla stoops out of the kitchen, our mother's phone in hand. I can see the grimy fingerprints all over the screen. She must have been eating chips or something, because how else could her hands have gotten so oily.

"Calla, you're going with Luke, okay?" Our mother tells her.

"Do I have to?"

"Yes Calla, he'll take you to the beach."

I nod in agreement, secretly knowing I'll make a stop at the docks first.

"Okay, hop in the car. Luke, here's the keys." My mother hands me the car keys, which jangle back and forth as they hang there.

I take them and thank her, heading for the restaurant exit. When I walk outside, I see the usual fog that blankets the town has thickened, covering the blue sky completely. I shiver as I unlock the car and slide into the driver's seat.

I twist the ignition and the car roars to life.

"Are you all buckled in?" I ask Calla. I twist around and see her strapping herself into the booster seat. She has the same brown with a hint of blonde hair I have, though it lacks the strong waviness mine shows. Her blue eyes match our father's exactly, just as mine do. Our mother's eye color must have been lost in some genetic soup, because neither Calla nor my eyes exhibit any trace of brown. We both have pale skin, though my skin is a bit darkened from all the days at the beach, despite the fog.

"Are we going to the beach?" Calla asks as her buckle clicks.

"Yes, I just need to check something first." I say, turning out of Main Street and the road that leads to the docks.

"Did mom say?"

"No, but I just need to check something. It'll only take a minute." I tell her. The road ahead of me is cracked so I slow down while driving over the damaged asphalt.

"I wanna go to the beach" Calla pouts, pulling her sassy face on, which she is well known for back at home.

"I know, and to the beach we will go." I say, making a right around a ridge overlooking the ocean. I drive past a small blue car racing down the street, presumably coming from the docks. I recognize the car to be Tammie the butcher's, because I saw it pull out this morning. What kind of news does she hold?

She's been at the docks all morning, maybe unloading the new supplies brought by the ships, or maybe waiting for the arrival of boats that never came.

Another right and two lefts, and we're finally there. Calla has been quiet for a while now, and I'm wondering how she managed it until I glance back to see she's got my phone clutched between her tiny fingers.

"Calla!" I exclaim, "How'd you get that?"

"I just got it." She says.

"From where?" I ask, engaging the parking brake and flipping the car key to the left, shutting down the engine. The constant noise of the car is replaced by silence.

"Your pocket." She says, pointing to my jeans pocket. "It was hanging out and I grabbed it."

I sigh and rub my forehead. "Okay Calla, you stay in here, okay?"

"But I wanna-"

"Calla, no, I'll be back in a sec, okay?"

She shoots me a glare, but argues no more. I unbuckle and open the car door, stepping into the empty parking lot of the docks. I adjust my shirt and walk over to the main entrance area. There is a chain strung between two posts, preventing me from entering the main boardwalk. A sign saying that this is a supplies dock only hangs from the shiny chain, warning that trespassers will be fined.

I lift the chain and step onto the wooden pier, looking down through the cracks to see the spot I stood in yesterday as I eavesdropped on the worried group.

"Luke you're going to be in big trouble." A small voice says behind me.

I whirl around to see Calla standing on the other side of the chain separating the two of us.

"Calla what are you-" I stutter. I glance over to our car to see the back passenger side door wide open. "Calla, what are you doing here?"

"I'm-gonna-tell-mom." She says in a sing-song voice. I quickly shake my head.

"Calla, get back in the car. I'll be there in a second."

Calla stretches her tiny leg forward and takes a step towards me. She lifts the sign hanging from the chain, turns it so that it faces me, and points at it lifting her eyebrows.

"The sign says don't go there." Calla says, giving me a 'duh' face.

"Calla, you don't even know how to read." I say knowing it's not true.

"Yes I do!" She protests. "You're going to be in big trouble."

"Calla-"

"I'm-gonna-tell! I'm-gonna-tell..." She taunts, using her sing-song tone once again.

"What if I let you come?" I say, panicking. She pauses and seems to think it over for a second, weighing if she'd rather get me in trouble, or investigate what I'm trying to accomplish by trespassing here.

"Fine." She finally says, stepping under the chain rope, a certain look of satisfaction on her face.

"Okay." I say, letting out the breath I was holding. "Follow me, this should only take a minute."

Calla follows me down the dock and to the end of the pier. From here, I can see far out into the ocean, though the fog interferes a bit. I see absolutely no boats on the misty horizon.

I look around, my heart thumping, trying to find any shred of evidence that the supplies had arrived. No boxes, crates, or trucks anywhere in sight. I even check the ropes, trying to see if there is any evidence of them being used recently. They are dry and have no details to suggest they'd been in use.

I make a sound that is a mix of a sigh and a grunt of frustration.

"So?" Calla says, widening her eyes at me sarcastically. "Why are we here?"

"Nothing Calla, just wanted to see the ocean." I grunt, examining the wood of the pier. That's when I hear it.

A low, extremely quiet, screeching sound, slowly escalating to a higher pitch. Like vocal cords being shredded. Almost like the sound of metal on metal, but very quiet.

I fall silent, staying still as possible. What is that? I can barely hear it...

I am interrupted by the loud sound of Calla screeching her head off. I whirl around and see her on the ground, screaming.

"What!" I get up and rush over to her. "What's wrong?"

"I-" She stops for a round of racking sobs. "I slipped!"

"On what?"

"The w-wood." She says, tears streaming down her little face. I see the loose board behind her she must have tripped on.

"Aww, it's okay Calla." I say as soothingly as I can. "Where does it hurt?"

"My- my knee and- and elbow!" She snuffles and rubs the snot from under her nose onto her hand.

"It's okay Calla, it's okay. Let's get you back home, does that sound good?"

She nods and wipes her snot covered hands on her sparkly pants.

I help her up and guide her down the dock, under the chain, and out to the car across the parking lot. She's still sobbing so loud it hurts my ears. I open the car door and hoist her into her booster seat. She sits there crying, her eyes squeezed tightly shut.

I buckle her up and get a good look at the injury causing all the crying. A small but heavily bleeding gash is on her knee, and I wince at the deep scarlet seeping from the cut. I examine her elbow, which is still bleeding a bit but isn't nearly as bad as the knee.

Calla opens her eyes for a second, sniffing, and takes in the blood on her knee. This, unfortunately, brings on a new round of hysterical sobs.

"It's okay Calla, it's okay." I whisper gently and close the door. I open the driver's seat door and slip into it, pulling the car key from my pocket. Once I have the engine going, I quickly pull out of the parking lot and out onto the main road.

Calla's screeches seem to be amplified in the car, it being such a small space, and my ears are bombarded with all the loud noise. I drive quickly and end up at our house in less than five minutes, the town being so small.

I quickly help Calla out of the car and into the kitchen of our house. She still wails, but her sobs are not as ear-piercing.

"Calla, Calla, It's okay. I'm going to get you a band-aid, sound good?" I console her, hurrying over to the cupboard that holds the small cardboard box of bandages. I pull it out and choose a particularly large band-aid from the depths of the box.

I peel the casing off and show Calla. "This is for your elbow, okay?"

She nods and wipes her tears away. I am about to put the band-aid on when I remember I need to wash the cut first, so it doesn't get infected.

"Wait one second." I say, and have her hold the band-aid. I rush over to the sink and wet a paper towel. I squeeze most of the water out so it is just damp, before bringing it over to Calla.

"I'm going to do your elbow first, okay?" I warn, pointing at the cut on her arm. She nods, and I press the damp paper towel to her cut. Calla squeals, but at least she doesn't shriek.

"Good job Calla, almost done." I reassure her, washing the blood away. Once I have the cut all cleaned up and bandaged, I look down at her leg again. I now see that I should have done her leg first, because a long stream of blood seeps down her calf, ending in a growing droplet of red.

I decide just a paper towel and water aren't going to do for the leg, it's too deep. I stand up and promise Calla I'll be right back. In the bathroom, I open the cupboard with the first aid supplies and shuffle it all around in my search. Finally, I find a small spray contraption labeled "Neosporin". I remember my mother using this very spray on my cuts as well.

As I walk back to the kitchen, something catches my eye through my bedroom door. Suddenly, I have an idea of how to cheer up Calla. My microscope sits on the dresser, slightly covered in dust because I haven't used it in forever. I remember Calla's interest in all the science experiments I would come home and tell her about once school was out for the day. The way her eyes would shine with curiosity even as I describe the most gruesome dissections. She's a character, I'll give her that.

I quickly slip into my room (a plain area with a bed, dresser, and closet) and pluck a particularly minuscule crystal vial from the small collection I have.

I walk back into the kitchen, Neosporin spray and tiny glass tube clutched tightly in my fist.

"Okay Calla," I say, kneeling in front of her. "I'm going to wipe away some of the blood and spray on some special stuff, okay?"

She nods, sniffing.

"It'll sting a little but I think you're brave enough, okay?"

Once again, she nods and there's a glint of determination in her eyes.

I dampen a paper towel and bring it back over to Calla. Before I clean the wound, I take the little vial and allow the stream of blood running down her leg to slowly fill the tube, giving it a moment so the dark red liquid reaches the very top.

"What's that for?" Calla asks me, cocking her head.

"You'll see…" I say mysteriously and the corners of my twitch up a bit.

I screw the top of the vial shut to prevent the blood from drying up, then wipe the rest of the blood away from Calla's leg. I spray the Neosporin onto her knee, and she winces but doesn't protest, possibly too intrigued with what I might use the vial of her blood for.

Three minutes later Calla is all patched up and no longer crying. She sniffles as I give her a high five for being so brave.

"What is that glass thing for?" She says and points at the small crystal tube of her blood.

"C'mon, I'll show you." I say and help her to her feet. Leading her to the counter, I have her sit down on one of the stools. I run over to my room and haul back my microscope. Calla's eyes light up when I pull the cover off the thing.

"I can use it!?" She says excitedly.

"Yup, and guess what…" I ask with a mysterious smile.

"What?" She says, stretching her neck to see what I'm hiding behind my back. Admittedly, this is a rare occasion. We almost never get along, but that's just how siblings are I guess.

I pull out the small crystal vial filled with dark red liquid. "We get to look at *your own* blood!"

Most seven year olds would probably have been grossed out or repulsed, but Calla gets so excited she squeals in delight. I retrieve a thin glass slide and place a small droplet of blood onto the smooth surface. I then place a tiny square of glass on top of the slide and the blood, flattening out the droplet. I set aside the small vial with the rest of the blood in it, the cap screwed on tight.

Putting it under the microscope and flipping the light on, I focus the lenses and gesture for Calla to place her eye to the eyepiece. She does and gasps.

"Woah!" She exclaims and laughs. "They're like little red polka dots!"

We spend the rest of the afternoon examining things around the house under the microscope. Planter water. House plant leaves. Toys. I don't even know our mother is home until she is standing in the doorway of the kitchen.

"Hey guys," she says, walking in with a smile across her face. "What's going on here?"

"Mommy! Mommy!" Calla calls, swiping through the pile of random objects we'd been looking at under the microscope. She pulls out a dead leaf we'd found behind the house outside. "Look, look!"

She hands me the leaf expectantly and I slip it under the microscope eye. Calla waves our mother over and gestures for her to press her eye to the eyepiece. She does and gasps dramatically.

"Wow, Calla! This is so cool!" Our mother exclaims and looks up. "Luke, is this your microscope?"

"Yeah, Jamie got it for me last Christmas." I shrug. My mother raises her eyebrows because she knows Jamie has had a crush on me for years now. I shake my head and look away grinning slightly. My mother knows full well that I have no feelings for her other than being her friend, and even that feels artificial at times.

"Cool." My mother says, then looks at Calla. Her eye catches the band-aid on her knee.

"Hey what happened here?" She asks and looks up at me.

A sigh escapes my lips. I open my mouth, about to spout out the entire truth, when Calla speaks instead.

"I fell on the rocks at the beach." Calla tells her, holding her knee and elbow up painfully. "Luke brought me back here and put my band-aids on."

My mother looks at me. "Really?"

I hesitate, not exactly keen on lying, but I say; "Yeah, I showed her her own blood under the microscope! Figured it might cheer her up."

"Really?" My mother asks Calla, "And you liked that?"

"Yeah!" She says enthusiastically.

"Well, good job getting her all patched up." My mother says, grinning. I feel bad about lying to her but smile.

"Thanks."

And the day moves on like any other. But it's not.

A tight bubble of dread slowly grows in the pit of my stomach. Something... foreboding is happening here on Eastrock Island, and I want to figure out what.

● ● ●

What does it mean?

I lie in bed thinking about what we're going to do now that supplies haven't come for the second night in a row. There's always the possibility they're still coming and have been badly delayed, but what are the odds of all seven boats being stopped from reaching our small town of Bluehill Ridge? All of them are coming from different places, so something closer to us must be delaying or flat out preventing them from reaching us. But what? What could be so major it's stopping the supplies that keeps us alive? We rely entirely on those shipments and they know that.

I know we can use our own boats to get off the island but then what? Demand our supplies be brought to the town? Or will whatever is blocking the supply ships prevent us from getting across the ocean too?

And what about the rest of us? The ones who *don't* own boats. I know plenty of people on the island who don't have access to watercraft, including my entire family. And, my father is out on the mainland. If no boats are able to get here-

We'll find him

At least, that's what I tell myself.

I clench my comforter in my fist and squeeze as hard as my knuckles will allow, making them turn white and leaving little red marks that fade away after a minute or so. The entire thing is frustrating. The mystery. The lack of an answer. The silence.

I sit straight up in my bed. Why is everyone keeping this silent? Every single soul on this secluded island has the right to know. Whether the supplies arrive or not directly affects everyone. Everyone, even the few rich people who live on the upper side of the island, will be hit by the lack of supplies and hit hard.

Food. Fresh water. Even electricity. All of these things and more will be gone in a month, probably less if everyone keeps silent.

The fact that people are keeping it quiet from the rest of the island is infuriating.

But then again, aren't I one of those people? I know all about it and haven't told a soul. I haven't even told my own mother.

Ugh, the whole thing is making me tie myself in a knot. See, that's what I do. I overthink things until my head is about

to explode, see all the things that could possibly go wrong, and then stress over all of them like they're guaranteed to happen. It's exhausting.

I resolve to make telling mom a priority. I plan to tell her tomorrow at breakfast, but I never get the chance.

● ● ●

The next morning, I rise and stretch my limbs as far out as my body will allow. It feels great. I quickly change into my clothes and rush down to the kitchen. I look around for my mom, thinking she may be in the kitchen, but the minute I step into the living room she practically pounces on me.

"Luke, go pack your clothes and everything you want to bring. One bag only, so stuff it all in."

"Wha- What?" I stumble on my words, "Why?"

"Calla is already packing; I was just about to go wake you up. Go back upstairs and pack, now." she says.

"Mom, what's going on?"

She hesitates a moment before hurriedly spouting it all out. "We didn't get our supplies a couple of days ago, the entire town didn't, everyone's taking boats back to the mainland today to see what's going on. They said take your stuff just in case we need to stay in hotels while we're there-"

So they finally made it public.

"Mom! Mom!" I say, trying to get her attention. "Why are all of us going at the same time? Shouldn't they send one person first? I mean, why is all of it so sudden?"

"They did honey," she says, and she looks like if we don't get out of the house in the next ten minutes we'll explode. "The phones to the mainland are dead, all of the internet for that matter, so they sent the sheriff last night. Things- things are happening. They said that if he didn't come back by morning it meant to start sending everyone over."

"Everyone?"

"Well," My mom says, twiddling her fingers. "not everyone. We need to go to make sure your father is okay."

"Why wouldn't he be-"

"I don't know, okay honey? Go pack please. Now." She says and shoos me up the stairs. I quickly pack my clothes, laptop, and a couple of books for the boat ride. They're finally acting on what's happening, but it's all a bit sudden. What did they do, go door to door last night telling everyone? I would have at least held a meeting about it, and I definitely would not have sent the sheriff, our only law enforcement, at least in *our* town.

We're out of the house in five minutes, Calla in her booster seat, me in the passenger seat, and my mom frantically driving to the resident docks. The resident docks are for the residents of the neighborhood, but is actually a good distance away. Nevertheless, we're speeding so we're there in less than ten minutes. When we arrive, we pull into the packed parking lot. There's a line forming on the docks, and we get there in time to not be too far in the back.

People are being directed into boats by a man wearing a bright green jacket. One by one, the boats drift out into the water. They float away slowly, but don't take off. They must be waiting for everyone to board before leaving.

"Mom, why is it all so urgent?" I ask. Calla is grasping her hand as we walk through the line.

"It's not, it's not-" She begins but I stop her.

"Mom, really, what's going on?" I persist. She looks at me for a second, then drops her voice to an urgent whisper once again.

"I don't know anything for sure, but people are saying the government is stopping transportation between the island and-"

"Why?" I interject.

"I don't know I don't know, we think the boats left the dock but were stopped. Not by a storm. Not by a mechanical problem." She continues in a hushed voice.

"What? *Our* government? As in Oregon state, or... what, Federal?"

"Yes, we don't know why but people are saying they interfered with the shipments."

What is this theory based off of? Solid evidence or panicked guessing. Given the state everyone looks to be in here at the docks, I'd guess the latter.

"When were you told the shipments didn't get here?" I push curiously.

"Late last night. All of this was last minute but they're taking anyone who wants to get off the island to the mainland." She says, glancing around. We're almost to the front of the line. "That's not all. They're saying people are going missing. Dissapearing."

She sees the look on my face.

"No, Luke, please don't freak out. Listen, it's all rumors, but things here... things aren't right, that's why we're leaving. Okay?"

"And they sent the sheriff last night?"

"Around one in the morning, I'm told." She mutters, looking up from Calla and at the man in green. "I think it's our turn."

My insides turn the wrong way. Is that the reason for the whole rush? Is it true, the disappearances? And *why on earth* would they send the sheriff? It's all wrong, seriously wrong. No shipments. No internet. No outside world. Now people are going missing?

"Next!" The man in the neon green vest tells us. My mother, Calla, and I all step up to the next boat available. Already, there is a family of three; A mother, father, and young son around Calla's age. We clamber into the boat and take our seats on the fancy upholstery. A man sits in the driver's seat, and he pulls out of the docks once the boat is untied.

We drift away from the docks slowly, and I watch the next group of people board the slightly larger motorboat behind us. We drift out into the group of boats waiting to depart from the island. We are actually leaving Eastrock, something I haven't done for far too long. I can't believe it. It's ironic how only these circumstances are pushing us out of our shell.

It's when the next boat departs from the docks that I see it. A large white object is washed up on the rocky shore a few hundred feet away from the docks. It's hidden by a slight corner, so you wouldn't be able to see it from the docks. In fact, the angle we're looking at it right now is the only way to see it, unless of course you were standing right above it.

"Hey," I say as we drift further away from shore, "What's that?"

At first, the driver ignores me, but when he hears the sounds of confusion and interest coming from the rest of the people on the boat, he turns his head around.

"Huh," He says gruffly, "Didn't see that yesterday."

I can see the object bobbing slightly in the water.

"Can we get a closer look?" I say, not sure what kind of answer to expect. What would the man say? Sure? Flat out no? Or would he give it some thought?

"Got nothing better to do, do we?" He grunts and starts up his engine. The boat roars to life and moves quickly towards the white object on the rocky shore. As we get closer, I can see now that it's some sort of watercraft. Maybe someone's boat came untied in the night?

The driver of the boat slows us as we pull up right next to it and my eyes finally grasp what they couldn't from a distance.

The white object is indeed an overturned boat, washed to shore. On the side, A single word accompanied with a picture of a golden badge is printed onto the white body of the watercraft.

SHERIFF.

CHAPTER THREE

The words are upside down because the boat is overturned, but they are large and easily recognized accompanied with the large imprint of the badge. This is the sheriff's boat, presumably the one he'd taken late last night and *attempted* to reach the mainland. Obviously, something had stopped him. What had happened? Had he gotten back onto the island?

"What the-" The boat driver whispers accompanied by a curse, "That's the sheriff's boat…"

"I thought the sheriff left for the mainland last night…" My mother says, leaning over the side of the boat to get a better look at the overturned watercraft.

"Hey," The boat driver says into the walkie-talkie. "We've got a problem over here."

On the docks, I see the man in the neon green vest raise a walkie-talkie to his mouth and speak into the device.

"What's the problem?"

"We've- found something you better take a look at."

I see the man on the docks sigh. The walkie-talkie on our end crackles to life as he speaks again. "Where are you?"

"We're to your left. You can probably just see the end of our boat." The boat driver says. I see the man on the docks lower the walkie-talkie from his mouth and look over at us. He spots me and waves. I wave back. He puts the walkie-talkie back up to his mouth.

"I see you, going to make my way over on land." The man in the vest says, starting to walk over to us, but then stops abruptly. He seems to remember something and raises the walkie-talkie one more time.

"This better be worth it, you're holding up all the boats."

He makes his way over here across the rocky shore. He stumbles once, and almost falls, but he catches himself with his hands at the last moment. He finally reaches us and takes on a shocked expression when he sees the sheriff's boat overturned on the shore.

"Wha-" he says, then rubs his temples in frustration. "What now?"

The boat driver stands up and jumps into the shallow ocean water to join the other man. The water goes all the way up to his waist. He stumbles for a moment, as if he had not expected it to be so deep, but then regains his balance and joins the man in the bright vest.

The man in the vest examines it for a moment, then speaks to the boat driver.

"Here," He says, "help me turn the thing over."

The two men work at it until the boat turns all the way over the rocks. As it hits the ground, there's a loud clattering and squealing sound. It bounced with a loud hollow *BONG*, and I am beginning to lean over the side of our boat to get a better look-

Something whacks me in the face and clamps over my eyes. I am stunned for a moment. What is happening? I am disoriented. Had it come from under the boat? I press my hands to my face and find another hand covering my eyes. Maybe my mother?

I pry at the hand until finally it releases. Turns out, it had been my mom. Her other hand is pressed firmly to Calla's eyes, unmoving though she struggles against it.

"What-" I say, whirling my head around. I see that the family on the other side of the boat is covering their child's eyes as well, horror-struck expressions playing across their faces. What's going on?

I look over the edge of the boat and see it. See why the parents are covering their children's eyes. Why my mother had tried to cover my eyes too. Because the deck of the sheriff's boat is slick with red sticky blood.

"What?" I say, stumbling back. The two men standing over the thing are frozen, shocked by the sight of the red splatters. I stand. Sit back down. What's happening?

"Any chance it's-" I say, my voice trembling slightly. "Fish blood? Was he fishing?"

It's a long stretch but maybe?

"Maybe." The man in the green vest says, eyeing the boat deck. The parents, who are still covering their children's eyes, stare wide-eyed at the washed-up boat. I myself am speechless.

"Everyone back to the docks," The man in neon says into the walkie-talkie. "Now."

He turns his gaze on us. "I'll have the island scientists test this blood to see what or who it belongs to. You guys get back to the docks and go straight home. I'll announce what's going on when I figure it out."

He then tells the same thing to the people on the walkie-talkies. I turn and see the boats all starting their engines and heading for shore.

"What about the Sheriff?" I ask.

"I'll search for him but if I had to guess-"

"If you had to guess you'd say he's already dead." I say flatly. Nobody loses that much blood and survives without some sort of life-saving transfusion. He nods and gestures for us to head back to the docks. We do and go straight home from there. Once we're there though, we don't get a bit of rest. Our mother orders Calla and I to open the refrigerator and jot down everything we have along with its expiration date, and how full it is. She gives us a blank notepad to get the job done. She starts marking down everything we have in the pantry as we get started. It takes us a full two hours to have everything accurately marked down. I have to ignore all the questions Calla poses to me.

"What was on the boat?"

"What blood?"

"What do you think happened?"

"What scientists?"

"Calla," I say for the hundredth time. "I have no idea, stop asking!"

She sighs and is about to say something when I check off the last item on the list. "Done!"

We tell our mother and she doesn't even smile. "Good, now you two get to bed. Go to sleep straight away. Tomorrow's going to be a busy day."

And with that, my mind whirring to its breaking point, I make my way up to bed and attempt to sleep for my third night of being trapped on Eastrock Island.

The next day, my life, past present and future, is destroyed, but it all begins when I wake up, and for a split second I think everything's back to normal. I have an unexplainable warm feeling of safety.

That feeling, of course, is stripped away the moment I remember my situation.

I sit up in my messy bed and stare around. I wipe some drool from my mouth and stand, moving in front of the mirror that hangs over my dresser. It had taken so long to fall asleep last night that I have heavy bags under my eyes.

I rub my face with my hands and push the unruly brown hair out of my eyes, which just falls back into its previous position. Images of the blood splattered across the white deck of the boat flash through my head. Thick. Sticky. Dark red. These last few days have been like a dream, everything off-kilter, but I have a feeling it's going to get worse and get worse fast. I don't know why I feel that way, but some feeling deep inside me says things are just getting started.

I walk down to the kitchen to find it empty and silent. My mother must be at work already, and who knows what Calla's doing. I go back upstairs but find her room empty, so I assume she must have gone to her friend Maddie's house.

I get myself a bowl of cereal and pour some orange juice into a glass. Once I'm finished with my breakfast, I leave the house and head to the beach for some sanity. I consider heading to the neighborhood docks to see if the boat is still there, but decide against it. I want one normal moment of silence.

Everything seems to be falling apart at my feet and I can't do anything about it.

Maybe I'll just spend the entire day at the beach winding down.

I walk through the quiet Main Street, but this time every single shop is open. They all have a depressed feeling about them though. I take the small path down to the little beach I go to every time. The damp sand refreshes my bare feet as I slip my shoes off. The fog blanketed over the ocean is as thick as ever, affecting even the vision thirty feet in front of me.

I consider just lying in the sand, but decide that would give my mind too much time to wander. Instead, I jog down the misty beach, the sound of the waves filling my ears. I'm able to clear my mind and it feels so, so good. The cool breeze sweeps across the skin on my face, and I feel refreshed; physically and mentally.

My feet dig deep into the dark sand of the shore as I run. As I run and run and run until I see it, and I instantly know that today will not be normal. No, my days spent relaxing over the summer are over.

Because when I see the crumpled form of a human body lying on the beach, I instantly know something is wrong.

I stand, frozen, for what feels like forever. What should I do? Leave, like I never saw it? Run over and investigate? When I choose the latter, I almost immediately regret it.

The body is lying face down in the sand, as if it had washed ashore not long ago. The ocean water occasionally touches its feet and sometimes makes it all the way up to its knees. The tide must be going down for it to have been washed up this far. I walk over to the lifeless body. It's not skinny, not large. Seems healthy enough- other than the fact that it's dead. I discover that when I work up enough guts to check the pulse. I feel nothing, and the skin is ice cold.

I shrink away from the form, terrified by the lifelessness of the skin. I'm about to check again, just to be sure, when I hear muffled footsteps in the sand behind me.

I whirl around, fists extended and backing away. A shadowed man stands ten feet away, examining me with his brown eyes. He sees the body and gives me a questioning look, tilting his head slightly.

"Look-" I stumble on the body and fall to the sand. I scramble to my feet and continue walking backwards, away from the man and the body. "I- I didn't do anything- I swear I- I found it right where it is-"

"I know," he says, and I am momentarily stopped in surprise. Not by his words, but by his voice. The person is not a man. He is a boy, maybe even a teenager. I strain my eyes and examine the features of his face more closely. Slightly hard to make out, because the fog has thickened considerably, but I am sure he must be my age, maybe a little older. Seventeen at very most. He stands at a slight angle, suggesting he may have a limp.

"What?" I say, shakily regaining my posture.

"I know," The boy repeats, and nods at the body with his head. "I saw you find it and all."

"You-" I say, and glance at the body, "You were following me?"

"No," The boy says, and looks away. "I just, came for a jog."

I eye him suspiciously. "Okay."

"So?" He says in a questioning tone.

"So, what." I say, baffled by the boy in front of me.

The boy shrugs his shoulder at the body lying face down in the sand. "Is he dead? The man." His voice shakes slightly "I mean, you just checked his pulse, right?"

"Yeah- yeah he's dead." I say, looking at the body. I hadn't even registered that it's a man, but now that I think about it, the form is distinctly male. Broad shoulders and straight waist.

"Okay then," He sighs in a way that sounds slightly intrigued, and slightly disgusted, scratching his head. He has loosely curled hazel hair and deep brown eyes. His skin has a slightly darker complexion, suggesting some sort of Latino descent. A tall scrawny figure. He looks taller than me for sure, though we could almost pass as related if it weren't for the eyes. My skin tans easily, and the hair is almost the same.

"Should we flip him over?" He whispers, eyeing the form carefully.

"Excuse me?" I say, looking at him in shock.

"Flip him over." He repeats, looking at me a bit closer now. "Huh, do I know you- from somewhere?"

"I get that sometimes." I say. Brown-haired, blue-eyed boy named Luke? I blend in pretty well, nothing special to look at. "Okay, let's flip him over then?"

The boy shrugs hesitantly and walks over to the man. He gestures with his hand for me to get over on his side of the body. I step over the thing and position myself to his right. "On the count of three, okay?"

I nod and slide my hands under the man's chest.

"Okay. One, two, three!"

We both grunt as we try to turn the man over onto his back. He is a lot heavier than he looks. We groan in effort as we try to flip him over. Giving the lifeless form a big push at the same time, the body shifts over.

We get it off the ground, and then gravity takes care of the rest, causing it to fall down to the sand facing up.

Immediately, I shriek and fall to the sand, scooting away on all fours. I close my eyes as I hyperventilate and continue scrambling away from the- thing. The other boy has a similar reaction, stumbling backwards as if smacked in the face. *What-what is that?* One thing's for sure, it's not alive, but the bigger question is whether it's even human. What in the world could- do that to a...

The boy trips over my legs and he falls to the beach beside me. He's breathing fast too, staring at the body. At its face.

Or at least, where the face is supposed to be.

CHAPTER FOUR

One time, when I was a kid, I'd gone to the mainland and visited an aquarium.

All of the miraculous sea creatures, gracefully gliding through the water in their crystal tanks. Watching the fish as they shimmer in the overhead lights, awed by the mere gallons and gallons of blue liquid on the other side of the glass.

My mother, father, and I had gone through the entire aquarium except for the deep seas area. We were running out of time, but I was begging my parents to take me there, just for a quick run-through. This was before Calla was even born, so I was an only child. Eventually, they agreed and set a timer on their phone for five minutes. They said when it went off, we'd need to be leaving.

I happily agreed and we rushed over to the "DEEP SEA EXPERIENCE" area. We had to step through a black curtain to get to the other side, and it was like stepping into a new world. Everything was dark, the only light coming from the tanks built into the walls.

We made our way through quickly, examining all of the creepy glowing deep-sea creatures. We were moving quite fast until I came across the little jelly tank. Their tentacles gracefully trailing behind them as they float through their dark tank.

When my parents tell me that the jellyfish have no brain or heart, I am immediately intrigued. But, as my kindergartener self, I am less interested by that, and more concerned by its lack of a face. Everything, and I mean everything I'd seen up to that point had had a face, no matter how normal or bizarre.

I feel that same twisting in my stomach now, as I stare at the man lying on the beach. He looks completely normal, until you notice the smooth skin that replaces the features of what normally would be a face. Just like the bell of a jellyfish.

I am slightly intrigued, but throw revulsion into the mix of emotions jumbling around in my brain.

"What… What do you think it is?" I ask the brown-eyed boy beside me in the sand.

"I- It's the sheriff…" He says, which catches me by surprise. What is he talking about? I look closer and again find that his eyes have picked up what mine had not. There is a shiny gold sheriff's pin on the body's left pocket tee. The badge is shaped like a five-pointed star, "BLUEHILL RIDGE SHERIFF" printed in blue across the metallic surface.

"What?" I say, but my brain is whirring away in my skull. What does this mean now? Everyone thinks the sheriff is dead, and clearly, he is, but what do these new developments throw into the mix?

What had happened? Did his boat overturn and he was stranded in the ocean? That wouldn't explain the blood on the boat, or what happened to his face.

"So," The brown-haired boy says, straightening his shirt. "What do we do with it? We know the sheriff isn't going to take care of it."

He gestures at the man. There's only one law enforcer in Bluehill Ridge, it being such a small town.

"Okay…" I shudder, "We could take it into the lab and have them do tests on it." I suggest. Eastrock Island has a huge lab hidden in the depths of the misty forest away from the shore. Our science industry is what keeps us running. It's mostly robotics and engineering, but I think they have a small biology sector.

"We could…" The boy says, thinking. "But then they'd take it and run all sorts of tests on it, and you can bet they won't tell us what's wrong with… it."

"Okay, but we do need to find out what's wrong with it." I say, pushing on.

"Okay, how about this," he says, examining the body. "We take a blood sample and take *that* to the lab. We can hide the body until we get some answers, then turn it in when needed. We'll make up some kind of story."

He gulps, obviously already having second thoughts. Apparently lying does not come easy to him. Yet, he suggested it. I know, I know, the whole thing is ridiculous. We should just turn the body in and be done with it. But what would that lead to? More secrets? The lab is well known for its secretive tendencies, all the workers there forced to keep a strict code of silence. I assume because of the sorts of innovation they do there. I've been told they're not just any old lab. Not that I would know what that means.

"Where are we going to get his blood?" I ask.

He gestures at the body.

"We are not cutting it open." I say, disgusted.

His face goes green. "No, that's not what I mean. Look, on the side of his pants… you can just see-"

I see what he means and I really have to admire his eye for detail. There's a thin red line in the blue jeans, and around it is stained a dark red.

"Can we even take it from that?" I ask hesitantly, "I mean, doesn't it have to be sterile to get good results?"

"I don't know, don't ask me." He shrugs. "I'm not a scientist or anything."

"Okay," I mutter, "so we'd probably need a syringe of some kind to get the blood correctly. Not from the cut, but maybe an arm?"

"Yeah, but before it clots up or whatever the heck it does after the body is dead."

"Okay," I say, my mind racing. "I have an idea, but it's probably the stupidest thing we could do."

●　●　●

The boy, who tells me his name is Griffin, kneels beside me.

We are behind a large bush that lines the edge of my high school. The full leaves cover us from any onlookers, but if there were any well-placed cameras, we'd be spotted easily.

"Okay, listen up," I tell the boy named Griffin, "We can get in through the biology lab window, Mr. Brown always leaves it open because of the smell."

"Won't the cameras see us?" Griffin asks, scrunching his brown eyebrows together.

"Probably," I say, repositioning my legs for running, "But with all that's going on, I'm hoping they won't be too pissed with a couple of rogue teens. Plus, they might run through the internet, in which case we're safe because it's down."

"Okay…" Griffin says, and I can tell he's not thrilled with the idea of breaking into the school. On our way here, he told me he goes to this school too, but when I asked if he recognized me, he shook his head and looked away (despite claiming to have earlier). I certainly don't recognize him.

"Either way though, we're going to run to get there. All the doors are locked over the summer, so the window is our only chance, okay?" I tell him. He nods and positions himself to run as well.

"Okay." He inhales sharply, "Now."

We both sprint across the grass lining the entrance of the high school. The mist has cleared up a bit, but not enough to let the place warm up much. I almost slip on the damp grass a couple of times, but Griffin seems to be having even more of a problem on the slick turf.

Finally, after struggling on the wet lawn, we're at the base of the school.

"This window?" He says, pointing at a second-story window above us. Oh shoot.

"It- it's open alright." I say, crossing my arms. I totally forgot that the biology lab is on the *second story*, much too high for us to easily climb to.

"Seriously?" He asks. "How are we supposed to get up there?"

"I forgot, okay?"

Griffin sighs and runs his hands through his brown hair.

"Luke, you said we could get in through the window." He says, looking at me carefully. "How exactly are we supposed to get up there?"

"A ladder?" I say sheepishly.

"And where are you going to get one of those?" Griffin asks, examining the brick wall of the school, testing for handholds.

"Okay…" I say, "Okay. So, we're going to break in."

"Excuse me?" Griffin outbursts, "What?"

"We take a rock," I tell him, already regretting what I'm about to say, "And smash the glass in."

"Where?" He asks.

"The front school door is completely glass; we can get in there. I know how to get into the biology lab once we're in, that's where the syringes are."

"And if the doors *inside* are locked?"

"Smash the doorknobs in too." I say. I keep telling myself it's serious. It's necessary. There is a literal human body hidden back on the beach, waiting to be tested. It's either now or never.

I sprint back across the slick grass, careful not to fall again. By the time Griffin catches up to me (Probably because he was frozen in place, stunned by the boldness of my suggestion) I am already choosing a particularly large rock from a pile of the stuff not far from the entrance of the school.

Griffin grasps one in his hand too, and we make our way over to the entrance of the school.

"Okay listen," Griffin hesitates, turning to me, "Do we have to? I mean-"

"Don't then," I say, and push my way past him and to the main glass door. I raise the rock and try to find the weak spot in the entrance.

"No, I'll go if you go," Griffin says determinedly, "But I'm just asking if we should."

"You really want to know?" I say, settling for the glass area right next to the doorknob, "No, I don't think we should, but I also think it's necessary."

I raise the rock over my head and prepare to bring it down on the glass.

Griffin nods. "Okay, here we go then."

I slam the rock down as hard as I can on the crystal glass of the door. A paper-thin fracture spider webs out from the impact point. This will be easier than I thought. I raise the rock again and bring it down with all my might on the most damaged part of the glass.

With a loud shatter, the glass breaks completely and the entire pane falls to the ground in a sparkling heap. A loud alarm goes off in the school. I look around nervously and so does Griffin. As I stare into the dark hallway, I realize how insane my plan actually is. I would never be doing this under normal circumstances.

But these are not normal circumstances, and I keep telling myself that I had no other choice.

A ladder. I should have just found a ladder.

We don't have that kind of time. Besides, it's done. It's either go in or out, the damage is irreversible.

"Well then." I say, "Let's go."

• • •

The seemingly endless hallways are dark and eerie. Our every footstep echoes loudly through the school. The only noise is the distant sound of the alarm at the entrance. I can't see any light switches in the area, but even if I could, there's no use in making it easier for the cameras to see us, right?

"Up the stairs," I whisper to Griffin, and I see him nod through the darkness. The only light source is coming from distant windows peering out into the thick, gray mist outside. My shoes seem to clap against the tile ground too loud, and even on the thinly carpeted stairs our movements aren't exactly quiet. All of it, the whole situation, doesn't sit well with me.

And I can almost hear some sort of soft screeching echoing up from the hallway below- is it my ears playing tricks on me?

"Luke," Griffin says, stepping up onto the top of the stairs. "We turn left, right? I took Physics not Bio, so-"

"Yeah," I say, shaking my head to clear it. "Two doors down."

We turn left and pass two doors before we reach the biology lab entrance. I'm already gesturing for Griffin to use the rock *he'd* brought; I'd tossed mine aside outside without thinking, but he twists the handle and it swings open freely, creaking slightly.

I step in. The dusty desks, and the squeaky-clean whiteboard give me a sense of normalcy. Sanity. I shake the feeling off and enter the room fully.

"Okay, I think they'll be in the closet." I say, quickly going to the back of the room. I open the heavy door and yes, there they are. A small box of tiny little empty syringes sits on the shelf. I pluck one from its depths and close the closet door behind me. It shuts with a *click*.

"Got it," I say to Griffin, "Let's get out of here."

• • •

The jog back to the beach feels like the longest trek across the island I've taken in a long time, but when we finally reach there, I am far from out of breath. The whole time I was looking back and forth over my shoulder, expecting someone to punish us for what we'd done to the school.

But nothing happens and we reach the beach in record time. The body is just where we left it, hidden under some thick brush at the edge of the sand. Griffin and I hoist it out by its feet and sit down in the sand, huffing from the effort of dragging the man.

"Okay, we're really doing this…" I whisper to myself.

"Are you kidding me? After everything we just did, of course we're doing this!" Griffin exclaims, and gives a pressured, forced laugh.

"Never said otherwise," I say, pulling the small empty syringe from my pocket. There is a small cover protecting the needle, keeping it sterile. "Know how to perform venipunctures?"

"No," He says, "We never did anything like this in school."

65

"I think there's a matter of sterilizing the area around where we're going to make the," I begin, but Griffin cuts me off.

"Screw danger of infection, he's already dead." He says, rubbing his hands together either from anticipation or the bite of the cold air. "Do we even need to find a vein to do it?"

"Well, I don't know," I say, "But the doctor always takes blood from my upper forearm. I suppose we should try to find the vein there?" I honestly have no idea what I'm doing, but neither would Griffin so here goes nothing.

Griffin turns away and I grit my teeth and do the best I can to get some blood. I'll spare you the details, but let's just say when you don't know what you're doing, it gets a little messy. After about three minutes of holding back my breakfast, I proudly hold up a syringe full of dark blood.

"See?" I tell Griffin, waving the tube of liquid in his face, "I did it!"

He sighs and takes it into his hand. "It's dark, isn't it? Is it supposed to look like that?"

I examine the bottle closely. The blood is barely red, more of a disturbing blackish color. You can still see the distinct maroon color on the side of the tube though, so I shrug the question off.

"Maybe it's because he's been dead so long?" I say, glancing at where his face should be. The smooth skin there still gives me the creeps, sending my skin crawling all over. Or does it have something to do with that.

"Yeah…" He says quietly, and then hands me the blood sample. "Let's get it up to the lab and ask about it."

"Can we just do that?"

"We can try," says Griffin, and gestures for me to follow. After we hide the body again, he leads me up into Main Street. He turns left, heading out of town.

"You don't mean for us to walk all the way there, do you?" I say, surprised.

"What else do you have in mind?" He says, turning back to me. I tell him about how my mother lets me borrow her car sometimes. He follows me back into the thick of town and to my mom's diner. The moment I walk in, my mother turns to me and smiles.

"Hey Luke!" She says and waves. I grin and jog over.

"Hey mom," I say, still shaken by the body on the beach but doing my best not to show it. "Can I use your car? I should be back within the hour."

"You and your friend?" My mother says, nodding at Griffin. I turn to face him and gesture for him to come introduce himself. He does so shyly, and shakes my mother's hand.

"Mom, this is Griffin," I say as they shake hands, "Griffin, this is my mom."

"Nice to meet you Mrs. Anderson." He says and smiles. That's odd. I don't remember telling him my last name. Weird.

"Nice to meet you too Griffin," My mother says, then turns to me. "Where are you guys going to go?"

"Oh, just inland a bit," I say vaguely. She raises her eyebrow. "To the lab area, we got invited for school."

"Both of you?" She says, looking back and forth between us.

"Yeah," I say, my insides twisting. I hate lying to her, but what am I supposed to say? 'Hey, Griffin and I found a dead body on the shore, it's the sheriff, and he has no face. Also, we broke into my school and stole a syringe to take his blood, just because we want answers.'

I have a feeling that wouldn't go over well.

She hands me the keys. "Be back in an hour and a half, I need the car to get home, you too, okay?"

"Okay," I say, taking the keys and heading for the doors, "Thanks mom!"

The moment we got out the doors, I sigh.

"Okay, I drive," I mutter, and hop into the car. Griffin swings open the passenger door and slides into the seat beside me. I jam the key into the ignition and turn it with my foot on the brake. The engine splutters to life and I pull out of the tight parking space.

"You know how to get to the lab?" I ask Griffin. He just nods and points down the road. Following his directions, we turn right and leave downtown.

I set the syringe down on the dashboard, the barrel filled with dark blood, and head into the forest.

CHAPTER FIVE

The road winds through the tall damp trees as we drive along it towards the lab. The fog seems to be just as thick inland, if not more so. The moist bark and dark pine needles that make up the trees loom above us. We both are silent, and I can hear the soft breeze through the window, see the branches swaying.

"Make a right here," Griffin says quietly, adjusting his seatbelt.

I turn the wheel right when the curve comes, and the vehicle moves as I steer it.

"Another left in maybe a quarter of a mile and we're there." Griffin informs me. We follow the road until the turn presents itself. When we take it, a long flat stretch of road sits in front of us, ended by a large, squat building with some sort of big satellite on the top. There is a small parking lot to the left-hand side, but only a few cars are parked there.

I slide into one of the spaces, pull the parking brake lever, and turn the engine off. Its purr dies as I open the door and unlock Griffin's. We both step out and admire the lab, much simpler looking than I had thought it would look. Concrete, textured walls. Two bushes on either side of the entrance.

I grab the small syringe off of the dashboard and slam the car door shut. Pressing the lock button on the keys, we both head through the parking lot and towards the most modern looking outdoor feature; The automatic sliding doors.

The glass slides to the side as soon as we get near enough for the sensors to pick up our movement. We step through the opening. Smooth white tiles make up the floor, and smaller white and gray tiles line the walls. There is a large wooden desk to the right of the entrance, but it sits empty.

"Hello." Says a voice to our left, and we both jump and turn to the speaker. There's a dark-skinned man standing in front of a metal door, clipboard in hand.

"Hi, uhm," Griffin says awkwardly, "We were wondering if we could get some samples tested."

I glance at Griffin, wondering why he had spilled the question out so quickly. Oh well. The man in front of us raises his dark eyebrows, straightening round glasses propped up on his nose.

"Tested?" He asks skeptically, "And you came all the way here for… what? Some sort of school project? I'm sorry but we don't just test samples for random people, this is a government run facility."

"No actually, we have some blood we were wondering about." I say, "Testing for abnormalities and such?"

"Blood?" The man says, examining the syringe I hold in my hand, "What makes you think it has abnormalities?"

"It's dark," I lie, because both Griffin and I know it's really the source's lack of a face that has brought us here. "It's almost black, see?"

"Yes," He says, "I see. Okay, we normally don't do this, but I'll take this in and test it real quick. I'll get results back to you as soon as possible."

He gently takes the syringe and begins walking away towards the door at the end of the room, but stops and turns around one last time "I'm only doing this because we have nothing better to do." He says, and looks like he wants to say more. A subconscious guilty look comes over his face, like a kid asked if they took anything from the cookie jar, but only finishes with "stay here, I'll be back with the results in a bit."

We thank him and he nods before disappearing behind the door. Griffin glances at me and I give him a thumbs up. That was easy. One moment it was a firm no, but for some reason I now sense- it's hard to place. Anxiousness? Eagerness? We take our seats on two plump red couches to the left of the entrance. There are magazines scattered on a small coffee table next to me, but I don't bother reading any. I'm too nervous about what the results will have in store, squirming around in my chair.

We wait maybe twenty minutes (Much less than I had expected) before the man reappears through the door. By now, both Griffin and I are dying for answers.

But the man doesn't bother greeting us, he just walks up to us and holds up the blood.

"Where did you get this from?" He says at once.

"What?" Griffin asks, clearly not anticipating the hardness in his voice. "Did you run the tests?"

"Yes, we did," The doctor says, and then furrows his dark eyebrows, "Well, at least, we tried. Now, where did you get this sample?"

"I, we-" I stumble on my words, "We found it."

"Found it?" The doctor mutters doubtfully.

"Yes," I say, struggling to create some sort of story, "It was a science sample in our school."

"You were at school today?" The doctor asks, "Wouldn't you be on summer break?"

"Not today," Griffin bursts, "We had it during the school year, but we wanted to have someone, uh, professional test it."

The doctor gives Griffin and I a strange look in response to his obvious nervous lying, but doesn't say anything.

"So," I say, trying to pull his attention towards myself instead of Griffin, who seems to be internally screaming for help, "you said you *tried* to run tests? Was there a problem?"

The doctor's gaze lingers on Griffin for another moment, but then turns to me.

"No, the test went fine," He says, "We just got… Strange results."

"As in?" I press, and he eyes me as if he knows something's going on, and he's not in on it.

"May I ask where exactly your school got this particular sample?" Inquires the doctor.

"We have no idea," I say, and Griffin nods to reinforce that my statement is true, "It was on the desk."

"Who is your science teacher?"

"Mr. Brown," Griffin responds, "I think."

"His full name, if you will." The doctor says, pulling out his clipboard once again. Okay, this is getting serious. If Mr. Brown somehow found out…

"Martin Brown, I think," I say, "Not sure about his middle name though."

"Thank you," he says, taking the name down in his notes.

"What were the strange results?" Griffin continues, "Of the blood, I mean."

"The strange thing about the results is that there aren't any." The man says, "The blood is completely lacking in DNA. The Chromosomes are gone too. Somehow, we can't tell what or whose blood this is. We can't even tell if it came from a male or female."

I look at Griffin. We know full well who that blood came from.

"And there's more," The doctor continues, eyeing us, "Blood cells, white blood cells, even some leftover skin cells. They're all degenerating."

"Degenerating?" I ask, surprised, "What does that mean? They're, like, disappearing or something?"

"No," The man says, "They're all dying. Shriveling up and turning to something of a black paste, that's why the blood's color is so dark."

"What do you think caused it?" Griffin says, and I can hear a note of worry in his voice. What does this mean? Will we be caught? Will it matter? What could have possibly been done that to the blood, because even the doctor is visibly shaken.

"I don't know but whatever, or whoever, this blood came from has similar side effects to someone given Chemotherapy, and are most likely immunocompromised, but that doesn't explain the degeneration of the red blood cells and skin cells. Maybe the red blood cells are dying from the host's lack of oxygen or problems with glycolysis? And who knows what happened to the skin cells. This is a very odd sample, very odd indeed."

I caught some meaning from those words, understanding some of the terms. Griffin, who mentioned he had taken physics, not biology this past year, looks a bit lost but does his best to remain composed.

"Thank you," He says, standing up, "We should probably get going." I stand as well.

"Listen to me," The doctor says to us in a quiet tone, "Are you listening?"

I nod, startled a bit.

"This is very serious stuff. If you know anything, *anything* about where this blood came from, take it straight to us here at the lab, okay?"

We nod again.

"Until then, keep the blood test results quiet, we'll be keeping the sample here with us to continue studying it."

So now we're keeping secrets. As if we needed more of those around.

"Will you tell us if you find anything out?" Griffin blurts out, then seems to regret speaking at all.

The doctor seems to think about it for a moment.

"If you swear to tell us if you find anything out about the source of the blood, then I will get your phone number and call you to the lab if there is any progression in our studies that we deem okay to tell you."

It's not exactly the best deal out there, but it's better than nothing and I don't intend to tell this man about the body anyways.

"Deal," I say, and Both Griffin and I give him our numbers, which he takes down in notes on his smartphone.

"Thank you." I say to the man and before we know it, both Griffin and I are driving down the twisty road through the forest, headed back for the body on the beach. The dark, moist, evergreen trees on either side of us stand tall and proud in the gray misty air, and the soil just off the road looks damp and rich with minerals.

When the trees finally open up around us, we're entering main-street. I can once again see the ocean through the cracks and alleyways of the buildings. We are no longer engulfed by the island.

I drive us up to my mother's diner and park the car. I flip the engine off and engage the parking brake. Unlocking the car, Griffin and I open the doors and step out onto the sidewalk. I lock the car via the keys jingling in my hand, then walk up to the diner.

But the closed sign hangs on the other side of the glass, and I am confused because the diner doesn't close for at least another two hours. Maybe my mom is still in there, cleaning. Maybe they had to close early for… I don't know, a medical emergency? Did somebody choke?

I rap my knuckles on the glass, but nobody answers.

"Is it supposed to be closed?" Griffin asks. I only shake my head and look around. Where could she be?

Then I see it.

Dark, thick smoke is drifting up into the air somewhere far down the road, behind lots of trees. My blood turns cold as I realize it's coming from the direction of the neighborhood. My neighborhood.

• • •

"What could have caused a fire?" Griffin asks breathily as our car races through the short quarter mile of foliage between Main Street and the neighborhood. The great big billowing cloud of smoke hangs over the trees. The mist has retreated enough for it to be starkly visible against the sky.

I just shake my head in response. It's a good question, but his guess is as good as mine. Fires are hard enough to start when you're trying, thanks to the constant dampness of the mist hanging over the island. The only way to get a fire around here that puts off that much smoke is probably soaking the whole thing in gasoline.

As we pull into the neighborhood area, I can see that an entire block is ablaze with red hot flames, eating up buildings as an animal does food. I can hear a big crash even through the car door as an entire roof collapses.

In shock, I stop the car just outside of the wall of smoke and get out. Why now. Why here. Why is everything I know so suddenly falling apart.

"Mom!" I call into the fire. I think I can see a shape in the smoke, pressing something to their face. "Mom! Are you there?"

Griffin steps up beside me and gazes into the great wall of smoke, undulating and spreading like a living thing. Like a virus trying to overtake a body, effectively entrapping and killing anything within its vicinity. It's probably not even that thick but my eyes water so bad already that it intensely blurs my sight.

76

"Mom!" I shriek, because I know she's here, I just know it. Why would she be in the fire? I have no idea, but all I care about is getting my family out of there. Making sure they're safe.

And then another thought strikes my mind, as if someone has swung a shovel at my temple. The thought is so nerve-shredding I crumple down to my knees. What if Calla is trapped in the burning house? What if our roof has already collapsed and-

I bolt up to my feet and sprint into the fire and smoke. I hear Griffin shriek my name, but I don't care. I sprint even faster, faster, faster than I ever have.

The heat. The heat is so overpowering I almost shrink back and away from the flame. What I do, though, is take a gasp of shock. Up until this point, I've been holding my breath, keeping the potent smoke from my lungs, so when I take the deep sudden inhale, I choke so much I can't breathe and my eyes tear up so that the flames dancing in the smoke become shapeless balls of light reaching through the haze.

It takes a moment for me to regain awareness of my situation, but I pull my shirt up over my nose and press hard. I try to make out my surroundings, but the place I'd walked through nearly every day for my whole life now has turned into a glowing wasteland. What I can manage to see through the thick smoke is either collapsed, or so badly on fire I can't tell what or where it is in relation to my own home. The wooden houses are so full of foggy moisture, the wood can't burn effectively so it's putting out more smoke and less heat. It's plenty hot enough though, especially in comparison with the cold temperature I'd just left behind.

Multiple shapes run past me in the smoke, but I can't tell who they are either because the smoke is obscuring them, or because they have shirts and rags pressed to their faces. But once, I could swear I spotted a big man holding a lit match in one hand, and a box of the things in the other.

I run blindly through the smoke until I ram straight into an object. I fall back for a second, stunned, and I try to look up to see what I had run into, but my eyes are so watery that I can barely make out a thing.

At first, I think it's a wall, but then a hand reaches down through the haze of smoke and reaches for me. In a daze, I grasp it and it pulls me up from the ground. I stand and it helps me regain balance on my feet. It takes a second, but I look up at the face of a person and recognize who it is.

"Mom?" I try to say, but the shirt over my mouth muffles my words so badly I doubt what I said could be understood.

She nods and gestures urgently for the both of us to get out of the smoke. I shake my head violently and try to say Calla's name, but I choke on the smoke before any words form.

"Where's home?" I rasp, my voice sounding horrible even to me. We must have crossed paths in search of our house.

My mother points down the road, but then urgently grabs my shoulder and tries to drag me out of the smoke. I shrug her grasp off and gesture for her to get out of the smoke. She nods and tries to pull me that way as well. What about Calla?

I shrug her grasp off again, holding my finger up as in "One second," before darting back into the thick of the pungent gray smoke.

The stuff is so thick as to be almost tangible, like I could reach my hand out and push it out of the way.

I look around, searching for anything, *anything*, to tell me where I am in relation to my burning home, to Calla. At least, I assume she's in the house. What if she made it out in time? Should I be leaving the area of the fire, because she'd actually gotten out safely, and that's why my mother was pulling me away?

No, I can't take that chance. What if she *is* in there? And if I even hesitated for a moment, it could well mean life or death for her. If there's even a possibility she's in that fire, I'm going for her. There's really no other choice is there.

I squint my eyes so tight, I can barely see, but at least my vision isn't completely gone. I make out a couple of dark silhouettes running through the smoke around me, backdropped by the red glowing fire. I wonder what they are…

Fire.

Fire!

From what I can remember, only the side of the street *our* house is on was on fire, I remember seeing that as we drove in. I squint even harder and realize that the unbearably hot glow is coming mainly from my right, though there are some visible flames to the left. Maybe the sparks leapt over the street? No, it's too moist for them to catch fire like that, this is intentional spreading. I don't have time to wonder about that though, I think I know my general location. So instead of wandering aimlessly through the smoke, I head towards the glow, towards the roaring fire. I'm no expert, but my guess is that the fire should be easy enough to put out with the next downpour coming this evening. At least, that's what my phone said a few days ago, because the Wi-Fi had given out the night of the sheriff's death.

The heat comes at me constantly, blowing in my face like a brick wall. I press on though, bunching almost my entire shirt up over my nose. I'm having trouble breathing though, even through the shirt, because the fire is eating up so much oxygen.

And then I see it. I recognize the front door by the black, melted plastic pots dripping down the concrete stairs, the numerous plants that had lived there long gone. I bolt towards the entrance, which I can see is wide open as I get close enough. For some reason, this panics me even more, and I call Calla's name through my shirt. Of course, over all the sounds of burning wood and crackling sparks, my words are lost among the chaos.

The main roof of our house is still up. I can see that now that I'm inside, but I'm still worried about it collapsing because a few burning beams seem to have fallen to the ground and lit the carpet on fire.

"Calla!" I rasp out as loudly as I can. I scan the living room, but I can't see her. If she's here, she'd probably gone up to her room. I search for the stairs and am relieved to find that they are almost completely intact.

I race up to them before they could collapse or something. The top stair is missing, but I easily leap over the gap. I run down the hallway, flames licking both sides. It's so unbearably hot that I want to lay down on the ground and curl up in a ball. But I don't, and I run to Calla's door. It's closed, and I almost reach out and grab the doorknob before I remember it's probably burning hot.

I reach my foot up and swing the silvery handle down with my shoe. I then reel back and kick the door in as hard as I can. It slams inward and I quickly scan the room for Calla. There's absolutely no sign of her, and all the walls are on fire too.

"Calla!" I shriek once again, but there is no response.

I run down the hallway a bit and prepare to open the door to my room the same way I just had to Calla's, but it's wide open. In there, however, the only flames visible are the ones climbing their way up my door.

I dash inside. The smoke is horrible, but the temperature drops considerably.

"Calla, are you in here?" I call out again.

Something grabs me from behind and I jump. My nerves, which were already on edge, leap sky high. I whirl around to find Calla hugging me around the middle.

"Calla!" I gasp, raising my arms to get a better look at her grimy face "You're okay!"

She nods, and I see she has part of her shirt pulled over her nose as well.

"What are you still doing in the house?" I say, my words muffled by my shirt's thick fabric.

"I was getting stuff!" She informs me loudly, and her words are more clearly defined than mine because she has less of her shirt over her nose.

"Calla! You should have gotten out right away!" I say as I sprint over to my dresser, grab one of my shirts, and wet it in my bathroom sink. I realize that I should have a wet shirt as well, but don't want to waste time, so I just drench the shirt I'm wearing.

"But I was getting important stuff!" She says, pointing at her pink glittery backpack, which is still muddy from the day she was playing with her friend Maddie.

"C'mon," I say, and press the wet shirt to her face, "Crawl on the ground, there's less smoke that way."

We exit my room crawling on the hard tile ground. The tile is hot, but both Calla and I have long sleeve shirts on, so our elbows aren't burning as badly.

The real trouble began when we got to the bottom of the stairs.

We risked standing as we made it down the partially burning steps, careful to avoid the tendrils of flame. When we reach the bottom, however, there's an immensely loud *crack* of wood above, and a flaming wooden beam falls from the ceiling.

Last minute, I shove Calla out of the way and into the living room, knowing that if the beam directly hit her, the hit would be fatal. Turns out, it's not much fun for me either.

The full weight of the beam strikes me in the side of the head and shoulder. Its weight forces me to crumple on the ground, groaning under the burning wood. The shirt has fallen from my face, and I'm having trouble breathing.

Everything is silent for a moment.

And then pain roars into my veins, tearing through my nervous system and into my brain. All my common sense has evaporated, and I am just lying on the ground under the burning board, my full consciousness focused on the agony.

I am no superhero from a movie, nor a physical wonder. I am not used to this kind of pain, and it hurts so badly my vision is spotted. The flames eating up the wood on top of me threaten to slide across my back, burning the flesh. I need to prevent that from happening. The only problem is, I'm so incapacitated that I have no idea what to do.

I groan again, and my lungs burn from the smoke.

"Calla…" I croak, my voice so raspy and quiet I can barely hear myself. I have to repeat myself to be heard, "Calla. Leave the house. Mom is outside of the smoke,"

I cough.

"You can meet with her there." I finish. Selfishly, I want her to stay and help but deep down I know what needs to happen. Maybe I can lift the thing off of my back myself.

And then I feel the wood beam become slightly lighter on my back. Not enough to allow me to slide away by any means, it's almost nothing. Still though, it's weight lessens slightly. I twist my head around to find Calla groaning in effort to lift the board. The damp shirt I'd gotten for her is lying forgotten on the floor.

"Calla," I groan.

She just shakes her head, holding her breath. She grunts as she attempts to pull the beam off of me. The attempt is so futile I almost just collapse on the ground again. But she's not leaving. Calla is not leaving, but still there, trying to hoist the board up, tear marks visible on her ash covered skin. How long has she been in the house?

I shift around best I can, and get my hands on the burning wood. Sometimes the flames lick my hands, but it's better than having my entire body burn. I push with all my might, helping Calla raise the beam enough for me to slide out from under it. The moment I'm in the clear, we both let go, and Calla collapses to the ground, panting into the shirt once again pressed to her face.

"Thank you," I gasp, "Let's go."

My hands are burning, the nerves on fire, but I help Calla up. I see that she's burnt too, all the way up her forearms. Fresh tears run down her pudgy face, and I am sure to help her up by only touching the un-damaged areas. We stagger through the burning house, not bothering to get on our knees because we're so badly burnt. Calla's face was spared, but I can tell at least a bit of my own hair is singed, and I think there must be a bad burn across my cheekbone because it hurts every time I change facial expressions. At any rate, both of our eyes are fine, which is what really matters.

We are struggling to even proceed a few feet, tripping over burning debris every time it crosses our path. We finally make it to the door and exit the house, though the heat and smoke barely let up. We need to go the mere hundred feet or so to get into cleaner air.

I try to squint through all of the smoke, but then I remember I only need to follow the fire on our left side, and it should lead us down the road. We do just that, barely seeing anything through the smoke. I think I see flashing lights through the haze, and vaguely comprehend that it may be the small Island fire department. It doesn't matter. Calla and I are almost there.

Just hang on a little bit longer...

Calla and I emerge from the cloud of fog... no, smoke. Everything is blurry. Griffin is standing there, horror-struck by our appearance. I am supporting Calla, but I feel like collapsing.

"Mrs. Anderson!" He calls, evidently to our mother. I don't know, nor do I care. My body hurts so bad. "Mrs. Anderson, they're over here! Both of them!"

I keel over onto the street, letting my grimy, burnt face press against the black pavement. How nice it would be to be gone. Gone from this awful situation. Griffin seems to panic because I'd fallen to the ground. He kneels and calls for my mother again, but I can't hear him.

"Is Calla safe?" I ask, though somewhere in the back of my head I know it's a dumb question. She'd been right beside me- is right beside me.

"Yes, she's okay," Griffin says, looking worried. "she's right here."

I'm not worried. I am relieved, and my body finally allows me rest, passing me into the dark oblivion of unconsciousness.

CHAPTER SIX

Mrs. Harlow, a tall thin woman with brown shoulder-length hair finishes applying the burn cream to the blistering pink areas of my skin. It is now morning, and the sun is rising over the slightly misty horizon through the window. It had been a long night of burning pain. I'd barely gotten any sleep.

Mrs. Harlow is the mother of Maddie Harlow, Calla's best friend. She and my mother have been friends for a long time. She graciously welcomed us into her home when she discovered our house was one of the ones that had burnt.

The smoke could be seen from all over the southern side of the island. When the small firefighter crew arrived, the flames were put out fast enough, but the primary question was who had started it.

Apparently, they discovered that a band of locals had been acting unruly ever since the sheriff's death was announced and we were cut off from the mainland. No rules. No consequences, since we have no jails on Eastrock. With no enforcers to enforce the law, they could do whatever they wanted. They, apparently, wanted to play with fire by setting houses ablaze.

They didn't even bother to check if anyone was inside. Because there was. My little sister, Calla, was still inside the house. I talked to my mom, who is feeling absolutely terrible that she would have left Calla in the burning house. She had been here at Maddie's for a play date. According to Maddie, Calla had left to go get stuffed animals from her room without telling Mrs. Harlow, because the two houses are within walking distance. As far as my mother had known, Calla was safe here in the Harlow's house. She'd thought I might have gone back to the house so she raced to make sure I was okay. Once she had found me in the smoke, she had tried to leave since, as far as she knew, Calla was safe at the Harlow's. We still don't have Calla's side of the story, because she refuses to talk.

The pink glittery backpack made it out of the fire with her. The adults had gone through it, mostly to find what a girl of Calla's age would find important. Two stuffed animals, her tablet, piggy bank… But there had been something in that bag I never expected. Calla, for some reason, had packed my microscope in the backpack, along with a bunch of little tubes (Which are samples of all sorts of random little things we'd found around the house).

Since I have woken up, my mother has tried to call my father at least three times, but like the night of the sheriff's death, all cell service is still out.

The ointment and cream Mrs. Harlow had just applied begins to make the burns feel better already. The deep cut from the wood is beginning to scab over just like the rest of the scratches covering my body.

The day has just been an endless stretch of lying on the couch, drifting in and out of sleep, and sitting up every few hours to have my burn cream applied. Now that everything is over, I have realized that my injuries aren't extreme. The cuts are already starting to close. The burns still hurt intensely when I don't have ice on them, but they're mostly first and second-degree burns. The closest thing to a third-degree burn is on my shoulder, but the skin is not blackened or white, and it's not numb either.

The television is on, but it's just playing DVDs and they only have old Disney movies. I guess it's more for Calla's entertainment anyways. She's sitting on the couch, ice pouches covering her arms, and blankly staring at the TV screen. I sigh and rest my head on the headrest behind me.

This is basically how my entire day goes. Sleep. Wake up. Medicine. Repeat. Until finally it is night and I am given the blessing of undisturbed rest. I am even able to change my own ice without squinting in pain by the end of the day. I've got to say, that burn ointment works like magic. The next day, I even insist that I'm fine, that I'm ready to get out of the house again and help. Though standing is slightly painful, I can even manage walking pretty well. I wanted to try running but my mother had shot down the idea immediately and sent me off to bed once again. So, now, I sit in the Harlow's guest bedroom, blankly staring at the walls, and eagerly awaiting any news of what has been going on out in the rest of the island. Everything seems to be shockingly quiet though, no more events like the fire.

The last I heard was our very disgruntled mayor forcing the fire starters onto a boat and basically banning them from coming back to Bluehill Ridge. Harsh, I know, but when they had tried to lock them up in a house, they'd broken through the windows and escaped again so they were left no choice.

How barbaric it feels to be banishing someone from our town, maybe even sentencing them to the same fate of the sheriff, whatever that may be. They'll probably head towards mainland. Not our problem anymore.

And it's night again. I sleep and only have to get up for ice once, so that's a major improvement. And, other than a little stinging, I can walk fine too. My lungs have pretty much stopped coughing up mucus and I feel pretty good despite it all. Tomorrow. Tomorrow I will leave the house, or I might lose my sanity. Everything has fallen apart and I'm just, sitting in bed.

Tomorrow.

● ● ●

The morning goes as usual. Sit up, stay that way for a bit while blankly staring at the wall, and leave, trudging towards the living room. I'm slightly sore everywhere but desperate to do something, tired of just sitting on the couch or lying in bed.

Elizabeth, the oldest daughter of the Harlow's, is standing in the kitchen. Elizabeth is a red-haired girl, her face covered in light brown freckles. Her eyes are a crisp green, and whenever she looks at me, there is a visible expression of annoyance. I wonder what that's about. She's been particularly evasive these past few days, always shut up in her room since she's not allowed around town after everything that's happened.

"Here you are sweetheart," Mrs. Harlow says, handing me a plate with over easy eggs oozing yellow yolk. I take the plate and dig in.

"Thank you," I say as I hand the plate back to her after finishing.

"Of course!" She responds, smiling brightly, "Would you like seconds?"

"Oh no, I'm okay, thank you though!" I say to her as she takes the plate. "I can wash it if you'd like, my burns are practically gone I'd love to help out-"

"Oh no sweetheart it's alright," She insists, smiling, "I've got it from here."

She nods with another smile and walks back over to the kitchen. Turning the faucet of the kitchen sink on, she runs the dish under the water and scrapes the food off with a sponge. Their ginger cat, who's name I don't know, hops up onto the counter and watches her intently until the job is finished. Those piercing hazel eyes turn to me, before it hops off the counter and darts away to hide in the depths of the house.

Later, when Mrs. Harlow opens the refrigerator door to retrieve some apples, she frowns and puts her hand on her hip.

"This won't last long, with everything going on." She mumbles.

"I can go to the supermarket," Elizabeth, the oldest child pipes in eagerly, standing from the table. "I can go pick up whatever you need."

"No, not with everything that's going on." Her mother says sternly, "Certainly not alone. Perhaps when your father gets home this afternoon…"

"I can go!" I blurt out, standing from the couch. My skin burns a bit from the movement, but I try not to show it, "I mean, I'd be willing to go if needed."

Mrs. Harlow shakes her head gently, "I'm sorry darling, but you're in no condition to be going anywhere at the moment. Besides, the same point stands. You both are just children, and by the sound of it things are goin' crazy out there."

I look to my mother, but she just weakly smiles and apologetically shakes her head before returning to treating Calla's burns. She's putting so much cream on them her arms look like they've been covered in layers and layers of sunblock.

Come on. It's been two days since I've even left the house.

"No, seriously, I'm fine," I say almost honestly, "I'm dying to do something other than just sitting on the couch. I'd love to go. We can go together, Elizabeth and I. We're responsible."

My mother and Mrs. Harlow seem to think about this for a little bit. Eventually, they agree that I can go with Elizabeth as long as I take some burn cream and a walkie-talkie, which they have in their mudroom. Mrs. Harlow offers to go herself, but Elizabeth and I both tell her it's okay, because it's obvious that she's preoccupied with helping Calla.

"Besides," I insist, "The crazies are gone right? It's safe now. I'd love to go with Elizabeth, really."

Elizabeth quickly glances at me, a sharpness behind that vivid green, and her mother notices. She furrows her brows for a moment, but then just tells us to be back within the hour. I thank her, and we finally leave the house.

The moment the front door closes behind us, Elizabeth turns on me.

"Listen," She says stoutly, "Don't think that just because you're coming means I want you here."

"O- okay," I blurt, momentarily stunned.

"Because I don't." She utters, and resumes walking normally, leaving me to try and catch up. Walking hurts but I don't complain. The fresh cool air feels amazing on my burns.

"Can I ask you a question?" I say, struggling to keep up with her pace.

She says nothing so I continue.

"Do you know where Griffin is?"

I expect her to ask who Griffin is, but she just nods,

"Went home after we told him you and Calla would be fine a couple of nights ago." She tells me. We turn left and into the short stretch of forest between here and the town. I can see a car down the road zipping through the trees and heading our way. The car is swerving left and right all over the place, like whoever driving is not in his or her right mind. I guess all the crazies *haven't* left.

"Let's walk there on the beach," Elizabeth suggests, and I happily agree. I don't know how many of the people on the island are exactly trustworthy in a situation like this.

We veer off the road and walk for a minute before emerging out onto the cold beach. It occurs to me that somewhere, on that part of the beach Griffin and I had been on, the body still lies hidden in the brush. I ignore that thought though. It's not going anywhere.

"So, Elizabeth… Liz? Do people call you Liz?" I ask, tilting my head and looking at her inquisitively.

"My friends call me Liz," She says, nodding, "Call me Elizabeth."

"Okay," I mutter, raising my eyebrows and turning towards the ocean. The always present mist is beautiful as it hovers over the dark blue Pacific Ocean. My shoes sinking into the sand reassures me somehow. I may not have my house anymore, but this island is more of a home to me than any building could have been. I'm familiar with its dark sand and beautiful waters lapping against the shore.

The sounds, smells, and even feel of the breeze pressing against my face comfort me beyond words. I let out an audible sigh, which Elizabeth ignores.

"We're about halfway there," She says, "I take this way a lot, I don't like walking on the road."

I nod. I've always walked along the road, but I can see how a stroll on the beach is more enjoyable. Besides, her house is closer to the shores than our house. It just makes sense to take this route instead, and I'm surprised I hadn't done this more often.

We continue along the beach until I come across an odd sight. Something I was definitely not expecting. A wedding, right on the beach, is being held. Rows of foldable chairs in the sand, and a path of flowers leading up to the arbor.

"I wonder why they're having a wedding. Now, of all times." I wonder aloud, because it is a bit out of place.

Elizabeth shrugs. "Back in the main part of town, everything's almost normal. I mean, sure, there's panic. But that fire was just 'a house that burnt down on the other side of the island'. Besides, if they really believe everything's going to end or something, better get married now, right?"

"Still," I say, examining the rows of chairs, split in the middle providing the row for the couple to walk down, "who'd come? With all the crazy people around and all. Why are they even acting up, chances are that we'll be back at mainland before long."

Elizabeth rolls her eyes dramatically. "Why do you think? They're taking advantage of all the lack of government. Rules. The three firefighters on the island are all we've got. Plus, who knows what's happening up in El Arnica. They sent someone up there to see but they haven't come back yet."

El Arnica. The only other town on Eastrock Island. Eastrock Island is split into two different sections by a small channel of ocean straight through the middle, East to West. The two land masses are so close though, that they're considered the same island. I have been to El Arnica twice, and I don't even remember what for. El Arnica is much larger than Bluehill Ridge, but there isn't much travel between the two towns. Sure, there's a bridge across the water so they could potentially come here every day for work or whatnot, but they don't really like our town, and I guess we don't really like them either. Tourist competition or something.

"Yeah," I say, "Almost forgot about them"

We pass the wedding completely, which looks like it's just about to start.

"Almost there," Elizabeth mutters under her breath. We walk for another five minutes before climbing a steep path scaling the seaside cliff. Soon enough, we emerge right beside Main Street.

"Perfect, you really know that trail." I comment. She just glares at me before walking to the road that leads into Main Street. I don't get why she dislikes me so much, but this isn't exactly the time to ask.

The supermarket is just about the biggest store in town. A large rectangle with rows upon rows of groceries inside. Tall ceilings and vast interiors, it's pretty much your average mainland Target or Walmart. They almost built one of those here, but it was voted against because it'd harm local businesses.

"Luke," Elizabeth mutters under her breath. Suddenly, I look around. We're here, and I'd been zoning out. "Let's go."

I am pulled from my thoughts, and follow her into the store.

• • •

Apparently, Elizabeth had only been right to a certain point. Things had deemed more muted in town, yes, but inside the supermarket, everything has been plunged into utter chaos. People are running around the picked over shelves, grabbing groceries and sprinting away. Merchandise is scattered all over the tile floor, and for some reason, the overhead lights of the store flicker on and off. Creepy sounds shudder from above.

"I was just here two days ago," Elizabeth says numbly, "Everything was normal. C'mon, let's get what we need and go."

The first place we head to is the refrigerated area, holding the foods that are on the list Elizabeth's mother had given us. The blinking lights of the glass-doored refrigerators give off an eerie feeling, and suddenly I want to get out of this store as soon as possible.

"Okay," I say, "What's on the list? I know there was carrots..."

We walk down the row, stepping over the boxes of frozen and refrigerated goods scattered across the floor. I scan the area and find the vegetables, quickly grabbing carrots and heading back for Elizabeth.

After maybe ten minutes, we have all the refrigerated goods in a plastic bag I'd found strewn across the cold floor.

"What else?" I ask.

"Flour, cornstarch, milk," She lists off, "And a bunch of canned goods if there are any left." So we head over to the aisle that's supposed to hold the groceries we're looking for. Instead, we find almost nothing. Across the store, all that is left of the canned goods are a few scattered canisters of peas and pickles. I scoop what's left into the bag and stoop down on my knees to check under the shelves.

That's when I hear it.

It's almost like a ringing in my ears. A silent, low screech that slowly is escalating to a higher pitch. It's so quiet though, that I almost shrug it off as my ears playing tricks on me.

But no… something's definitely there. I pull my head out from under the shelf and look around. Elizabeth seems to have noticed the noise too, and is looking around to see what the quiet sound could be. Where is it coming from? It is raspy and constant and… tinny. As if it is coming from inside a thin metal tube.

The noise sparks some memory in the back of my mind, but I can't place it.

My thoughts are interrupted when the entire store is plunged into darkness.

At first, it is as if I am blinded by the darkness, squinting and feeling my way around. The constant hum of electricity dies.

96

The noises of people running around and shouting have vanished, replaced by utter silence.

Except for the noise. The noise echoing around the giant store. Bouncing off of the walls.

Where is it? *What* is it?

My eyes are trying to adjust, but I can barely make out anything.

"Elizabeth?" I whisper, "Are you there?"

"Of course I'm here," She whispers back, "what do we do?"

I stay silent, listening to the sounds… a chattering has now been added to the growing orchestra of foreboding sounds. Quiet, persistent chattering. The chattering is also echoed and tinny, which suggests it's coming from the same source as the silent screeches. Yes, screeches, as in plural, because the entire store seems to be filled with the quiet noise. The quiet noise that seems too loud in my ears.

My heart is thumping against my ribcage as if it's a rabid animal trying to escape metal bars. I strain my ears to pick up all of the noise. All of the screeching and chattering…

But in an instant, it is all gone, leaving me to the darkness.

We wait a moment.

"Elizabeth?" I whisper so quietly I barely even say it.

"One second Luke,"

"Elizabeth." I repeat.

"I said one second, I think I have a flashlight on my phone…" She whispers back much too loudly.

"Elizabeth, I'm not sure that's such a good idea."

"Here," She mutters. She quickly activates the flashlight function on her phone and shines the glow down the aisle we'd just walked through.

Instantly, as if triggered by the light, something comes flying down from the dark above and lands in the beam of light, a black blur of motion.

I shriek in surprise and stumble back. Elizabeth has fallen and her flashlight/phone has slipped from her grip, skittering across the floor. In that instant, I can make out a flash of red mouth and teeth on whatever is in front of us before it is plunged into darkness once again.

I hear it breathe. I hear the heavy, wet breaths of the thing in front of me. I hear Elizabeth dragging herself away from the thing, and can actually see her at the edge of the light beam her phone is still giving off, because it landed with the camera facing upwards.

Chattering fills my ears and turns my bones to ice. A low screeching sound emits from whatever had just…

My eyes follow the light casted by Elizabeth's phone, which is aiming straight up. The light is so illuminating, that it shines a cold glow up on the high ceiling of the store.

Black… things, crawl along the square ventilation shafts, emerging from the holes they'd torn in them.

"Holy-" I begin to whisper.

And it's as if a bomb goes off.

The dark shapes rain down around me, hitting the cold tile with loud rhythmic thumps. I see them. I can actually see them detaching from the ceiling and falling to the ground in blurs of darkness.

I hear the screeching and chattering louder than ever before and I want to cover my ears to drown out the noise. I reach my arm out to try and find Elizabeth in the darkness, but all the light is extinguished when something lands on the phone and audibly shatters it.

Chattering is coming from all around, like bone hitting bone, or teeth chattering together.

There's another sound too. Something more muted than the low quiet screeches and chattering though. There are small pulses of sound every now and then. They sound like a small noise made in the back of one's throat.

"Elizabeth," I groan.

Something grabs my arm and I jump. A hand quickly cups over my mouth and I realize it's Elizabeth.

The sounds, the horrible sounds emanating around me are too much.

The first scream echoes from across the store, and I can hear the chattering stop as the… whatever they are, listen intently. When a second scream calls out, there's the loud sound of them all making their way towards the noise. I can hear them skittering across the tile and slithering over the aisles, knocking them down.

And that's when the rest of the noises join the chorus. Yells and shouts of terror, people trying to get away from the things echo loudly through the otherwise quiet store.

I stand quickly and find Elizabeth. She grabs my hand and I help her up to her feet. I also pull my phone out, not turning the flashlight on, but having it ready if I need to.

We sprint down the aisle, running as fast as we can, tripping over the objects scattered across the floor as the shouts and screams ring through the building. It is when I run straight into a shelf that I give into the temptation of the light. I can see other flashlights around the store too, bobbing up and down as people run.

What is happening? What are these… things? Surely some sort of animal… maybe? I mean, I did see a red mouth with teeth. And all those noises definitely sounded organic.

I flip my flashlight on and wave it around cautiously. We are in the pharmacy area. I can see that the shelf I'd run into was a spinney shelf that used to be filled with prescription glasses, but is now smashed against the hard floor. We turn away and to our right, and I can see the glow of the entrance. I'm about to run that way when I see someone sprinting into the light, about to reach freedom, when a dark shape falls from above and lands on the man, knocking him to the ground.

I jump back and run the opposite direction, shining the light above us and onto the ceiling to see if there are any… *creatures* hanging from the ventilation shafts as they had before. So far, I don't see anything, but I can just make out the tears in the large, squared, metal ventilation tubes that the creatures had torn, evidently to crawl through.

I can see the flickering red glow of the emergency exit door to the far back of the store. It stands out brightly in the almost tangible darkness.

Not knowing what is lurking just beyond the beam of my light is unsettling. I feel as blind as when it had been pitch-black. Echoes of scuttling come from behind me every now and then, but I am determined to not look back. Elizabeth is just behind me, probably going slowly as to not run into any shelves. We are now in the row of the exit door, and I slow. I hear some sort of sound ahead of us, between me and that red glow of freedom. A scraping, maybe against the tile, coming from the row to the right.

No, no we are so close, we have to keep going.

"Elizabeth." I say in a dead calm voice, "Walk over here. Slowly."

She does so, her quiet tread can be heard until it stops right next to me. I don't look at her though.

"Keep your eyes forward." I say quietly. I slowly grab her arm and we walk down the aisle. "I'm going to turn the light off now."

She says nothing so I pull my phone up and extinguish the light. Now, the only thing I can see is the eerie maroon glow at the end of the store. There is more scuttling behind us, but I don't look. I can't look. They might sense it.

Low, excruciatingly quiet screeches come from somewhere near. Above maybe? I keep my eyes on the red glow of the exit sign. One step at a time, proceeding quietly as possible.

"Something's behind us." Elizabeth whispers. There's a breathy panic in her voice hidden by a mask of calm.

"It's okay." I say. "Keep going."

"Luke," She whispers, "It's above us too,"

"Keep walking." I say, taking deep breaths. I shiver all over my body.

"I can hear it," She chokes. In the dim light of the exit sign, her face is a mask of terror. Mine must look the same way.

I grasp her arm tighter to the point I'm sure it must hurt but she says nothing.

"They're behind us." She says. "I know it. I hear them."

Low, deep, wet breaths can be heard behind us. Maybe fifteen feet back. I can't tell. And chattering. Always a silent chattering as they scuttle across the tile floor of the store.

"Look forward." I say, my eyes can now make out the door beneath the red "EXIT" sign. "We're almost there, promise."

"Luke," She says, and she must be quietly crying. I just hope it stays quiet. Her arm jumps around in my trembling hand as she shivers. Her voice drops so quiet it's almost haunting…

"I can hear them… I- I can hear them…"

And then, in the dim red glow of the exit sign, I see her slowly turn her head around. Around to face the things behind us.

In a split second, I hear the creature launch itself off of the tile. I tighten my grip on Elizabeth's arm and yank her out of the way just as a dark blur flies past us, right where Elizabeth had just been. She screams and we fall to the ground. Something across the aisle had slid into the shelves and caused them to collapse into the next aisle. It waves long shadowed limbs around as it struggles to get back up, a haunting shape dancing in the dark, maroon gleam.

"Let's go!" I scream at Elizabeth and I help her get off of the floor. I can hear things behind us, down the aisle sprinting at full speed, knocking down shelves and screeching loudly now.

I run for the exit door, Elizabeth by my side. A few more feet. We're almost there. Almost…

I slam into the door and press my full body weight into the bar that causes it to open. It bursts outward and instantly a deafening alarm begins to ring through the store. Elizabeth runs through the exit and I turn around to shut the door.

A black mass of shadows push down the aisle, like a tidal wave of indistinguishable tar-black bodies surging forward. The blinking red alarm lights in the store illuminate the shadows, long-limbed, slim-bodied, before I slam the door shut with all the might I can muster.

Elizabeth stands, stunned, staring at the shaking door.

"C'mon Elizabeth!" I shriek and grab her hand. She shakes her head and seems to come to her senses. She slaps my hand away and sprints forward faster than I was running. My burns are on fire, but I catch up as quickly as I can.

"To the beach," I gasp. She nods and we turn onto Main Street. Behind us, there are the terrifying sounds of the low screeching and haunting chattering. We ignore it and sprint as fast as our legs will allow.

The fog overhead is so thick that everything has taken on a dark gray color. We run down the road until Elizabeth spots the turnoff to the side. She takes a sharp turn and we veer onto the steep sandy path that clings tightly to the side of the cliff.

When we reach the bottom, she suddenly spins around to face me.

"We go straight home, lock the doors, and hide, okay?" She tells me, and it's not a question.

"Let's go." I say, and she nods before we take off across the beach. Are the things following us? I'm not sure, until I hear low, silent screeching coming from behind.

"Faster," I whisper as we run. If it's even possible, we speed up.

Running on the sand is difficult, but I can only hope it's just as difficult for the animals behind us. Animals? Creatures? Monsters?

We sprint along the foot of the cliff for maybe two to three minutes before we come to the wedding. Way down the beach, I can see the rows of chairs and the marrying couple under the white arch covered in flowers. Fancy white-clothed tables line the back of the area, steaming with heaping servings of food.

I don't care what Elizabeth thinks. This is literally the worst time to have a wedding. Ever.

I run towards them, waving my hands and screaming my head off; "Run! Run!"

Elizabeth is right beside me, doing the exact same thing. When we're finally within earshot over the loud waves of the ocean, I can see some people turn their heads to face us.

Then, a black blur of a shape flies off of the top of the steep cliff and down into the midst of the wedding. First, there is confusion. Then, screams erupt as everyone runs from the thing, which I can't see clearly because it is crouched down low behind a table.

Screams, lots of them, are coming from the wedding as the people run from their seats. There is another steep trail up the cliff, and everyone is scrambling over themselves to reach it. I'm guessing that's our best chance too.

"Elizabeth, c'mon." I say and we turn to the left, to the side of the cliff. We finally reach the path after the first wave of people. Everyone is desperately scrambling up the sandy trail, which I think leads to a parking lot.

The man in front of me, dressed in a black tuxedo, goes flying off of the high trail as a *screeching* blur hurls itself at him from above. I keep running. Everyone around is frantic, slipping and sliding on the steep trail, pushing forward and causing other people to nearly fall off of the cliff.

A large black shape leaps down from the ledge above our heads and lands in the thick group of people behind us. Some are knocked right off the trail, plummeting down to the sand below. I am frozen, horrified, but some of the people below seem to be alive, groaning in the sand. I keep going.

We still push forward. Up the trail. Up the cliff. Another man, formally dressed but not in a tuxedo like the other man, is swept away by the black shape two people ahead. He falls down and down and down, until he's unlucky enough to miss the beach by mere feet, and land in a patch of rocks. Everyone behind him surges back and Elizabeth and I are almost pushed off of the edge.

Elizabeth grabs my arm and violently pulls me forward, passing the rest of the people. When we reach the parking lot above, everything has already been thrown into chaos. Waves of people running to their cars, being picked off by the... *things*.

I see one person hop in their car and start the engine, only for one of the things to jump right on top and send the vehicle plummeting down to the sand below. There's a loud *bang* and smoke begins to pour upwards, reaching for the sky.

A deafening screech erupts to my left and I jolt my head around to try and place it. A creature stands, right there, roaring, its head facing the sky. I am desperate to make out the details, but before I can, something tosses me to the side. I feel the impact in my left ribcage and I go flying through the air. I land in a tall scratchy brush at the edge of the cliff. I squeeze my eyes shut as the sharp ends of the twigs dig into every inch of my body.

And then Elizabeth is there, reaching her hand into the bush, helping me climb out. The first car I've seen leave pulls out of the parking lot and screeches onto the road.

To our right, a man runs up to his car and unlocks the door. He sticks the key into the ignition and is about to hop in before a swift black creature launches itself towards him. It slams into his chest and they both fall out of sight over the edge.

"Eliza-" I begin, coughing.

"I know," She says, "Let's go."

We run to the car. She jumps through the open door into the driver's seat, and unlocks the passenger door for me. I yank it open harshly and jam myself inside.

"Go!"

"Yeah, I know-" She says, and is about to call me a foul name when the car thumps. I feel the bottom of the metal frame scrape against the pavement as the car bounces up and down on its suspension.

"What is that." She whispers.

"Go!" I yell. She turns the key and the engine roars to life. She shifts it into reverse and slams on the pedal. We jolt backwards and something flies off of the top of the car, landing on the pavement in front of us.

Elizabeth makes a two-point turn and rotates us around so we're facing the exit of the parking lot. People are running around in front of us, in the way.

"Move!" Elizabeth shrieks, leaning on the horn. "Move! Move! Move!"

A dark shape flies down from above, landing right in front of us.

"Run it over!" I shriek. "Go!"

Elizabeth puts the car in drive and slams her foot down on the pedal. Once again, I feel the jolting sensation as the car jumps forward. This time though, we aren't going anywhere. The dark creature has it's, I don't know what to call them… claws? Hands? On the hood of the car.

And now is when I finally get a good look at the thing right in front of me.

A slim, bony, pitch-black body. Rough, leathery, almost scaly skin is stretched tightly over its skeleton. If I had the mind to, I could count every rib on its body. The arms, slim and muscular, look much too long. The wrist is too far up the arm, and the long fingers end in sharp claws.

You could say it's humanoid, with four limbs, a torso, and head, but the similarity ends there. The hind legs, also long and muscular, have weird joints, like a dog's or goat's hind legs. They look like they are built to run quickly and leap high. Attached to its back, are maybe five to seven long, thin, curvy spines that twitch back and forth, left and right, with no apparent rhyme or reason. They slant back, facing behind the creature, and they remind me a little of keratin shark fins.

The most haunting feature though, is the face. Or, rather, where the face should be, because instead, there is smooth, featureless, tar skin stretched over the head.

I hear the engine of the car violently rev up as Elizabeth tries to run the thing over, but it is pushing back, and I hear the rear wheels screeching against the pavement. Thick, rubber smoke is coming from behind as Elizabeth fights against the creature. In a moment, the only thing I can see of it is the dark shadow amongst the haze of light smoke.

And then the car lurches backward. We are pushed out of the pungent cloud and back into the parking lot.

The monster moves closer to the windshield and opens its jaws.

Okay, I take back what I said about the blank face being the most haunting part.

To open its mouth, the front of the entire head swings upwards, as if on fleshy hinges, exposing the sets of razor-sharp teeth, going back in rows all the way to the dark hole that is the throat inside its head.

Red saliva sprays on the windshield as it shrieks at us. More of a roar, really.

Then, it positions its legs in a bracing stance, and pushes the car in one huge burst of strength. Our vehicle slides backwards, despite Elizabeth practically standing on the brakes.

And then there's a swooping sensation as everything I see through the windshield tips and spins. I can see the edge of the cliff above us, getting farther and farther away...

'We're falling' I think.

And then the back of the car hits the ground. Instantly, my body screams in agony. Everything hurts, all at once. I cry out and I feel that feeling in my stomach again. The cliff's edge, which is right in front of me but still straight up (The car must be standing on its back end.) Starts tipping away. The top of our car begins to fall down to the ground, only upside down.

Since neither Elizabeth or I have our seatbelts on, we go flying into the bottom of the car, then are slammed back down onto the hard ceiling as the top of the car hits the ground.

A loud, long groan escapes my lips as my body tries to process the pain it's going through. My bones feel like they are compressed together from the impact.

"Elizabeth?" I croak, and then break into a coughing fit. The rough landing had stolen the air from my lungs and I'm struggling to regain it.

"Yeah," She groans. "I'm fine."

"Are you hurt?" I ask, struggling to regain my voice.

"I said I'm fine." She says, rubbing her head groggily. Screams echo through the broken windows of the vehicle.

A face appears in the driver's side window beside Elizabeth. The face is panicked.

"Are you okay?" The woman says, frantically looking around. Her face is contorted in fear, but there's something more behind those eyes. Something I don't like. "Here,"

She reaches her hand in, evidently to grasp Elizabeth's. Elizabeth pulls her hand away from the woman's.

"We're okay, really."

The woman reaches in again, and tries to grasp Elizabeth's hand. She gets ahold of it, but Elizabeth jerks her hand away once again. "We can do fine on our own."

The woman grunts in frustration. "Fine then, open the back door."

"No," I say, finally seeing the woman's intentions clearly. She thinks it is safer inside the car wreck.

"Open it, now." She says calmly. She then reaches into the vehicle and feels around for the unlocking button. Should we just let her in?

"No!" Elizabeth shouts, apparently also seeing what the woman is trying to do.

"Let me in!" The woman shrieks. She begins banging on the door, rattling it on its damaged hinges. Then suddenly, before either Elizabeth or I can react, she is jerked backwards and away from the car, sliding away in the sand, a sleek black creature ahold of her foot. She violently thrashes, clawing at the ground but it's no use.

Elizabeth shrieks and backs away from the crushed door.

"Out! Out!" She yells, panicking. I oblige and kick the damaged car door beside me out. I quickly scuttle onto the sand and help Elizabeth climb over the upside-down ceiling of the car.

We stand, slightly crouched, behind the overturned vehicle taking account of all our injuries. I know there is no time to spare but I need to know exactly what to worry about.

I am covered in scrapes from the bushes, bruises from the car's fall, and bloody from a few spots broken glass had penetrated my skin. I pick out a few shards and take a look at Elizabeth.

She holds her arm at an awkward angle, but it doesn't look broken, thank goodness. She also has glass shards sticking out of her arms, which she had used to crawl across the ceiling of the car.

"We need to go," I say. Elizabeth nods, and it's as if the volume around me is turned up once again.

Screams and shouts of panic ring out as people run across the beach, attempting to reach their cars up on top of the sea cliff.

Despite all my injuries, I feel the urgent need to run. Run far and away.

I grab Elizabeth's good arm and am about to pull her into a sprint when she points out something on the side of the cliff.

"You're a genius-" I gasp, already changing direction.

The large, metal, circular drainage pipe sticks out like a sore thumb on the face of the coastal cliff. Elizabeth and I do the best we can to quickly scramble up the rocky surface and into the large tube. Just as we make it inside, I can feel the start of cold raindrops splattering on my skin.

We climb into the space, and lean up against the side of the pipe, catching our breaths.

"Some errand." I say after a moment of breathing heavily.

Elizabeth just shakes her head.

"What do you think they are?" I say, picking another crystal shard from my calf.

Elizabeth just shakes her head again.

I slouch down to the bottom of the pipe. Maybe we could just rest here- but no, it is much too close to the beach. Much too close to those… things. The clear image of what they exactly are is already fading from my brain.

They had been quadrupedal, right? The nerd side of me struggles to make a reappearance as I try to classify the creature. To no avail.

"We," I pant again, "We need to keep going. Get back to your house and warn the others.

Elizabeth nods and crawls over to the edge of the pipe, poking her head out to observe what is going on outside.

"What's happening?" I ask.

"I don't know." She says slowly, "I think they're above us, at the parking lot. The only things down here are… people."

"Dead or alive?" I ask, knowing the answer already.

Elizabeth just shakes her head. "Let's find the other end of this pipe and get back home."

Painfully, I raise myself to a crawling position and we make our way down the progressively dark tube. It is much longer than I could have thought, and a thin stream of water has begun to flow through it, most likely due to the new downpour outside.

It isn't long before we can't see anything at all, only able to feel the cold edges of the pipe and hear only our own heavy breaths.

"There has to be an external end." Elizabeth says. "The water only started flowing after the rain started."

I notice she neglects to point out the danger of the entire pipe flooding, or that the end could be a completely vertical pipe, which would mean we'd have to turn around.

Not that it matters, but the pipe we are in seems to be much longer than every other drainage pipe I've seen. I don't care though. The longer we crawl, the farther away we get from that beach.

Unless one of those things are in here with us, which would be even worse.

I put the thought out of my head.

"Here," She sighs, "I can see the end. It goes up but it's not too steep. I think we can crawl up that no problem."

It turns out that Elizabeth is right. The exit is very close, and the only thing between us and daylight is an upturned slope about as steep as a playground slide. We are easily able to scale it, using the corkscrew design of the tube as footholds. When we finally emerge, I simply stand for a moment, appreciating the fresh air, and now heavy torrents of rain pounding against my body.

We had emerged right beside a road, at a slightly lower level for the drainage pipe to run under the pavement.

The icy cold spray of rain against my face invigorates me, filling my body with a new energy. The swelling bruises covering my body are doused into relief as I am soaked with the water pouring from thick, dark, silky gray storm clouds above...

I pound my fist as hard as I possibly can against the wooden front-door of Elizabeth's house.

Doubling over, both Elizabeth and I press our hands to our knees and try to banish the painful rawness in our lungs. I haven't run that fast, much less in that kind of weather, for years. Not to mention the soreness acquired from the car crash, *and* my burns.

Adrenaline works magic I guess. My side absolutely cramps, and I can tell Elizabeth's does too because once she catches her breath, she presses her right hand to her stomach, keeping her left one to her chest, wrist limp.

"Putting your arms over your head helps." I pant to her.

"What?" She says, exhaustedly turning to face me.

"Your cramps." I say, "Putting your arms over your head helps. Stretches the muscle or something, which is supposed to make it go away? That's just what my track and field coach told me at least."

She looks at me for a moment, as if I must be stupid, but just sighs and lifts her arms above her head. I rap my knuckle against the wood once again, and this time, the door opens instantly.

"Oh, I'm sorry dears, didn't mean to make you wait, it's just that…" Mrs. Harlow begins, but stops dead as she gets a clear look at the two of us. "Oh my dear me! What's happened to you two?"

"Tell you later mom," Elizabeth whispers. "Let us in."

"What?" Mrs. Harlow stutters.

"Please Mrs. Harlow," I say, glancing behind me. If the creatures had a mind to, they could be here in minutes. It just depends on how determined they are. "Let us in. We'll explain everything."

Mrs. Harlow takes a shaky look at the two of us before stepping aside and letting us in. Elizabeth seems to worry her even more when she locks the door once we're inside.

After doing so, she nods to me and I set about the house, closing curtains over windows and locking all back doors.

"My!" I can hear Mrs. Harlow shout shakily, "Elizabeth! Why are you putting the table in front of the door? How do you expect us to get out?"

I jump on Elizabeth's idea and move the large heavy couch in front of the back door. In doing so, I pass the kitchen, where my mother, Calla, and Elizabeth's younger sister Maddie Harlow sit.

"Elizabeth!" I call, "Do you guys have a basement?"

"Yeah!" She shouts back, "Entrance is under the stairs!"

"Mom," I say, "Calla, Maddie, get down in the basement."

"What?" My mother protests, "Luke Anderson. Why would you-"

"I'll explain, promise." I say, "Just get down in the basement."

I finish covering every entrance to the house, even going to the extent of checking their small attic, which features a large circular window. I cover it up with boxes, which the attic is in abundance of.

Together, Elizabeth and I do one last check of the house, turning all the lights off, before creeping down into their basement. I shut the door quietly, flip off the single overhead light, and place my index finger over my lips, but then remember no one can see anything.

"Shhh," I whisper.

It turned out that the creatures from the supermarket either were too lazy to come all the way over to Elizabeth's house, or they'd just had enough violence for the day, because everything seemed peaceful after the scene at the beach. Nothing whatsoever tried to barge into The Harlow's house, not even Mr. Harlow, who was supposed to be home from work with the newspaper company.

"He works up in El Arnica, you see," Elizabeth had told me, convinced that her father is still alive. Unfortunately, the topic brings up thoughts of *my* father. What is happening back at the mainland? Is he searching for us? A way to get across the ocean and to Eastrock Island? Or is he unaware that anything has gone amiss? He's not scheduled to arrive home for another week and a half.

I push the thought aside. *Our* current predicament seems to be more pressing.

After thoroughly explaining what had happened back at the supermarket and on the beach to our mothers, (And convincing them we aren't fibbing) We decide it is safe enough to go above ground and poke our heads around. There is no food in the basement, so we want to search around and see what happened. Maybe even see what is going on in town, because despite what they tell us, neither Elizabeth nor I seem to think our mothers are completely convinced of what has happened.

Really though, until the moment we stepped out of the basement, I wasn't very keen on searching town. It wasn't until my mother brought Griffin up that I feel a surge of determination.

"And what ever happened to your friend? What was his name… Griffin?"

"Griffin?" I say suddenly, jerking my head up. I feel a wave of guilt pass over me. I hadn't even given Griffin a thought. I know for a fact that he lives much closer to town than any of us, might as well live on Main Street. I know this because he'd mentioned it on our drive up to the lab.

To the lab…

I am suddenly stuck with inspiration. Dangerous, risky, inspiration, but it could potentially result in an abundance of information I'm desperate to get my hands on. That doctor there had seemed awfully suspicious when we'd shown him the sample. The two events, the body and the creatures, they have to be connected somehow.

I'd bet he knows something. Something we don't.

Griffin. Griffin first, then we can discuss the lab.

"I-" I stumble over my words, "I don't know. I haven't seen him since-"

"The fire." Elizabeth finishes, before looking at me and rolling her eyes. "You know where he lives too, right?"

"I think I know the general area." I mumble. "We'd only met a couple of days ago."

A couple of days ago? Could it really only have been-what, two, three days? I don't know what he thinks of me, but we've already gone through far more than I have with any of my other "friends". Is that what he is now? A friend? Yet, I hadn't given him a single thought since I'd conked out the day of the fire. You'd think that he'd merit at least a concerned thought, me knowing that he lives right in the middle of the whole mess I was running from.

My brain seems to be playing tricks on me though, so maybe I'm not fully to blame. For some reason, I must keep reminding myself that the creatures back at the beach were real. *Are* real, because my brain doesn't seem to want to process it. It keeps changing the story, twisting the features of the monsters. Luckily, though, I know what I saw, my eyes had not deceived me. Plus, Elizabeth had been there.

"Okay then," Mrs. Harlow says worriedly, grasping Maddie's hand firmly, "Lead the way."

"Are you sure some of you don't want to stay back at the house? With the little ones?" Elizabeth asks, and I have to admire her bravery. The thought hadn't occurred to me, I had only been glad we finally had adults with us. Her willingness to head back out, alone, is quite admirable.

"No." My mother says harshly, then switches to a more mellow tone. "No. I am sorry. We are not splitting up again. We are staying together, okay?"

I nod. "It would probably be safest to avoid the main road, but going through the forest would take much longer, especially with the littles."

"We could take the car." Mrs. Harlow suggests hopefully. "That way we'd be sheltered and much quicker."

"Yes, but then we'd be trading that for stealth." Elizabeth mutters, "Especially because the motor is diesel. Dad took the hybrid, so the car we'd be driving would be much louder."

I see the skepticism in the adults' eyes again, of our entire story, but they push it aside quickly and nod. "Through the forest it is."

● ● ●

The trek through the forest was nowhere near as bad as I thought it would be. I had expected the whole place to be swarming with the creatures, lurking just out of sight. But instead, I find tranquil silence. I am also pleasantly surprised by how quickly the little ones were able to move over the knobbly roots and slippery pine needles.

The forest. The forest is so beautiful that I can almost forget the circumstances we are trekking through it under. The low heavy mist seems to blanket the forest floor, dampening all it touches. A cloud of water droplets that moistens everywhere it lands. Gentle, quiet birdsong reaches us through the twisted branches and thick pine needles overhead. I think I can hear a woodpecker pecking away at a tree somewhere.

It is almost as if I am transported to a different world, where pain and suffering are merely words with no meaning behind them. A world washed clean of danger and violence, consisting of the tranquil forest around me, insisting I take in it's beauty with all senses. The curvy, damp wooden branches. The

120

quiet birdsong wafting through the misty, cool air. The smell of nature so fresh in my nose.

All is interrupted when we come to the edge of the forest. It is as if we are literally jolted back to reality.

Main Street, which lies a mere 150 feet in front of us, is the exact opposite of the forest. Stop lights and signs lie smashed on the abandoned paved streets. Shop windows shattered and empty, allowing the cool air to waft freely into the buildings. Broken- things are scattered everywhere. Merchandise. Restaurant plates. Glass, of course, is all over the place. Puddles in the road reflect back up on the abandoned buildings.

The most haunting developments, however, are the few bodies that lie strewn across the area.

I can see any doubt of what we have said has happened leave the two adult's eyes.

The bodies seem to be untouched though, as if they have dropped dead of their own accord. Well, that's how they seem, at least, until we check a couple of them and realize all of the bodies have at least a small to medium size wound. Not big enough to kill them, almost definitely, and not enough blood around to justify their death as bleeding out. As if they'd caught their arm on barbed wire and gotten scraped.

And I am reminded. Reminded of the body on the beach Griffin and I had found. It had had a similar wound on its side. We'd almost taken a blood sample straight from there, but there was too much of a chance of it being infected or some such.

"Where from here?" My mother whispers dismally, turning away from one of the bodies, and I recognize this one. Jane Winter, a woman who would always come to my mother's cafe in the evening for a warm cup of cocoa. Surely my mother must recognize her, they had chatted often. Mrs. Jane. Gone. Ended, forever. I had spoken to her too, on multiple occasions. She'd always smile at me brightly and tell me "What a nice young man" I'm turning out to be. Gone.

"I, uh…" I look back up to everyone else. "I think they live down the street a bit, above the little Coffee shop his dad owns."

We continue on, the little one's hands grasped tightly in their mother's, Elizabeth and I walking slightly ahead. I want nothing more than to be closer to my mom right now, but if Elizabeth isn't, then I'm not either. I don't know why this is important but I feel it is. To me, anyways.

We walk down the empty street, which echoes of the days when nothing had gone wrong. Happy shoppers and tourists visiting for the summer and fall months, sometimes bundled up in jackets and sweaters, arms full of souvenirs, gift bags, and warm fudge from the candy shop at the edge of town.

"Here," I say, stepping onto the sidewalk that lines the road. Small weeds poke out of the crevices in the cement. "I think he said he lives here."

"Do we knock?" Elizabeth whispers, and suddenly I am much too aware that all the creatures couldn't have just disappeared. That they're hiding somewhere, waiting.

"The window's broken," I say, "We can get in quietly."

"Who'll go?" Mrs. Harlow whimpers. "Surely not just you two."

"We'll be fine." I tell both parents, "It looks like they're all gone now anyway."

"You will not be going alone." My mother says sternly, then passes Calla's hand to Mrs. Harlow, "Now you stay here. We'll be right back, okay?"

Calla nods, still silent. I don't know how much she'd talked when Elizabeth and I were in town, but she seems to have lost her usual backtalk and sass. Maybe she'll be back to normal when her burns heal.

My mother rolls up her sleeves and clambers into the window before either Elizabeth or I can even react. She reaches her hands back out for Elizabeth.

The inside of the house is an absolute mess, everything scattered across the hard tile floor. It seems that the complete bottom level is devoted to the coffee shop, because little round tables stand around the place, some overturned. There is a counter with a fancy light up menu above the cashiers, flickering in the dank silence.

"Griffin?" I whisper into the emptiness. "Griffin? Where are you?"

"He's probably upstairs." Elizabeth mutters, "That's where he lives, right?"

"Yeah," I say slowly, because I don't remember mentioning that to anybody.

I sweep aside the shattered glass on the counter, and climb up and over, landing on the other side. Everything on this side is broken too, but no one is hiding under the counter's ledge.

"Just checking,"

My mother makes a hand gesture for me to get back over to the stairs. I do, as silently as possible, and join Elizabeth and my mother at the foot of the stairway.

"Griffin!" I whisper as loudly as possible, calling up to the second floor. "You there?"

And then suddenly, a shadow rounds the top of the ledge.

"Who are you." Says a voice. The shadow slowly begins to walk down the staircase.

"Griffin?" Elizabeth whispers.

"*WHO ARE YOU?*" The voice roars suddenly, and I almost stumble backwards in surprise. The shadow advances down to the bottom of the stairs, and a faint light illuminates its features.

The figure, a human, holds a long metal pipe in their hands, their face almost unrecognizable due to the layer of dirt, grime, and blood that covers it.

"Griffin-" I gasp, stepping forward subconsciously. "You're okay! I was so worried that-"

"Go away." He says in a dead quiet voice.

"What? We came here to-"

"You came here too late." He says, wiping his nose with his sleeve. "Now go away."

"What do you mean we came her too late?" Elizabeth insists, "You're still here! Dirty and scraped up, but you're alive! Griffin, you're alive!"

"You're too late." He repeats coldly, and I notice the tear-streaks down his face for the first time. "He's dead."

"Who's dead?" My mother asks in a gentle voice, "We're here to help you, Griffin."

"The only other person he lives with." Elizabeth says, tears filling her own eyes now, "Oh Griffin, I'm so sorry."

And suddenly Griffin launches himself at Elizabeth, wrapping his arms around her and burying his face into her shoulder. I am so unprepared for and shocked by this move that for a moment, I am speechless.

The metal rod drops from his hands, landing with a clank on the tile.

"He's gone." Griffin sobs, his words muffled by Elizabeth's shirt. "He- he's gone."

Elizabeth hugs him back and he sobs again into her shoulder, sniffling madly.

I give Elizabeth a questioning glance.

"He lives... lived with his father." Elizabeth whispers to my mother and I, "His mom died a while back."

"You guys know each other?" I ask, too stunned to realize how insensitive it sounds.

"It's a long story," Elizabeth sighs, and sniffles madly, attempting a smile, "Well, not really. School."

"Oh," I say, "School."

"Yeah." She says.

Suddenly, Griffin jerks his head back and away from Elizabeth. "I- I'm so sorry. I didn't mean to- to-"

"It's alright." She says and squeezes him in one last hug before letting him go completely. "You're with us now. You're safe."

I refrain from adding that he is nowhere near safe, even with us. In fact, by joining our group, he is accepting that he will be traveling with a bigger target. If I were him, though, I'd rather be with us than alone.

And then he turns to me.

"Hey."

"Hey." I say. "I know this may not be the best time for you, but we have a plan."

We go outside and I tell him everything. Everything since I passed out at the fire. How we'd stayed at the Harlow's house after our own home had burnt to ashes. How Elizabeth and I had gone to the supermarket to find it an absolute mess, and then being attacked by the things that had killed his father. The wedding scene on the beach. The car, falling, and then Elizabeth and I hiding in that drainage pipe. Finally, I get to how and why we'd ended up here, and our plan to get to the lab. When the moms ask about it, I shrug it off by saying if anyone knows what those creatures are, it'll be them. They obviously think it's a dumb assumption, and I know what a stretch it is, but what am I supposed to say? Besides, I tell them it'll be safer there anyways, away from the action. It's a secure facility. And just like that, the conversation continued.

"...But we didn't want to take the car because it would be too loud and draw too much attention to ourselves." Elizabeth finishes.

"Well you should've." Griffin says flatly, then, realizing how blunt he sounded, evaluates. "All of the things left ages ago. Here one moment, gone the next. Like a wave in the ocean. I don't think they're coming back."

"Why not?" I ask, curious as to why he thinks it'd be safe enough to drive a car. In the dead silence of the town, it'd be like a beacon to anyone or anything that cares.

"After they'd left, everyone started milling around the place, helping other people. I thought it was dumb and stayed inside, but the things didn't come back, and then everyone hopped into their cars and left. As far as I could tell they were safe. At least the ones who were still alive"

"Huh," Elizabeth grunts, "But the lab is all the way to the middle of the lower island area. What if they moved there instead."

"It's possible," Griffin shrugs half-heartedly, "But they looked like they were headed towards the east of the island, not the north."

"At any rate," Mrs. Harlow interrupts timidly, "We didn't bring the car, so that's that."

Griffin shakes his head and gestures for them to follow. It turns out that there is a large garage at the very back of the coffee shop, holding a medium sized silver car. It would be a tight fit for all of us, but I assume we could do it.

"Well," Elizabeth sighs, louder than the quiet whisper we'd all taken on, "If they don't come to the sound of the Garage, I think the car might be worth a shot."

Griffin grabs the keys off of a rack and slumps into the driver's seat, gesturing for everyone else to get in. For some reason, I end up in the passenger seat, which really isn't fair because there are two adults in the car, but I guess they both have the little ones and the back seat is safer anyways. Elizabeth, who sits in the back row as well, comforts her little sister.

"You have your license?" I say doubtfully. Griffin just grunts, and I'm not sure if that's supposed to mean yes or no.

The engine of the car roars to life and the car silently backs out of the garage. We make a two-point turn and head onto Main Street. The joyful vibrant baskets of flowers that had hung from the lampposts sit smashed and dejected on the sidewalk curb. Broken glass crunches under the car's tires, and I hope we don't get unlucky and have a tire pop.

We go slowly down the silent street, leaving the engine at a low purr. My hand sits on the locked door handle, trembling slightly. Nothing seems to have taken notice of us yet, but we haven't even made it to the forest.

"Griffin," I whisper, even though we're in an enclosed car, "I'd go faster."

He looks back at Elizabeth and the adults to see what they think of the suggestion. They just slowly nod and keep their eyes out the windows. The car picks up its pace and the engine takes on a higher, louder pitch. Within a minute, we are out of Main Street.

For some reason, I take a deep satisfying breath of relief, when really, in reality, I should *start* holding it. We knew relatively well that Main Street had been empty, but the forest holds far more unknowns than what we are leaving behind.

"You remember how to get there, right?" I ask him.

"Yeah." He sniffs silently, making a left and rounding the side of the cliff that looks down on the ocean. Half the town lies atop this cliff, which I assume gives it the *ridge* in its name. I have no Idea where the *Bluehill* came from. Possibly the last name of someone important? I wouldn't know, I'm not into history much.

"Have you two been to the lab before?" My mother asks.

"Yeah, remember?" I tell her, "When we borrowed your car."

"Oh yes," She exhales, taking on a comprehending look, "For school. I remember. So much happened that day, with the fire…"

More than the fire though. The body, sitting on the beach. The first of many. Or is it? How many other bodies lie hidden on the island? With that many of those creatures, there could be tens, even hundreds already. It all depends on how well they've been hiding, if at all.

"I didn't even know they had a lab on the island." Mrs. Harlow mutters quietly, looking out at the damp forest beyond the road.

"Yeah." I say, "It's farther inland. And I don't even think it's a proper lab, they're more focused on robotics than biology."

"Then why are we going there?" My mother asks.

I sigh. I owe her of all people an explanation anyway. I tell everyone the whole story. The body. Stealing the syringe. Taking the blood and noticing it's blackish color, then bringing it to the lab. I tell them about the man's odd line of questioning, and the even more odd test results. When I'm finally finished, my mother is too stunned to even reprimand me for keeping the story of the body from her, stealing the syringe from the school, and even taking the car to the lab under *false* pretenses.

"Why didn't you tell me?" She says finally.

"With the fire and everything…" I mumble guilty, running my hand over the growing number of injuries I have acquired. Man, these bruises and scrapes really hurt. I guess I should be thankful they're as minor as they are. "I never really thought of it. Everything's been happening so fast, one thing after another."

My mother doesn't even respond, just sits silently, trying to process everything I have just said.

"Are we going to die?" Calla says suddenly, shocking both my mother and I, "Are we going to die like those people back in town?"

"Oh, no Calla." My mother says firmly and wraps Calla in a tight embrace. "We're all together now. All safe and together."

Calla shrinks back into our mother's arms and closes her eyes. My mother shoots me a worried look. Calla never talks like this, always acting above it all. Too cool. The thought of her annoying attitude almost makes me smile. The fact that it's gone, though, makes it all the worse. In a matter of days, I have already started to miss what I had thought her most annoying quality is.

"We're here," Griffin announces suddenly, and I see we are pulling into the large empty parking lot. He pulls into one of the many open parking spaces, then flips the key off and the engine dies. I notice he keeps it inside the car.

I shoot him a questioning look.

"If we need to make a quick escape." He says blankly, "I don't want to have to fish around in my pocket."

"Good idea." I nod. "How's it look outside?"

Everyone peers through the windows, examining the building and the forest lining the parking lot. Everything seems still. The automatic glass doors of the otherwise plain building stand unused and silent. I can see that the inside is lit with luminescent lights.

"I think it's safe." I whisper to the silent car. "You think those *things* even came here?"

"Sure doesn't look like it." Griffin whispers back, "Looks just like the day we came here. Do you think we can go in?"

"I guess."

I slowly pull the car door handle towards me, and there's a click as the lock disengages. I hold my breath as I push the door out, keeping my hand on the handle just in case I need to slam it shut. Nothing happens, and the quiet sound of breeze and birdsong fills the inside of the car.

Slowly, one by one, everyone opens their doors and carefully steps onto the black pavement. I consider leaving the doors open in case we need to get back in the car quickly, but I decide against it just in case one of those things wanted to crawl inside. I silently shut my door, and everyone else follows in my lead.

Elizabeth, though as far as I know she's never been here before, leads, gesturing for all of us to follow her. Slowly and cautiously, we do, our heads swiveling left and right scanning for danger. When we approach the sliding doors, they open smoothly, allowing us inside the lab.

I look towards the front desk, but it stands forgotten and empty. Once we're all inside, the sliding doors glide shut once again, closing us off from the outside, and silencing the breeze and birdsong.

There is a heavy metal door at the other end of the room.

"Should we go through there?" Elizabeth asks, gesturing towards it.

"Last time we were here, they just came out to greet us." I tell her. Elizabeth, being Elizabeth, marches over to the door anyway and tries the handle. It doesn't budge. She pushes against it. It still doesn't move an inch. She even throws her weight against the door, which clunks loudly with the impact, but still goes nowhere.

Elizabeth loudly grunts in frustration and walks back over to us. At first, her expression is neutral, or somewhat frustrated, but then her eye catches something outside, through the sliding glass doors behind us.

Noticing that *she* noticed something, we all turn around and gaze out the glass doors, searching for anything out of the norm. Bushes rustling, trees swaying, but nothing out of the ordinary catches my eye.

"What." I whisper to Elizabeth, "What did you see?"

"Near the power line," She murmurs, "At the base of the pole."

I sweep my eyes across the parking lot, and spot the place she's indicating. A wooden power-line stands tall and proud at the edge of the parking lot. Behind it, the forest is so thick that anything could be hidden just out of sight, behind a thick bush or a large redwood trunk.

"I don't see anything," Griffin mutters.

"It was probably just the wind," Elizabeth whispers back, dead still, "But I could have sworn I saw something."

I strain my eyes. What had she seen? What is there?

Suddenly, a large hand from behind clamps down hard on my mouth. I give a muffled yelp of surprise and try to whirl my head around to see what is happening. I can't. The person with their hand over my mouth is restricting my body movement, pressing hard and firmly. I claw at the hand, raking my fingernails down the skin. By now, everyone around me has noticed all my movements and, shocked looks on their faces, move to free me from the attacker.

Finally, after a silent struggle, the person behind me lets go and falls to the ground. I whirl my head around to see- the scientist. The dark-skinned man Griffin and I had talked with last time we were here.

"What are you doing!?" I yell, breaking the silence. The man's eyes widen at the noise I'm making. He shakes his head vigorously. Scrambling to his feet, he gestures slowly towards the heavy metal door that Elizabeth was trying to get through. Evidently, he'd just come out from the room behind.

"Do we go through the door?" Elizabeth whispers, beginning to regain her bearings, wiping the look of shock off of her face.

"Yes." The scientist whispers back, and gestures more urgently for us to go through the door.

"But why?" I ask.

"Did you just hear all the sound you just made? And all the motion that could be seen through the glass door." The scientist gasps exasperatedly.

"But they're not here," My mother tells him, "We just walked through the parking lot."

"They're here alright." The man whispers, and nods towards the glass doors which are now behind us. I turn and see that Elizabeth was indeed right. The bushes are most definitely moving, and a pitch-black figure is beginning to emerge through the greenery.

As soon as we see it, we hurry through the door. The last thing I catch before it shuts, is the black creature slowly slinking onto the pavement, and curiously circling our car.

Then the entrance seals against the world, and we are encased in inky darkness. I can hear multiple locks engaging, and then the man saying; "Okay, you can turn the lights on."

I am temporarily blinded by the bright fluorescent lights that fill the small room we are crammed into. It is about the size of a large walk-in closet. Enough space for us all to fit, but not comfortably.

The area we are in seems to be similar to some sort of… airlock or decontamination chamber. Two doors. One on the side that we just closed, and one opposite to it. I expect the second set of doors to open, but they don't.

"Sorry about the small space." He says, and gives the unopened doors a bitter look. I notice that three other scientists are in the room, all doing the same thing. "But the higher-ups won't let us into the that area of the lab."

I am curious as to why, but I have a much more pressing question on my mind.

"What are those things?" I ask, cutting to the chase. "You seemed to know something we didn't about that blood." I press the man before he can even say a word more.

"What? That's what you came for?" He says seriously, "What makes you think we'd know?"

"Because I'd be willing to bet they're connected. Somehow. Strange things don't usually happen on this island Mr.-"

"Robert Wilkins."

"Mr. Wilkins then." I say, "Why are these things here?"

Mr. Wilkins looks at me as if deciding something, before dropping his eyes down to the floor and sighing. "You're asking the wrong guy. We don't know much, but here's what we do. We don't know where all of them came from but-"

"Great." Elizabeth rolls her eyes, "So you don't know anything about them, do you?"

"But," Mr. Wilkins continues indignantly, "We have our theories. Odd things have been happening at the lab recently."

"Like what?" Griffin asks, momentarily dropping the expression of hopelessness he'd been wearing since we'd picked him up. We're all eager for answers.

"There's been a classified project at the lab." Mr. Wilkins says, "Some important people just came here one day and dropped off the thing. They wanted our lab to study it, whatever it was. We didn't see it. Us lower-level scientists have been restricted from the bio lab ever since. We aren't supposed to know anything, but sometimes we can hear sounds out of the eastern side of the building."

"Sounds?" I ask.

"Sounds like... Chattering and heavy breathing. Like they have- had something alive but not human in there. We thought it might be some kind of animal? They're studying it. But I could swear there was only one. We only heard one. Yet, there could be hundreds out there, we've already seen at least twenty. The two things have got be connected somehow, but I just can't figure out *how*."

"Did anything else strange happen here at the lab?" Elizabeth presses, like a brick wall slowly advancing.

"Yes." One of the other scientists says, "My friend, Tobias, he's in higher level research; he went missing just a few days ago. No one's seen him since work then, not even his family. He stopped video calling them even before the service went out"

"Why won't they let you in?" Mrs. Harlow asks shakily.

"I don't know," Mr. Wilkins says, "But we haven't been permitted inside the biology lab for weeks. The door is always locked, and it's like they live in there. They never come out, even to go home. That's why Tobias could only *video call* his wife and kids. Now, they're locking themselves in, protecting themselves from the things outside… unfortunately at our expense."

I think for a moment. "Is there another way into the biology sector? You tested that blood for us somehow."

"I specialize in the robotics lab." He says, and I detect a hint of bitterness in his voice, "At first I graduated college with a biology major, but the scientists here deemed me- unfit to help with the task at hand."

"Okay," I say, seeing the predicament but not how he tested the blood. "How'd you test the blood?"

"I-" He stutters, a guilty look playing across his face, "I snuck into the biology lab through the back door. I was curious as to why the blood was so dark, and, why not admit it, a bit bitter about my exclusion from the project. I have dedicated my life to science after all, why shouldn't I be a part of it? When I went in there, my suspicion increased because, well…"

"Well what?" Elizabeth says, crossing her arms.

"There were identical blood samples in there too."

PART TWO:
THE BLOOD

CHAPTER
NINE

I grip the crowbar firmly in my hands, feeling the cold metal against my warm, sweaty skin.

The rest of the robotics lab is too dark to see, but I run my hand down tables blindly, looking for other potential weapons. I'd taken the chance of crossing the lobby over to the door of the robotics lab to get weapons. Anything really, that could help protect us from the creatures outside.

By the time I leave, I have a crowbar, screwdriver, and long metal tube that could pass for a club. I poke my head out the door, before darting out into the lobby.

My mother had wanted to go with me, but as soon as she let go of Calla she started screaming and crying, so she had stayed back. Everyone else, Elizabeth, Griffin, Maddie, Mrs. Harlow, and the lab scientists had wanted to go as well, but I slipped out of the door before they could protest any longer.

I hop on my tiptoes through the lobby, my eyes on the empty parking lot through the sliding glass doors. Everyone had considered just staying in the robotics lab instead, but it only had a flimsy wooden door that wouldn't even keep out a dog if it had to.

140

I knock three times on the metal door, and it swings open, revealing everyone standing inside. I scamper in and they shut the door behind me with an audible bang, the lock loudly engaging.

"Okay, listen," Mr. Wilkins says, a determined glint in his eyes, "The back entrance of the biology lab is at the very north of the building. It's a large metal door that should be locked. We have a key for that door if we need it, which I'm guessing we will-"

"Absolutely not." My mother says suddenly.

"Pardon?" Mr. Wilkins says.

"Absolutely not!" My mother repeats. "I have been silent for quite some time, but I am putting my foot down here. We are not sending these children, *our* children, out to be slaughtered!"

"Ma'am," Says another scientist, with dark brown hair and skin as pale as a sheet of paper, "We'll be with them. The only reason you can't go is because of your daught-"

"I am fully aware." My mother says firmly, nodding at Mrs. Harlow. For the first time, I see Mrs. Harlow's eyes light up in an intense, fiery glow.

"I agree." She says in a tone that suggests she will not be persuaded otherwise, "Sending our children out there would be absolutely wrong."

"Mom!" Elizabeth protests, but Mrs. Harlow shushes her.

"If you really want to get into that lab, you can do it yourselves. We, on the other hand, are waiting for the attack to pass, and then we will be on our way."

"But-" Mr. Wilkins begins.

"Our children will not be leaving this room and that is final." My mother says. My mouth hangs wide open. What? What is she thinking? Elizabeth, Griffin, And I have the most experience with those monsters out of anyone in the room. How could she possibly think getting to that lab wouldn't be worth it? We could open the doors and let them in! We'd be safer inside the secure biology lab. With all those other scientists selfishly locking themselves in there, I'd bet they even have food.

She checks her watch. "At any rate, it will be getting dark now. We'll sleep here and leave in the morning." Apparently, she senses our protests coming, because she adds, "No arguing."

"Boys on that side, girls on this side." Mrs. Harlow says, pointing at opposite sides of the tiny room. I sigh, thinking splitting everybody up is ridiculous, but decide I don't have the energy to say so. I head over to the designated area for the boys. Unfortunately, there are more males than there are females. They are also much larger, and smellier. Also, unfortunately, I am right next to the door that heads out into the lobby, which means I can hear everything going on through the crack at the bottom. The eerie silence somehow scares me more than if there had been noise. To top it all off, Griffin is on the other side of the four scientists, which means no hushed conversations can take place.

I adjust my body, trying to get comfortable on the hard tile floor. Eventually, despite the loud snoring and deep breaths of the others, I fall asleep.

●　●　●

"Luke,"

I groan, already drifting back into unconsciousness

"Luke," A voice says quietly. "Luke, get up."

I swat the empty air above me, trying to shoo whatever is disturbing me. Or, at least I thought it was empty air. When my hand connects with something, there's a gasp.

"What is wrong with you?" Elizabeth says in a harsh whisper, "Get up you useless piece of-"

"I'm up, I'm up," I say, sitting up abruptly, "Sorry. Is it morning-"

I am silenced by Elizabeth's hand over my mouth. I stare at her through the darkness, slightly panicking.

"Be quiet." She whispers.

I look around the room, registering all the sleeping bodies on the cramped floor. I pull Elizabeth's hand away from my mouth, and listen. The only thing there is the occasional snore.

"What time is it?" I whisper to her as quietly as possible. I can almost sense the eye roll in response.

"It's one in the morning."

"Geez," I breathe, "Why-"

I am stopped by the sight of another form behind Elizabeth. At first, I am alarmed, but then I recognize it. Griffin stands behind her. I can mainly tell because of that sideways slant he always stands with. I assume it has something to do with his limp. For a moment, I think hard, trying to put a reason to why they'd be waking me up at this hour.

And then it clicks. They plan to sneak out and go over to the lab. Just us three, before the sun even rises. They want to do it secretly, so that the rest of the group can't prevent us from doing so.

"I'm in." Before they even say a word.

Elizabeth nods and hands me a weapon. The heavy metal crowbar drops into my hands. I heft it up and down a bit, getting a sense of its balance once again.

"Okay," Elizabeth whispers, "the outside is crawling with them. I opened the door a minute ago and saw one poking around in the parking lot. I have no idea how many there are, but there has to be at least ten. I might have seen a couple picking around the bushes, I don't know."

"How do they see?" Griffin asks suddenly, "They don't have eyes. Maybe they can't see us."

"Yes, but from what we can tell they don't have a nose or ears either, and they have to be seeing people somehow. They can't just be roaming around, running into trees and such. They're coordinated. Somehow, on some level, they can see." I assess.

"Okay." Elizabeth says, "I'm not exactly sure where the other entrance is, but we know it's around back, and we know we need a key."

"In the desk." Griffin says at once, "When Luke and I were here, I saw Mr. Wilkins take a key from the front desk. I am assuming the key we need is in there."

"Okay." I say, "Key in the desk. That's not hard."

Elizabeth and Griffin nod vigorously, hoping against hope that it's true. That we can do this without any problem.

"Are we sure about this?" Griffin says warily.

"Getting cold feet Griffin?" Elizabeth says tauntingly.

Griffin crosses his arms indignantly, marches over to the metal door I'd slept next to, and pushes it open. It swings into the dark, silent lobby with a much too loud squeal. I whip my head around to see if any of the adults had heard, but they are all sleeping soundly.

Griffin scampers over to the front desk on the tips of his toes. He reaches it and opens one of the drawers. He frowns and opens the one below it. Glancing up, he begins opening all of the drawers in the desk. Getting frantic now, he checks the small cup that holds pencils, but comes up empty handed. He searches quickly around in the drawers again, and only calms down when he emerges with a key ring holding 15 or so keys.

Elizabeth scoffs and gestures something at Griffin. He doesn't understand.

Elizabeth pinches her shirt, and then gestures at Griffin. He cocks his head and grabs his own shirt, pretending to pull it off. Elizabeth shakes her head, frustrated. she gestures again, and this time, Griffin must get it because he grabs his sweatshirt and Elizabeth nods. He takes the sweatshirt off and hands it to Elizabeth along with the keys. Gently, she places the keys in the sweatshirt and wraps it up in the thick fabric.

Smart. Just in case they *can* hear us. If we needed to run, both Griffin and I's pockets are too loose, which would allow the keys to jingle. Elizabeth's pants have no pockets, which she seems to be quite peeved about.

In the moonlight, I see her tuck the sweatshirt under her arm and head towards the sliding doors. The motion sensors detect her and slide open. The breeze wafts in, running across my face and effectively refreshing my senses and ridding me of my sleepy sluggishness. All the night sounds, crickets, owls, and trees swaying in the breeze fill my ears once again.

We all wait, seeing if the sliding doors had attracted any attention, but nothing presents itself. I step out onto the pavement of the parking lot, the others following my lead. We stand there for a bit, surveying the moonlit parking lot. We all cringe when the sliding glass doors shut behind us.

"Okay, let's go then." Elizabeth whispers so quietly, I can barely hear. I follow, and Griffin does as well, though I notice he hesitates before walking along with the rest of us. For some reason, his limp is more noticeable than ever. Maybe because he's scared, though I don't know what even causes the limp in the first place. Earlier though, I couldn't even tell he had one. Sometimes he can be good at hiding it.

The night sounds around us fill my ears, the buzzing of the crickets like static in the background. I can barely see where I'm going as we round the corner of the lab. There is a small sidewalk here, but it's so cracked and damaged that I'd be less likely to trip over a rock or stick. Still, though, it's quieter than breaking branches and crunching pine needles, so we continue on.

Elizabeth ahead, Griffin behind, I feel pretty sheltered, though I feel bad about it because it's at the expense of them.

The *clamp clamp clamp* of our shoes on the cement scares me, especially whenever one of us stumbles and makes more noise than even the constant grasshoppers up in the bushes.

When I'm not looking down at the floor making sure I won't trip, my eyes are on the tree line above us fixed to the slight hill that lines the building. I wait, shaking, for dark shapes to emerge from the bushes or the inky darkness beyond, deep within the heavily wooded forest.

Still though, it's not until I hear the chattering that I begin to really worry.

Clacking sounds are emitting from just out of sight. Low, haunting, wet screeches can barely be heard over the chatter of the crickets. As if to make the situation worse, a cloud moves over the moon, shadowing us in temporary darkness.

"Up here," Says Elizabeth quietly, "I think I feel a door."

What are they doing, just beyond our line of vision. Watching? Waiting for us to make a sudden move? And how are they making that horrible chattering noise? Like teeth clacking together as a person shivers. So is that it? Their teeth? From the outside, they don't seem to have a mouth, but I certainly remember that large, red, toothy maw through the front windshield of that car, just before we'd plummeted off the ledge.

I rub my bruises at the thought, wondering if that might have caused a mild concussion.

"Yes, this is the door he was talking about," Elizabeth whispers, unwrapping the keys.

Griffin is looking at the forest just like I am, but when a bush starts wavering, he presses up against the wall of the building. I gulp, wanting to follow in his lead. Elizabeth is trying the second key now.

"C'mon, c'mon," She's muttering. Her hands shake so violently that it takes her a few seconds to even pick out the third key.

Something in the shadows is moving. Maybe it's just a swaying bush.

"Stupid keys," Elizabeth spits, struggling to pick the next one and try it out.

Something is sliding through the bush and out into the open, still shrouded in darkness as it stalks closer. I hear sniffing, which must mean it has a nose somewhere.

A key slides into the door and I hear a click as Elizabeth twists it with her jerking hands. She gasps a little as it pushes inward, squealing slightly. The shape is still moving closer and closer.

"Inside," I hiss, "Get inside."

Griffin is just staring, petrified at the sight of the moving shape as it nears us. I have to actually grab his upper arm and jerk him towards the door before he even realizes it's open.

I slip the door shut behind us right as I see the creature slither down the steep hill, and crawl to the cement on all fours.

As the door slams shut it produces a loud echoing clang through the pitch-black room we now stand in.

"Is this the lab?" Elizabeth whispers after a moment.

"Must be." I whisper back, "You wouldn't know it. Suppose there's a light?"

I hear Griffin shuffle around for a moment, then run his hand along the wall, evidently looking for a light switch. I join him, disliking the darkness as much as he does, running my hand along the textured paint.

"Careful," He says, his voice echoing through the dark lab, "There's spilt water up here. Slippery."

Completely blind, I blink, willing myself to see something, anything, but to no avail. The darkness almost seems to mute my other senses as well, like it's trying to drown me in my own helplessness.

I do step in the little puddle of water, and follow Griffin farther down the wall. Well, I follow him until I slam right into his back.

"Oh- Sorry!" I say, backing up into another solid object. Elizabeth gives a grunt and stumbles back a bit. "Sorry!"

"It's fine," She mutters and reaches her arms out. When her palms hit my upper back, she uses me as a point of reference as she makes her way around me.

"I think I found it," Griffin says, feeling the wall, "It's a switch anyway. Should I flip it?"

"Do it," Elizabeth says, her voice echoing through dark space, "I'm sick of being blind."

I can hear the flick of the switch. At first, nothing happens, but then lights dangling from the ceiling flicker to life, making little electric pulses as they do so. Even once they're on though, they flicker on and off occasionally.

The lab, to say the least, is in complete disarray. Microscopes litter the floor, shattered glass and vials lie broken on the tile. Chairs are overturned, cupboards open, and medical equipment is strewn everywhere. The room is empty.

Elizabeth gasps loudly, looking over my shoulder. I whirl my head around, expecting the door to be wide open, a creature standing in the light of the lab, but the metal door still sits firmly in place.

"What?" I say, alarmed, but then I see it. The water we stepped in isn't water. It's blood.

Red shoe-prints follow us to the spots we are at right now.

"What?" I gasp, stumbling away from the red.

"It must be from one of the scientists," Elizabeth says darkly, looking around. Griffin stares at the small puddle, his eyes blank.

"You think they're still here?" I ask, "I thought the biology sector of this lab was small, but I guess I was wrong. See that hallway? Who knows how far it goes after that turn."

"Should we search?" Elizabeth asks weakly.

"Are you crazy?" Griffin says, shuddering, "Or do you just have a death wish? See that blood?"

I stare at the maroon puddle. A light dust has settled on the liquid and the tile around it, but it still hasn't dried up. Blood, when exposed to air, will clot and dry up. This blood has been here for a while, but is still liquid. It's also dark, just like the sample from the beach. Why?

"I say we poke around a bit here before we search for them." I suggest, and then think of something to add. "And I also say we keep the door leading to the adults, and our sisters, shut. For all we know one of those things is in here with us. We'll make sure the area is safe while looking for the scientists."

They both nod.

And with that, in the flickering glow coming from the hanging lights above, we all begin to search. We rummage through the trashed lab, opening cupboards and boxes, tossing aside useless items and tools that I can't even name. It isn't for another five to ten minutes that we find anything remotely useful.

"Guys," Elizabeth says, staring at a paper and waving us over, "here's something."

Interested, I scramble over to her, abandoning the empty cupboard behind me and trying to ignore the blood on the other side of the room. I approach her, and Griffin does too, looking over her shoulder at the paper. She apparently finishes reading it and hands it to me, deep in thought.

I take the paper from her and begin to read, Griffin looking over *my* shoulder now. The paper is handwritten, the scraggly handwriting suggesting the writer was in a hurry. It speaks of strange blood samples from what is labeled as "the project". It says the DNA and chromosomes have "degenerated" from the blood, and that it's turning a disturbing black color. At the end, it also mentions that all their previous research is being transferred onto paper, for fear of losing power.

"Losing power?" I ask, because the blood sample bit isn't news to us anyways, "Why would they be worried about that?"

"This must have been written after the internet gave out, when the shipments didn't come." Elizabeth says, then gives it some thought, "Maybe they were worried about whatever is running the power on this island. Probably some big generator, eating up gasoline. What happens when that runs out?"

"Generator?" Griffin asks skeptically, looking around as if he thought it'd be in here.

"I don't know," Elizabeth shrugs, "I'm not an expert, but we don't have a power plant here."

"Yeah, but-" Griffin stops, "The computers! We can check the computers! The power hasn't gone out yet, and with any luck there are offline files too."

I'm about to jump up and agree, calling him a genius, when a thought strikes me.

"Griffin, that's a great idea," I say apologetically, "But... um"

I point over to one of the counters. On it, lies a smashed computer, broken bits of electronics poking out from deep crack in the screen. I feel bad when Griffin's shoulders drop pathetically. I pat his back, and look to Elizabeth to see what she thinks of it all, but she has her nose buried in another paper.

"What is it?" I ask her, the lights above flickering out, then turning back on again.

"It's an experiment record." She says. "They were testing on rats."

"Doing what?" I ask, forgetting the computer predicament and growing interested once again.

"You know how the scientists said they heard a creature? Something not human?"

"Yeah?"

"They refer to it here," She says, "only briefly, and they call it a *cancer*. That might be what those things outside are."

"What were the experiments on the rats?" Griffin asks, apparently eager to get whatever is coming, over with. Elizabeth shoots him *the eye*.

"I was getting to that part." She says, "Apparently, it had a habit of licking its... *Claws*, then scratching the walls, so they decided to test why it did that. They sent a pig into the cage to see what it would do-"

"That's horrible," Griffin says, cringing.

"Yeah, I know, now shut it," Elizabeth says, and then shoulders him to take some of the sharpness from the blow, "it says the thing just scratched the pig, and let it be. The thing just fell asleep, and stayed in the cage until it died, but the, uh, *cancer* didn't eat it. Unable to safely remove the pig, they..."

Elizabeth flips to the next page.

"They somehow got it to scratch a rat instead, then extracted the rat out of the cage to run tests on it. They say its blood started degenerating into the black stuff we were just talking about. That's the end of this paper."

Is there another one? For the next day?" I ask, frantically searching.

Griffin is the one to find the next paper.

"It says," He starts, but then stumbles on the first sentence, his face taking on a look of surprise.

"What?" I say, grabbing at the paper. He holds firm to it though, and keeps reading.

"It says the next day they came back, the rat had no face." he gives me a significant look, "It says no bloody mess or anything. Just, it was gone. Smooth skin under normal, if new looking fur. It was dead though, and they say it was because some sort of virus overtook its body, and it wasn't able to handle it. They had cameras though, and monitors. It mentions that before it died, it fell asleep. Like a hibernation."

Griffin flips the page.

"They studied the, uhm, *cancer's* saliva and found that it had traces of all sorts of stuff like propofol, pentobarbital, and thiopental. It also says it acts like cancer to any blood exposed to it. I guess that's why they call it a cancer." He grunts.

"What are those chemicals?" Elizabeth looks to me. Great. Apparently they know about the whole "science geek" thing.

"I think those are the chemicals used to put you in a coma, though I'm not one-hundred percent sure- I'm more into biology than chemistry."

What is the purpose of all of it? The saliva acting like a cancer. The disappearance of the face. Let alone the obvious question of where the thing even came from? Some freak crossbreeding? *Aliens?* And how did there get to be so many of just one thing. Just one cancer in this lab somehow multiplied into…

Wait a minute. What are the two things animals will do anything to achieve? Number one, survival. Number two…

"Elizabeth," I say suddenly, "Is there a subject on that paper?"

She picks a paper up again and reads the top. "This one is under *Saliva*"

"Look for a paper under the label *Reproduction*." I tell them, already looking around. She and Griffin seem to notice I think I'm onto something and begin searching vigorously. Griffin holds up a single paper, only filled quarter way with hurriedly scribbled words. At the top, the word "reproduction" is scrawled in hasty handwriting.

He hands it to me and I read like my life depends on it.

"They have no reproductive organs." I tell them, "None. So then how do you think they reproduce…"

"cancer…" Elizabeth nods slowly, "What if its saliva is really it's way of reproducing…"

"It only scratches it's victims." I say, "Remember? In Main Street? All those bodies with only a scratch…"

"And that body on the beach," Griffin says, visibly putting it together.

"Why the coma though?" Asks Elizabeth. "Why put it to sleep?"

"It must put the person into more of a hibernation." I say, having a strong sense of all the puzzle pieces coming together. "It needs the new host's energy to make it go through the change. So, it can't kill it, but it can't let the host use up its energy on its own either."

"Then why the death?" Elizabeth says suddenly, "The rat died. The pig died. All those people on Main Street... Well, we didn't really touch them, did we."

"The rat..." I say, thinking hard to try and piece the puzzle together, hoping for the full picture. "The rat must have been too small for the cancer to spread through. Its virus just ran right through it and killed it in the process."

"And the pig?" Griffin asks, his face slightly green but he's keeping it together so far."

"The pig." I say, "It was larger than the rat, but maybe it wasn't the right body type. You saw the cancers out on the beach and at Main Street. They were somewhat humanoid. Four limbs, a head and a torso."

"We have- no, *we are* the resources we they need to spread." Elizabeth says darkly, "It's like Goldilocks."

"So..." Griffin says slowly, "if we get scratched, we turn into one of them, like... what. A werewolf? A zombie?"

"No, I don't think so." Elizabeth says, rummaging through more papers. She grabs one and quickly scans the thing, holding a finger as in *'wait a sec'*. "Not according to what the scientists thought anyway. Think of it more as play-dough. We are about the right size and shape of play-dough they need, so they use us. We are just the materials. From there on, it's just them. I'd assume anyways, I don't want to think about the alternative."

"They're like seven, eight feet tall though," Griffin moans.

"They're also skinny as heck." Elizabeth adds, "You could count every bone in their body from the outside."

"So, first the face, then the blood, and then..."

"Then we're dead, and they're alive." Elizabeth says, a dark look crossing her face. "There's another thing, though, that we still don't know."

"What?" I ask, thinking all the puzzle pieces have finally fit together.

"Where are all of them coming from? They didn't have as many scientists here as there were cancers." She says, "And the attack just happened. Where would they have gotten at so many people?"

"That scientist," I say slowly, "The one they mentioned who went missing? Tobias? He could have been infected. And then, maybe he left and went to…"

There's only one other place on the island that could support a cancer population of that size.

"El Arnica." Griffin says, looking at Elizabeth, "They've already been there."

"It's okay, Elizabeth, it's okay!"

Elizabeth is in a state, panicking and rifling through the papers violently, ripping them occasionally in her search for any information to prove the claim true.

"My father is there!" She says harshly, "If he's alive I'm going to find him!"

I remember hearing that Elizabeth's father is in El Arnica for work at the moment. Griffin and I keep telling her it's fine, that he's going to be fine, but she is throwing all the papers around in search of who knows what.

"Elizabeth," Griffin says exasperatedly, a paper flying into his face as Elizabeth chucks it over her shoulder, "Elizabeth!"

She stops, looking up at Griffin and I.

"We're going to go find him." I say firmly. "Us three. Tonight."

She looks at me, trying to see if I'm serious. Am I joking? Would I really do that for her? She looks at Griffin, who nods solidly, though his face has gone a bit pale. El Arnica is all the way across the island, which is split in two by a channel of ocean. The only reason they're considered the same island is because the land masses are so close together, and had originally been conjoined before some sort of earthquake long ago. There is one bridge across the water, and that is the only way to get to the other side, unless of course you want to swim.

"Really?" Elizabeth almost whispers, staring at me with suspicious eyes.

"Of course." I say, "Our parents are as safe here as anywhere on the island, frankly."

Elizabeth's shoulders droop in deep relief, the papers dropping from her hands and sliding onto the floor. She slowly stands up and *hugs* both Griffin and I. Despite everything going on, I feel blood rush to my cheeks and butterflies stirring deep in the pit of my stomach.

"W-" I say awkwardly, "We can leave as soon as we check the rest of the lab."

She lets us go and steps away from us, clearing her throat. I look at Griffin and he looks back at me, his face red as a tomato.

"We uh," Elizabeth says, clearing her throat *again*, "Better get to it then."

We all split up, searching the entire biology sector of the lab, which is quite extensive. I'd always thought the biology part of the lab would be small, thanks to its primary focus on experimental robotics, but the biology lab has plenty of its own surprises. While searching the echoing hallways, I find a few smears of blood on the wall, broken glass everywhere, and even the containment cage they talked about in the papers. It reminds me of an interrogation room, because there is a rectangular window looking into another, heavily enforced room. The glass of the window is broken, and it seems to be extremely thick. From picking up a large piece, I also find that you can see through only one side of the crystal barrier.

Other than that, though, I find no scientists, or *cancers* anywhere in the building. I do find an exit door in some sort of office, and it's even open. I panic and quickly close it, looking around. I don't think any cancers have found this particular entrance just yet. Everyone, including the cancer, must have exited through this door. Or had all the scientists become cancers by the time they left the building, slowly hunted down through its dark corridors?

When I'm done, I head back into the main room we'd come from, to find Elizabeth and Griffin waiting for me. I join them and tell them what I had found. They tell me they found nothing of interest, and I am relieved that we now are sure nothing had gotten in through the door. We are indeed alone.

"Okay then," I subconsciously pick at my fingernails, procrastinating on having to go outside into the dark again. "I'll unlock the door everyone else is sleeping behind."

On the other side of the room, I find the door leading to the small room that everyone else is in. Once I'm certain it's the correct one, I unlock the door, but leave it closed, not wanting to wake anybody.

"Okay," I let out a long sigh, walking over to the light switch and picking my crowbar back up, "Let's go."

* * *

Elizabeth carefully shuts the door behind us. We're back outside, the darkness still as pressing as ever. For some reason, inside the lab I'd almost forgotten it's night outside. Now, though, in the inky darkness and eerie night noises, I'm reminded more than ever of how helpless and blind I am.

"Do you think they're gone?" I whisper.

"I think," Elizabeth whispers back, "The Main Street wave didn't last that long. They've probably moved on by now."

"Probably?" Griffin asks, gulping.

"Most likely." Elizabeth says, straightening up, "Either of you have your phones on you? Mine got broken in the store."

"Oh," Griffin pulls out his phone. The screen glows a faint white light as Griffin clicks the power button with his thumb. "Yeah, It's only fourteen percent though."

"Here," Elizabeth says, taking the phone from him and clicking on an application at the bottom of the display. A compass pops up on the screen. The arrow spins for a bit, but then points a certain direction, evidently north. "El Arnica is on the northern part of the island, right on the coast. We'll go north until we hit Pirate's Avenue-"

Pirate's Avenue is the nickname for the channel of water that splits the island in two.

"-and then follow it west until we hit the bridge. The GPS on the phone will drain the battery too fast, so the compass should work just fine." She finishes, visibly taking note of where north is, before turning the phone off to save battery life. Unfortunately, because we are conserving the phone's power, we are unable to use the flashlight either, but maybe that's for the best. A flashlight may draw too much attention.

I take the first step off of the sidewalk, my step crunching slightly on the layer of pine needles that covers the ground. The fog drifting across the forest floor is only barely visible in the moonlight reaching through the thick foliage above. The floor is damp, but thanks to the pine needles we leave no shoe-prints. This is for the best, so that the parents don't try and follow us very far.

A pang of guilt slams me in the gut, but I'm able to rid myself of it by thinking of *why* we're leaving. Mr. Harlow, Elizabeth's father, may already be dead. I hate to admit it, but we're hanging to a thread of hope. It disturbs me to think that one of those cancers from the supermarket could easily be him.

But, as long as there is any hope at all, we're going to search until something proves otherwise.

My father is off the island, both of Griffin's parents are dead, and now Elizabeth's father may be too. If there is any chance at all of one less tragedy, I'm on board.

Elizabeth pulls out Griffin's phone again and checks the compass. The arrow points slightly to the left now, so we follow in that direction. The light fades and she puts the device back into her pocket.

The damp tree trunks and moist air around me somehow lessens my fear. Despite everything that is happening, the island is still the same. It couldn't care less about what comes next. Whatever happens, it will continue on, the same as it is now, and always has been.

"Listen, "she says, stopping in her tracks. I still, freezing in place. I hear it, up in the trees. Branches rustle as something above stirs. Are the cancers like leopards? Will they scuttle up into a tree and wait for someone to pass by, jumping down and pouncing on them when they do?

The leaves above rustle again, and this time I'm able to actually see the branches moving.

Then, suddenly, something swoops out of the branch and straight towards us. We all yelp and stumble back. My hand instinctively latches onto Elizabeth's-

And the *owl* pulls up and into the sky again, hooting at the noise we'd made.

I make a nervous sound between a laugh and a sigh of relief. Elizabeth notices our hands, and pulls hers away quickly, avoiding my eyes. I hold my palm up in front of my face and flex my sweaty fingers. I think I squeezed her hand a bit too hard in my fright, she's examining her palm as well. My face, once again, becomes warm despite the cold air as blood rushes to my cheeks. I almost chuckle.

What is getting into me? I've known this girl for *one* day. *One!*

Has it really only been one day? It feels like forever. I've already gone through more with her than I have with any of my so-called friends from school.

She's made it clear she can barely put up with me, much less- what? Am I developing a crush? Now of all times? The word seems out of place in this thick, lifeless, freezing forest.

"Pull yourself together." I mutter to myself, and then make sure nobody has heard. They haven't, and are already beginning to walk on. I jog to catch up with them.

"Not a word." Elizabeth says to the both of us, and this time, I do laugh.

• • •

"This should do nicely for the night," Elizabeth says, not even bothering to whisper. If those things were around, they'd have already attacked us. "I don't suppose we have to set up a shelter or anything, but we do need food."

"Yeah," I say, suddenly realizing how hungry I am, "I haven't eaten since this morning. Well, I guess that'd be yesterday morning, since it's past midnight."

"I haven't eaten since the day before that's lunch." Griffin says, which shuts me up.

"I can set up some padding on the floor," Elizabeth volunteers. I'm about to say I can join her, when Griffin says he'd be happy to help her too.

"Great," She says, already gathering some soft, thick grass from some particularly overgrown areas, "Luke, you can get food, if you don't mind."

My mouth is open, my tongue still hanging with the offer to help with the beds, "Yeah. Sure, no problem. Except what am I supposed to get? Fish? There's bound to be a stream somewhere, right?"

"No," Elizabeth says, looking around the dark, cold forest and fidgeting absently. "Either of you have a knife?"

It so happens that Griffin always carries a pocketknife with him, telling both Elizabeth and I of the time his father had recommended it. His eyes turn a little glassy and he looks away, holding the knife out for Elizabeth. She takes it and pats his hand before walking over to the nearest tree.

"See," She tells me, placing the knife on the bark at a very steep angle, "You take your knife and slide it down the bark until you get to this pale stuff, you see?"

She slides the blade under the bark and skins the tree until reaching a layer of thin, very pale wood.

"Now, there are three layers," She continues, "First is the outer bark, the stuff you see when you just look at a tree. Then there's the core, which is what makes up the rest of the inside of the trunk. Now, in between the two layers…"

She peels away some bark on a different part of the tree, careful to go slightly shallower than her last cut…

"There's a softer layer just below the outer bark, and before the core. It's kind of soft, see?" Elizabeth gestures for me to feel it. I do, and the layer is very fibrous, and a bit spongier than in the core she'd shown me first.

"Elizabeth, "I begin, "Are you-"

"Liz." She says.

"What?" I say, confused.

"Liz." She repeats as she pushes her bright red, slightly wavy hair behind her ear, pulling the knife away from the tree "You can call me Liz."

"Oh," I say, dumbfounded., "Um…"

"Unless you don't want to," she says, looking back to the wood, cutting a square shape out of the softer inner bark and peeling it away from the tree.

"No-" I stammer, "No. It's just that, I thought you said only your friends call you Liz."

She looks at me. "Shut up and go get us some dinner. I'm starving."

As I go deeper into the woods while cutting strips of inner bark away from trees, I scout out the location around the campsite. I could have just harvested off of one tree, and trust me, I'd have rather stayed at camp, but I thought it would be a good idea to create a little mental map of what's around us. I am particularly desperate for a stream, because I'm extremely thirsty now that I think about it, but the closest I get to water is the fog hanging above the trees.

In no time, my hand is clenched full of inner bark strips, but I haven't dared try one in case there's a way we need to prepare them before they can be eaten safely. I finish carving a small piece of bark from a tree and head back towards camp. For a couple moments, I think I'm lost, but then find a bare spot on a tree where I'd harvested inner bark, and backtrack the way I'd come.

When I finally approach the camp, I see that the beds are already made of green grass pulled from an area just to the left of where I'm standing. Elizabeth and Griffin sit together, talking. I walk towards them, but stop at the sound of silent sobs wafting through the breeze.

"I'm really sorry about your father," Elizabeth says, "I truly am."

"I'm fine." Griffin almost whispers, raising his hand to his face, probably to wipe away a few grimy tears, "It's fine."

"You know, you don't have to hold it all in just because of Luke. We're all in this together."

"Luke is fine," He says, "But it's not- he's not-"

Griffin sighs, apparently unable to say what exactly I am.

"How can you not have a problem with traveling with him?" He accuses suddenly, his head perking up, "Do you remember how he was? How he probably still is?"

"Well, yes-" Elizabeth admits.

"Well then how can you not have a problem with him? How can we be friends with him, now of all times?"

"I-" Elizabeth stutters, "He's different when he's not around them. I don't think he's like his friends."

My friends. The "popular" group at school. I don't even know why I had bothered with them. Maybe because they were willing to accept me, so I let them. Simple as that. It wasn't like elementary or middle school, where you could hang out with whoever you wanted. There are- were cliques. The *delights* of being a high-schooler.

All that doesn't matter now though, does it? School? Friend groups? Not now, when all of our worlds have been ripped apart at the seams.

"Elizabeth. He doesn't even recognize us." Griffin insists.

"So what?" She argues exasperatedly, "I saw you two. You guys are friends now!"

"I've had a change of heart." Griffin snaps, slumping.

Elizabeth looks at him. "I know what this is about." She looks down at her lap, "You're jealous."

"I am not!"

"Then what?" Elizabeth asks, raising her hands into the air. "What is it that bothers you so much about him? We haven't even known him for two days and you think- what, that I'm suddenly in love?"

"You remember how he treated us-"

"He didn't treat us badly! His friends did!"

"Yeah, and he didn't have the guts to stand up to them!" Griffin says, standing up. Elizabeth stands up too, looking him in the eye.

"Yeah, and I didn't see you having much guts tonight either! I saw your face when Luke suggested to look for my dad, you didn't want to go did you? You've always been such a coward, Griffin! Always having me fight your battles, why, because you can't do it yourself? Get a grip!" Elizabeth shrieks, angry tears flowing from her eyes now. Then, a second in silence passes, and she immediately backs off. It's too little too late though. She's struck a nerve.

"That's unfair! You're only defending him because *you* like him and *you* know it!" Griffin spits in her face.

"No, I do not!" Elizabeth says indignantly, "Griffin, do you really think I'm that shallow?"

"We've been friends for years!" Griffin yells, his voice echoing through the forest.

"So does that suddenly mean I can't talk to anybody else?" Elizabeth asks angrily.

"Just," Griffin says, dropping his voice to a hurt whisper, "next time, remember who you're talking to."

He turns around and sees me. He wipes his nose and stalks past me, hitting his shoulder against mine as he enters the forest, disappearing into the mist. I stare at Elizabeth, at a loss for words. She just shakes her head and turns away.

I walk to the beds and set the pile of inner bark in the center.

"Anything we need to do to prepare these?" I ask. Elizabeth shakes her head, so I pick one up. It reminds me of chicken in color and jerky in texture. I take a bite.

"Ugh," I say, chewing the stuff. "This is horrible."

The bark is so bitter and fibrous it's hard to get down.

"You can boil or fry them with salt, but we don't have that option. I don't even know if this is the correct tree." She mutters dryly, wiping her nose and still not looking my way

I stare at her.

"Desperate times call for desperate measures. You're not dead yet."

I down three more strips before settling down in my bed. "What was that all about?"

Elizabeth ignores me.

"Liz?"

"Go to bed." She says, "I don't want to talk to you right now."

"So, you like him?" I ask, unable to stop myself.

"I like no one," She hisses harshly, "so both of you need to stop tripping over yourselves and butting your heads, and realize we are in this together whether you like it or not."

I am silent. Somehow, the danger of the night seems distant in light of these recent events. As I fall asleep for the remaining hours of the night, I think of how I had thought Griffin was actually becoming my friend. I thought I had finally found an uncomplicated friend group at last (as uncomplicated as things can be, given the circumstances).

This throws a wrench in things.

In the morning, I find that Griffin had come back after I'd fallen asleep. He lies behind me, facing the other way, dead to the world. Elizabeth, however, is nowhere to be seen.

I stand groggily.

"Elizabeth?" I call out, "Liz?"

She emerges out of the forest, placing a finger to her lips. "Are you out of your mind? Don't yell!"

I think of how she and Griffin had yelled the previous night, but decide not to bring up the whole ordeal. Luckily, no cancer had taken notice of us while we'd slept. Most likely because all of them were too preoccupied with the remaining people in town.

"Okay." I say, putting my hands up, "Okay. I was just worried about where you had gone."

"I can manage myself, thanks." She says, "I went to get more bark to eat on the road. I'm assuming we're maybe two and a half miles from Pirate's Avenue."

I stretch, extending my limbs as far away from my body as my bones will allow. It feels amazing. I stand, and scoop up the remaining pieces of inner bark lying on the grass bed. They are dried out now, but I take it just in case Elizabeth's supply runs out.

Griffin breathes heavily in his sleep.

"What time did he get back?" I gesture at his limp body.

"Must've been late. I was asleep too." She says, "But he's got to wake up now if we want to get to El Arnica at a decent time."

"Yeah," I say, moving forwards in his direction.

169

"Maybe, I should do it," Elizabeth suggests, giving me a significant look.

"Yeah," I say again, stepping away, "he's all yours."

Elizabeth places her hand on Griffin's shoulder and gently shakes him. He groans, and shifts to his side. Elizabeth shakes him again, and this time, his eyes lazily flicker open.

"Wha- what." He says, bolting upright, "Are they here? Where?"

"No, no," Elizabeth says, squeezing his shoulder, "We're fine. We're going to get going now, okay?"

Griffin nods, then catches sight of me staring and looks away. I look at Elizabeth. She just rolls her eyes and stands, brushing off her pants and pushing her frizzy, grimy hair out of her face.

I kick around the bed so that the grass is dispersed instead of all being in one area. I'm not sure why, but it just feels right. Elizabeth checks Griffin's phone, and then confirms which way is north, before walking on.

"That's it? We can just leave?" I ask in disbelief.

"You see any bags to pack?" She says without looking back. I walk over to Griffin, who is on the ground, and extend my hand for him to grasp. He looks at me suspiciously, before grabbing it and accepting my help. Now on his feet, he looks around the forest.

We walk maybe five feet behind Liz, but don't talk at all. We both are silent. I find this cold behavior odd for Griffin. Sure, I've only known him for a couple of days but he always came across as kind, or at least not solemn. He has soulful brown eyes and a kind composure.

The forest seems less foreboding now that the sun is shining through its thick foliage. As if the universe decided we deserved a day of beauty, it had removed the usual fog and let the sun shine brightly down upon us. Its warmth fills my insides with hope and thoughts of the future. Back at the lab, the adults would be waking to find our empty spots. They would discover the door unlocked, and can figure things out for themselves. Now though, for better or for worse, we're on our own.

I allow myself to enjoy the sudden warmness, despite not knowing what could be stalking us at this very moment. Elizabeth had given both Griffin and I strips of inner bark. I slowly snack on them, chewing the fibrous bitter stuff. It's better than starving, I guess. Elizabeth says it's a good source of vitamin C, so maybe It'll pay off anyway. Everything would have actually been fine, almost like a hike through the woods on a normal day, except my tongue feels like a dry piece of sandpaper in my mouth. I want water more than anything, but I try to focus on the cheerful turn of weather. Unfortunately, this isn't enough. After another hour of walking, I need to sit on a tree stump.

It's not just me either. The other two sigh and collapse on the pine needle strewn forest floor as soon as I stop. They're just as dehydrated as I am. It's another few minutes before we're on our feet again. We'll be fine. We can deal with the side effects for another couple days before it becomes serious. If everything goes according to plan, we'll make it to El Arnica before that. If we only had a road to follow… I'd check the map on Griffin's phone, but once again I'm afraid that firing up the GPS would take too much battery. It isn't going to last much longer as it is. Its percentage has already gone down to five, leaving us with limited compass checks to come.

We walk and walk and walk, and all I can think about is water. The way it moves, sliding over rocks and pouring off of cliffs in magnificent waterfalls. How I can have anything but. My lips are chapped and have started bleeding multiple times already.

"How far?" I croak.

"Not far," Elizabeth says back in a voice equally husky, "This is taking longer than I thought."

And so, we continue onward, through the forest. The only thought in my head is; I haven't had water since I left the Harlow's place yesterday.

CHAPTER ELEVEN

The moment we reach the bridge, any hope of reaching El Arnica without error evaporates into thin air. It's an absolute disaster.

The story forms together in my head. The scientist that disappeared, Tobias, made it all the way to El Arnica. Whether he was human or not at that point is a mystery. He became a cancer and started attacking the inhabitants of the town, which is much larger than Bluehill Ridge because it's the main tourist area. In response, everyone tried getting across the bridge and to the other side of the island, throwing the two-lane road spanning over the salty water into chaos.

Cars are smashed into the guard rails. Some open spots lead to where they had apparently plummeted off the edge. Other cars still sit with their doors open, apparently from when the inhabitants could no longer drive forward. Shattered windshields, popped tires, overturned vehicles. They go past the bridge and down the road which probably leads to our town. I guess none of them ever reached their destination. Well, they did, just not in the form they'd have preferred. They'd just been material at that point, the building blocks the cancers needed.

I look down, trying to ignore how horrible it all is. How morbidly horrible and wrong everything that is happening is. I look at Elizabeth, who takes a deep breath and continues onto the bridge, a determined look in her eyes. I try to admire her bravery, but all I can see is the horrible scene spread out in front of us.

Griffin looks at me, gulps, and continues on to follow Elizabeth, his apparent hatred of me temporarily forgotten. I follow him, no more excited than he.

My shoes crunch in the shattered glass as I weave through cars with open doors, shattered windows, and dents so bad it could have been a soda can, not a car. The bird song drifts away as I near the middle of the bridge, overtaken by the sound of the ocean. To the left, I can see the expanse of water leading into the horizon. To the right, I see Pirate's Avenue wind slightly and out of sight.

"What happened here," Griffin whispers, crouching down to check an overturned car. He whips his head up suddenly, "Don't look under there."

The bridge is pretty long, so when we finally reach the middle, I'm far enough from each shore to be nervous. I don't like the damaged state the bridge is in, but what am I supposed to do? The bridge is the only route to El Arnica, and I can hardly ask Elizabeth to turn back over this. I'm just overthinking things, as I always do.

Something clatters to the asphalt, making me jump out of my skin, and whirl my head around in an attempt to see who or what had created the noise. I hold up the crowbar that I've been lugging around, its weight feeling good in my hands. It makes me feel in control of this out of control situation.

"Sorry," Elizabeth says, putting her hands up, "Just me, sorry."

I sigh, and lower the heavy crowbar, the metal cold in my hands. Elizabeth is peeking into a car, almost getting all the way in. She scrambles onto the nice leather seat, leaving dusty footprints across the interior of the vehicle. When she walks back out, she holds a large *water bottle* up into the air triumphantly. I feel my face light up immediately. Water. We have water!

I shake Griffin's shoulder, as he had been busy looking over the side of the bridge, and point to Elizabeth. His face breaks out into a grin and we both jog over to her. I feel my mouth explode with the little saliva it can produce. My mind is occupied by the thought of the wet, cold liquid sliding against my tongue and down my throat, filling me with the energy I've been lacking all day.

When I near Elizabeth, I see the fairly large bottle is even almost full, which brings up my morale even higher. Elizabeth smiles and marches around, holding the bottle in the air as if it's gold. I smile with my dry, cracked lips and she brings the bottle down and unscrews the plastic lid. It is tossed it aside, because surely us three will finish the bottle in no time.

Elizabeth holds the excessively large bottle up to her mouth and cautiously takes the first sip. The sound of the water sloshing around in the bottle is torture and heaven at the same time. She slowly swallows it, before taking another big sip, swishing the water around in her mouth, and gulping it down, handing me the bottle.

The water tastes so good, I squint and blink as my eyes try to produce tears. The feeling of relief spreads through my body, just as the water does now. I quickly take my serving and hand the bottle to Griffin. He takes a huge gulp and burps in a satisfied way. We all start laughing and I realize how dumb, how childish the argument last night seems now in the bright warm sunlight. I've never felt closer to any group of people in my life. We spend the next few minutes just standing on the bridge, passing the bottle around until it's bone dry. Still not as much as I'd normally drink in a sitting, but I couldn't be happier. It's amazing how much dehydration has affected my mood.

"Ah," Griffin sighs as he gets the last drop out of the bottle and tosses it aside, "That felt good."

I couldn't agree more. Any quarrel I'd had the previous night is wiped from my mind, as it seems all three of us have forgotten the whole ordeal. Dehydration and hunger had twisted our feelings and judgment, but for now, we are lost in a cozy bliss.

It can almost make me forget our current predicament.

Almost.

Because in the warmth of the sun, relief from dehydration, and chatter, we've all let our guard down. The sound of a car bouncing on its suspension, squeaking and creaking ringing through the air, cuts us all off. I freeze, the smile on my face falling as I listen intently. I see Griffin wipe his mouth of the newfound moisture and stand still as a statue.

The sound of something leaping from one car to another, impact on metal followed by bouncing of suspension, causes us all to quickly crouch down in the shadow of the car the water had been in. My heart is beating in my chest, my throat closing up. I feel the trickling sense of fear and anticipation filling my body, slowly washing away the comfort I'd experienced moments earlier.

The suspension of another car bounces up and down, slightly squeaking. I hear heavy sniffs and stiff footfalls on metal. I dare to look around, but I don't see anything so whatever it is must be on the other side of the car.

Whatever it is?

I know what it is. A *cancer* is on the bridge.

I look to Elizabeth and Griffin. They stare back at me, wide-eyed. The heavy sniffing coming from the animal is punctuated occasionally by a short guttural bump of sound coming from deep in the animal's throat.

"What do we do?" I ask, daring to whisper to the others. They just shake their heads. I look around frantically. Behind us, there is a long stretch of road before the next car, which is smashed into the side railing. No use in backtracking anyway. I turn my head forward, towards the other end of the bridge. *There!* Just a few feet away is a car, maybe we could-

A dark blur launches onto the car I'm looking at, the windshield shattering into a million pieces under its weight. Its front appendage falls through the glass, and into the interior of the car. It lifts it up, examining the shattered window with no eyes, making those pulses of sound deep in its throat.

Those long, thin, curvy spines protruding from its back twitch back and forth.

I take advantage of its confusion and scramble into the car we're next to, pulling Elizabeth and Griffin after me. We all climb over each other in our haste to get inside, and when I close the door, I accidentally slam it.

At the loud sound, we all freeze. I am in the driver's seat, and I look in the rear-view mirror to see the cancer's smooth featureless face looking straight at us through the rear windshield. It cocks its head slightly, before stepping onto the hood of the other car, and slinking down and out of sight, off of the vehicle behind us...

We lose sight of it for a moment, before it rises up again, right in front of the rear windshield. It rises up and up, until, I realize with a start, it's up on its hind legs, a disturbing human quality about it.

It leans in towards the window, putting its freakish closed mouth inches from the glass. It seems to stare into the car, before lowering out of sight again, presumably onto all fours.

We all wait, not daring to breathe, as the creature slowly makes its way around the side of the car. I can see it. I can get a horrifyingly accurate look at its starved body. The dead, leathery skin shrink-wrapped over an inhuman skeleton. Its tail (if you can even call it a tail, for tail seems a too normal word. It doesn't quite capture the horror the creature invokes inside me…) waves behind it as if it is a large, smooth eel swimming in inky black water, just waiting to glide out from the murky depths.

Its hands, because hands are the closest way to describe them, are long and clawed, the human-like wrist seems to far back and up its arm. Its legs, constructed like a dog's, stretch far back as it slinks towards us slowly.

"What do we do?" Elizabeth whispers, dread seeping through her tone.

"I don't know," I say, and every second we don't do something, the creature gets closer. I suddenly realize how defenseless I am. I'd left the crowbar outside the car, as I'd dropped it when we were drinking the water.

The cancer is at the hood of our car now, lifting itself up onto its hind legs again. I press against the seat, trying to put as much distance between myself and that thing.

The cancer moves its face closer to the windshield, and I can hear those pulses in the back of its throat through the glass. The glass… It's almost like it can't see us through the glass. Like it can see the crystal surface but not through it…

I keep my eyes on the creature through the glass, and whisper to the other two, "It can't see us. It must be using echoloca-"

Apparently, although it can't see us, it can most definitely hear. Its head jolts straight towards me, the disturbing blank face swinging upward as if on hinges, the top of the mouth from the chin up, revealing its massive set of yellow, razor-sharp teeth. I can hear it roar through the glass. It brings up its hand, and slams the largest of its three fingers into the glass, its dinosaur-like claws puncturing and shattering the windshield into a shower of sparkling shards. It's as if the sound is turned up and its screeching fills my ears. I kick the passenger side door open and we all fall out onto the pavement, the tempered glass digging into our arms.

We scramble away, only daring to look around when we're at a safe enough distance.

It's as if the cancer still thinks we're in there, screeching and clawing around the seats, searching for us. Then, for a moment it stops. It makes a series of pulsing sounds again and lowers itself from the hood of the car, evidently realizing we are no longer in it.

The cancer looks around, making pulsing sounds. It seems to see us, and crawls towards us on all fours. It stops ten feet away from us, low in a pouncing position, but staying still. The only sound it makes is the pulsing in its throat, and the chattering of its face/mouth bobbing up and down, clicking the teeth together in fast repetition. Its teeth are oriented in such a way that they seem to be sharpening each other.

It just watches us.

Griffin is squeezing his eyes shut, his face screwed up into a grimace. He is shaking and I can see the droplets of sweat beading on his forehead.

The cancer lunges at him, soaring through the air and extending its claws towards Griffin. I throw myself at him, hefting all my weight into the move, and knock him painfully to the ground. I fall with him, landing on top of his body as the cancer soars overhead, missing both Griffin and I.

It hits the guardrail of the bridge face first, crumpling against the metal on impact and letting out a deafening screech. I take a moment, stunned, before pushing myself to my feet and beginning to sprint. Frantically, I try to get the others to do the same. If we can only get into the forest, we can hide. Run. Get to El Arnica.

Elizabeth and Griffin scramble to their feet and hastily follow me, sprinting towards the only hope of survival. We need to get off of this bridge.

One foot in front of the other, I run as fast as I can towards the end of the bridge. My lungs already hurt. Almost there... Almost-

Something heavy launches onto my back and I fall to the ground face first. My chin and cheekbone scrape across the rough asphalt. I try to cry out, but my jaw is against the pavement, jamming my mouth shut over my tongue. I can taste coppery blood fill my mouth.

I scramble to turn over and face the cancer, struggling to avoid the claws at all costs. When I turn over though, it repositions its hands to be right on my chest. Not digging into the flesh, but able to if needed.

Its head is inches from mine as the face swings upwards, almost like the trunk door of a car, revealing its vast array teeth inside its head once again. Low screeching and inhuman sounds fill my ears as it nears my face even closer. Its saliva sprays me in the face.

Just when I think that it's over, that it'll either scratch me with its claws or flat out eat me, it yelps almost like a dog and staggers to the side. Above me, I see Griffin with my crowbar gripped in his hands, positioned like he just hit a home run.

He reaches his hand down to me, and I grasp it. Quickly pulling me up, Griffin turns to face the cancer once again. I wipe my face, making sure the saliva didn't get into my mouth or eyes. Hopefully they can't spread like that.

Elizabeth is by our side now, panting, her hands on her knees. I turn my eyes towards the cancer.

It's creeping towards us, slowly extending its clawed arms and its teeth chattering like crazy. A low screech is beginning to build in the back of its throat, and-

And Griffin launches himself at the creature. I cry out in surprise, reach for him. He's too far though, the crowbar raised above his head. Apparently, the cancer is surprised too, because it freezes for a moment.

That, is its fatal mistake.

Griffin swings the crowbar underhand, slamming the curved, sharp tip right up into the monster. It staggers back for a moment, before slipping over the guard railing and plummeting far down and out of sight.

I limp over to the edge, expecting to see it being swept away by the Pirate's Avenue current. Instead, I see its emaciated form on the shore, mere feet away from the water that could have saved its life.

I see its body twitch for a moment, before going still.

Griffin pants, dropping the heavy crowbar to the firm asphalt, where it loudly clanks against the surface.

"I hate those things," Griffin says warily.

I gingerly rub my chin and cheekbone, both of which are bleeding liberally. My face feels like it's on fire, and I attempt to pick out the bits of pavement and rubble from the open scrapes. I also check my body for any scratches caused by the cancer. Nothing on my chest that I can see, and I don't feel anything on my back so I assume it's alright. I'd rather not have Griffin or Elizabeth check it for me since I'm grimy as heck, and probably smell like a rotting pig carcass, so I shift my shirt behind me uncomfortably.

"C'mon," Elizabeth says, tearing her gaze away from the cancer's dead body far below, "We need to go."

I take one last look at the creature, and turn away, picking up the crowbar and patting Griffin's shoulder, "Thanks." Then follow Elizabeth, who is already walking off of the bridge. I catch up with her, then look back to see if Griffin is following. He is still looking over the edge, frowning.

"Griffin!" I call, "You coming?"

For a moment, he does nothing, but finally relents and joins us on solid ground once again, limping slightly. I look at him, trying to see what's wrong, for surely, he's not acting normal. I consider asking, but then I remember his and Elizabeth's argument last night and keep quiet. We're all on edge emotionally, and I don't want to push anything.

"Off we go then," I say, looking at him.

"Off we go." Griffin walks ahead, leaving Elizabeth and I behind.

The road off of the bridge is crammed with cars too, but the farther we go the less thick it gets. I keep expecting to run into another cancer, but nothing presents itself so I guess we're safe for now. It isn't long, though, until the winding road is empty of cars and broken things.

"Liz," I finally say, looking to Elizabeth to see if the name is still okay to use. She says nothing, so I continue, "About last night,"

She looks at me with those crisp green eyes and I'm startled by their sharpness. "Last night..."

"I just wanted you to know," I shift around awkwardly, "You know, to clear up any complications..."

She looks at me in a way that makes me want to shrink into my shirt and hide. I'm so nervous I'm going to say the wrong thing. I just need to get it over with. I need to clear the air between me and Griffin, who I know is listening in from ahead. I need to confirm that I have no feelings for Elizabeth, at least not in the way Griffin suggests. I open my mouth to continue, but trip over something on the ground.

I fall forward, this time able to catch myself with my hands rather than bloodying my face up more, but my hands are already grimy and scraped, so I stifle a curse as I hit the ground.

Elizabeth, startled, rushes to help me up, and grasps my hand, causing me to yelp slightly. She apologizes over and over again, trying to pick the bits of rock off of my hand.

"I'm fine, I'm fine," I say, pulling my hand away, "Thank you, but I'm fine."

She nods.

I brush my hands off on my filthy jeans and try to see what I'd tripped on. Three sticks lie on the ground right behind me, awkwardly positioned. The first two, smaller, are shaped like the top of a triangle, and the bigger of the three-

"Griffin, come here real quick," I say. In seconds, Griffin is by my side, his tawny-shaded face turning a notch paler.

"What," He says, examining the sticks I had tripped over.

"Did you see these sticks before I tripped?" I ask.

"No," He says, tilting his head this way and that to see what is strange about them. He seemingly is unable to place what about them is intriguing me, so he eventually asks me what I find weird.

"If I replace the stick I tripped over to where it was," I begin, "It sort of looks like an-"

"Arrow," Elizabeth says excitedly, "You think it was just a coincidence?"

"I don't know," I puzzle over the sticks, "If it is, it's pointing straight into the woods. Do you think someone intended it that way? It *is* too far from the edge of the road to be there by chance."

"What's the harm in following it?" Griffin muses as he examines the sticks.

"If we follow it for too long, my dad could die." Elizabeth says flatly.

I think, for a moment, on how true that statement is. We don't know that Elizabeth's father is even still alive. For all we know, he could be dead in a ditch, or even worse, already a cancer. If he is alive though, wasting any time in searching for him could ultimately lead to his death or infection. Following this arrow is essentially gambling with his life.

Still though, if the arrow is intentional, we could maybe find people that could help us. Point us in the correct direction. It's a risk.

"I say we follow it," Elizabeth says suddenly, surprising both Griffin and I. "There may be someone who can help us find dad."

Griffin sighs, "I hate this island more and more every day."

They both look at me for my opinion. I shrug, "It's up to Elizabeth. If you think it's worth the risk, then lead on."

We follow the arrow, which leads us to another, leaving little doubt they were made by human hands. This arrow, however, points north, traveling parallel to the road, so at least we're going the correct direction. We walk north for maybe twenty minutes to half an hour, before turning east and away from the road once more.

185

Now that everything is warmer and dryer, my footsteps are no longer muffled by the pine needles littering the forest floor, but give loud crunches with every footfall. It isn't long before we come across another arrow once again pointing north. We follow that for maybe ten minutes, before finally coming to something of interest.

A large shack, or more of a barn, stands alone in a clearing. The front doors are shut tight and all visible windows are boarded from the inside. I look to Elizabeth and Griffin, raising my eyebrows. They shrug and continue on.

The barn doors are tall and wooden. I place a finger on the structure, running it down the peeling brown paint, revealing even browner wood underneath. It's old.

A sliver slides into my finger. I wince and remove it, examining the little droplet of blood forming where the puncture had been. I'm so scraped up already I hardly notice it.

"You think anyone's inside?" Griffin asks Elizabeth, avoiding my gaze as if one look might turn him to stone.

"Only one way to find out." Elizabeth whispers, before knocking loudly on the creaky wooden structure. At first, there is no response, so Elizabeth raises her hand to knock again, but freezes in place when a small hole in the door is unblocked from the other side. A rifle barrel slides out, pointing straight at her chest.

For a moment, we're all frozen, Elizabeth's fist in the air, inches away from the door. What now.

"Back up." Says a gruff voice from the other side of the door. We all stand still until I hear the click of the gun's safety being flipped off. I put my hands in the air, slowly backing away from the wooden barn, keeping my eye trained on that rifle barrel sticking out of the door. Elizabeth and Griffin follow in my lead, raising both hands and slowly backing up.

"Drop the crowbar." The gruff voice says harshly. I let the metal tool drop from my fingers and hit the ground, kicking it away for good measure.

The large barn door slowly swings open, revealing the man holding up the gun. He scowls at us, slowly stepping out of the old, worn-down shack. Somebody from inside quickly steps out from a corner and closes the door behind him.

The man keeps the rifle trained on us, looking around the forest for who knows what. He's definitely on the older side, the hair remaining on his head gray as asphalt. He looks tired and worn, his face grimy and wrinkled. White stubble on his chin suggests he hasn't shaved for a while.

"Who are you?" He says, looking back at us.

"I'm Luke, uh, Luke Anderson." I stumble over my words, "This is Elizabeth Harlow and Griffin, uh-"

Apparently uninterested, the man grunts and shoulders his rifle with the strap attached to the weapon. Not putting it away, just making both of his hands available

He steps up to us and reaches one of his hands out to Elizabeth's face. Griffin and I begin to step forward in protest, but Elizabeth violently slaps his hand away before either of us could even say a word.

"Relax," The man says, trying again, "Trust me."

Elizabeth reluctantly stays still as the man examines a cut on her face, gently running his thumb over the red line. He then turns towards Griffin and examines the cut that runs down his arm.

"Have you run into any of them?" The man grunts.

"Any what?" I ask, stalling for time so I can think of what answer to give.

"You know what." The man says, raising his red, baggy eyes to meet mine. "By the looks of it, I'd say you have."

"Oh," I say, watching the way the man goes back examining the scratches on Griffin's arm, "No. Not since yesterday anyway."

"Hmm," The man says, furrowing his bushy eyebrows, "You'd already be gone. But you know what? I don't believe you." He nods at the scratches on Griffin, then turns to me.

"Oh boy, you're a mess." He says, examining my face.

"Thanks." I say dully.

The man gets closer and examines the cuts on my face. He nods, as if he determined they're fine, then moves on to my arms.

"May I ask what you're doing?" Elizabeth asks indignantly, throwing me a concerned look as the man examines the glass cuts covering my arm, picking away a couple pieces I missed. It's tempered glass, so thank God there's no splinters.

"Checking to see if you got scratched. If you're already going through the purge." He says, "I think you all are good though. *I think*."

"The purge?" I ask, massaging my cuts, "What's the purge?"

"We got some fancy scientist here, says that those monsters spread through us. Says it all starts with the purge."

"What's the purge?" I ask again.

"You can ask him yourself." The man says, gesturing for us to walk towards the barn door. "Got somethin' to do with blood being infected or some such, do I care? No. If you want answers you gotta ask him."

"Um," Griffin says slowly, "I think we'll pass, thank you though-"

The barn doors slowly swing open, revealing a large group of people that must have been hidden behind corners when the barn first opened, because they seem to have appeared out of nowhere.

"Nonsense," Grunts the man, "We ain't gonna hurt you. We're safe here. Got the whole place boarded up and everything."

I begin to walk forward, curious and interested. The others follow. We walk past the man, so when he gives a startled

189

exclamation, we whip our heads around to see what has happened. At first, I don't know what's wrong, but then I see the man staring, horrified, at... *me*.

"What."

"You ain't goin in. Your friends can, but you are not to go near those people. Not like that." He says firmly, staring as if I had just sprouted tusks. I point at my chest to confirm that he is speaking about *me*. In doing so, I'd turned my back to the people in the barn, who have all let out an exclamation as well, and have backed away to the farthest wall from me.

"What?" I ask again.

"Luke!" Elizabeth gasps in surprise, "Oh God, Luke, what happened?"

"What!?" I turn to Elizabeth, "What is it? Elizabeth, tell me."

"Why didn't you... Oh God" Elizabeth says with her hand over her mouth, ignoring me, "I can't believe I didn't see it! How badly does it-"

"Didn't see what?" I exclaim, throwing my hands in the air, turning to Griffin. He just shakes his head and backs away a little. "Oh just tell me!"

The man walks towards my back, but I spin around, my hands up in defense.

"Boy, do you really not know?" The man asks. I shake my head, still not allowing him to get any closer.

"Okay, okay," The man says, putting his hands up and backing away, "Let your friends show you."

I look to Griffin, who shakes his head, his face a bit green, and backs away even further, looking down at his feet. I look to Elizabeth, who gulps, her face a bit green herself, and walks towards me.

"Turn around." She says, taking a sharp intake of breath when I do so. She slowly takes the back of my shirt, and tugs part of it around my body. It is now twisted in a way I can see the part of the shirt that covers my back. It has a huge ragged tear in it, and it's soaked with blood.

•　•　•

I stand inside the small outhouse behind the barn. In the small, scratched mirror, I examine my bare back. There is a long, disgusting, rip in my skin, revealing muscle tissue beneath. The sides of the wound are messy, torn and ragged. There are spots where the flesh takes on a greenish tinge, sickening me to my stomach. I use a damp piece of toilet paper to clean off some blood dribbling down the bare skin.

The weird thing is, I feel nothing. I feel absolutely nothing from the wound or the skin around it. It is as if the nerves beneath the skin have decided to stop working, keeping the immense pain I should be in from me.

It's unnerving, not being able to feel it. Unable to gauge how bad it actually is through pain.

They're not letting me into the barn, but Elizabeth and Griffin had gone in to gather as much information as possible, and to maybe find any extra rags to help patch me up. I am unconcerned, though. My real problem is coming from what is running through me at this very moment. If our theory is right, which the man had even confirmed, I am turning into a cancer. Why my body is not responding to the chemicals trying to put

191

me to sleep is a mystery. A curse, really, because I'd rather be ignorant of the world around me right now.

I take one last look at my torn back, before unlocking the outhouse and stepping outside, scanning the forest around me to make sure no cancers are in sight. They aren't, but Griffin leans against a nearby tree. He sees that I'm out of the outhouse and walks over.

"Hey," He says, bundled pieces of cloth clutched in his hands.

"Hey." I brood dully. All the hope has drained out of me. For all I know, I'll be worse than dead by the time the sky goes dark.

"They, uh, sent me out here to patch you up." Griffin says, holding up the cloth, "And, they had a shirt for you, since yours is, uh-"

He nods at the bloodied mess of a shirt in my hand, and I nod in recognition. "Thanks."

He steps up to my back and helps me wrap the cloth around my torso, covering the ragged wound. I still feel nothing. He gives me a pin, and I pinch together the two ends of cloth flat to the front of my body, before running the needle through both and securing the fabric tightly around myself. I tear off the extra, stuffing it into my pocket.

"Here," Griffin hands me a shirt. It's dark green, and poorly fitting, but it works. It looks especially odd with the fabric beneath it.

"Thank you." I say, sitting down on a log.

Griffin takes a big intake of breath, looks around as if deciding something, and then sits down on the log next to me.

"Luke, about last night…"

"It's fine." I say flatly.

"No." Griffin says, a tone of frustration in his voice, "I shouldn't have said what I did. I'm sorry. It's just that-"

"I said it's fine." I say dully, "I'm-"

"No!" Griffin yells out of the blue, standing up, and causing me to look around, waiting for some creature to jump out in response, "No! It's not okay! I see the way you two look at each other! The way you talk! And I was selfish, Luke, okay? There, I said it. I thought that… It's just that-"

"Griffin." I interrupt, stopping him in his tracks, "It's not like that. We're- not like that. We only met yesterday, I swear it. And plus, it doesn't matter. I'll be gone by tomorrow anyways."

Griffin stares at me, taken aback. "Luke!"

"It's true." I sigh, slouching back, "You know where that gash came from. It's not normal. I can't even feel it."

Griffin stares at me, his mouth attempting to make words, but only able to open and close like a fish out of water.

I manage a weak smile.

CHAPTER THIRTEEN

The others, of course, forbade me from sleeping in the barn, but had the good will to lend me an ugly wool sweatshirt to keep myself warm through the once again cold night. I feel like a pariah, rejected from this small society they have going here. It's not even anything I've done, but I guess that's how the world works now. Survival comes first, and everything else is chucked out the window. Decency. Hospitality. Kindness. There is no room for such things anymore. At least not in this tiny, isolated bubble of an island we have here. Deep down, I can't help but loathe those people in the barn, at least a little bit. I can't even tell why. I think way back to school, when things were simple. Wasn't that what I had always worked so hard at? Being liked? Not becoming an outcast? Or am I making this all up in my head? I don't know, maybe it's just because my skull seems to be full of constantly buzzing bees, because my focus seems to float this way and that like driftwood in a vast ocean.

Elizabeth and Griffin insisted they wanted to sleep outside of the barn with me, and I had tried to persuade them otherwise to no avail. Now, in the cold darkness, we sit in a circle and discuss what they'd learnt from the people in the barn.

"Luke." Elizabeth says, snapping her fingers in front of my face, "Luke, are you listening?"

"What-" I say, waking from my mind of emptiness, "Yeah. Yeah, I'm listening."

"Tobias was there." Elizabeth continues, "*Tobias*. You remember who that is?"

"Yeah," I say, trying to make my brain work properly, "Yeah, I think."

I see Elizabeth give Griffin a concerned look. "You don't seem surprised."

Tobias. The name is familiar, and I can sort of grasp what it's tied to. I'm trying to push away the mist surrounding it... It's tied to the lab... to the lab and the scientists- the scientists.

"We thought he was dead." I say slowly, "That he was already a cancer."

"Yeah," Elizabeth sighs in relief, nodding her head vigorously, "You do remember. That's good. He says the cancer from the lab escaped. He says it's different than the ones we've seen somehow, but refuses to say anything more about it. He mentioned something about the cancers we've seen being some sort of- result of its spreading. What he did say, though, is that it followed him all the way to El Arnica."

The cold wind of the dark, starry night presses against my face. The same breeze that ruffles the leaves on the trees and ripples the grass I sit in. I shake my head, ridding it of its fogginess.

"So he's alive." I say slowly.

"Yes," Elizabeth says, "Yes, he's alive! We asked him why you aren't going into the coma like everyone else, but he says he doesn't-"

"I wish I was." I say, rubbing my temples as a pounding migraine had just entered my skull. Another sign of the infection I suppose. "in a coma, I mean. I wish I was asleep. Maybe it'd go faster."

Elizabeth flat out slaps me in the face.

I don't mean an endearing, comforting, concerned touch. Not even a playful push. She flat out slaps me in the face, leaving me shocked and very much awake.

"Luke!" She gasps, making me look at her as I rub my stinging cheek, "You're different, okay? You're not responding to the disease, and that's good! I absolutely forbid you of doing anything rash, like running off into the woods, or wishing you were succumbing to the disease, or whatever else goes through your mush of a brain!"

I am taken aback. There are tears in her eyes reflecting in the moonlight, and I realize she's actually concerned. The truth is, in the back of my mind, I'd been planning to flee into the woods as soon as both of them were asleep. I thought they'd be safer that way. Is that still my plan, or are am I being swayed? Do I even have a choice *not* to go?

"You don't mean to say that you actually care, do you?" I say, regaining my senses enough to make the weak joke. The corners of my mouth twitch up a little. Oh how my head hurts.

She sniffs indignantly, "No. I do not. I only thought it would be good to warn you, since you have a habit of making poor decisions."

A hint of a smile.

"Oh," I say, "That makes more sense. For a moment there I thought you actually had a heart!"

She laughs weakly and pushes me in the chest. Griffin chuckles, and I attempt a laugh myself. The result is a pounding wave of pain beneath my skull.

"Seriously, though." Griffin says, "Don't leave, okay? We need you."

Need me? That's pushing it. What have I done to help? Not read and interpret the papers back at the lab. That was Elizabeth. Not swing that metal crowbar into the cancer, pitching it off the bridge. That was Griffin. What have I done? Ultimately nothing.

"Even if I did, I don't think I'd be in any danger. This sweatshirt could scare away anything." I finally respond, tugging on the rag I'm wearing. It's too big for me, horribly wrinkled, and smells like B.O.

This time, neither Griffin or Elizabeth laugh. They are not amused.

"So," I clear my throat, "you guys find out anything useful? Did you ask about your father?"

"As a matter of fact," Elizabeth says, giving a look to Griffin, and I think I see a glint of joy, no, not joy, more like hope, in her eyes, however drowned in other emotions it may be, "We did. It so happens that he had spoken with Tobias."

"Tobias?' I ask, surprised. That grabbed my attention, "Why?"

"The newspaper company he was- is working for sent him there to try and investigate some odd happenings in El Arnica. He was searching around, according to Tobias, to try and find the source of what was happening. They were having disappearances and such. He found Tobias, who was desperately trying to tell everyone about the cancer that had escaped. Well, long story short, the fact that he looked like a nutjob, torn clothes, crazy hair, didn't help his case."

"Until your father came along." Griffin interjects.

"Yes, until my father came along." Elizabeth nods, "He says that dad found him and questioned him. Tobias said he ended up spilling out everything he knew to him, the first person to actually listen. He says my dad kept asking where the thing had come from."

"And?" I ask expectantly, "Did he tell him? Did he tell you two?"

Griffin shakes his head, "No, he didn't know. None of them knew where the thing had come from. All he said is that the government sent it to them to study."

"The government?" I ask, throwing my hands into the air, "Our government? What, is this some sort of ridiculous… conspiracy theory? Why? And why us? We don't even have that big of a lab, I mean-"

"We don't know." Elizabeth says to me, her hands up, gesturing for me to be quiet and calm down. I suppose I should. We have been a bit careless about letting the cancers around hear us, but I'm guessing they would have attacked by now if they were here. Probably still in El Arnica, or maybe Bluehill Ridge. I sure hope they're not back at the lab. We left our families in good protection, right? Unless they're out looking for us. Or maybe they already had looked for us. Maybe they're already dead, or in a coma, becoming a cancer.

I shake my head. I need to avoid going down such rabbit holes.

"We don't know," Elizabeth continues, looking around the dark, cold forest, "But Tobias said something about it being built differently. How it really wasn't suited for its external conditions. His exact words were 'at least not the original one' whatever that means. Anyway, he went into this whole rant on how it says so much about where it came and a bunch of other scientific things that I couldn't care less about. He said they were just getting to studying it's ideal environment when it escaped, so it's a mystery."

"And he has this theory." Griffin says quietly.

"It's a trash theory." Elizabeth says, crossing her arms.

"Elizabeth, he's a scientist, he knows what he's talking about." Griffin says, "It's at least worth thinking about. What else would it be?"

"It's ridiculous." Elizabeth says firmly.

Griffin looks at me seriously. "Tobias thinks they're extra-terrestrial."

I actually laugh out loud, snorting, which makes my migraine even worse, "Aliens? All of this, and he seriously thinks they're aliens. Like, what, the little green dudes flying around in a magical saucer?"

"That's what he says," Griffin mutters, frowning. "What else would they be?"

I roll my eyes, "I think he's got a couple of screws loose."

"Yes, but-" Griffin begins.

"I'm not being pulled into some crazy scientist's conspiracy theories." Elizabeth scoffs. "What would the aliens want? I don't see any 'we come in peace' signs."

"It's the most logical solution." Griffin argues weakly.

Elizabeth sighs. "That doesn't always mean it's ri-"

"Back to the important things," I say, cutting both of them off. I swear, sometimes they argue like an elderly couple. Too much thinking, my head hurts again. "Where did he say Elizabeth's dad is?"

Griffin, put out, responds; "Vavinto's. Apparently, it's a seaside hotel, supposed to be nice. Tobias said that he'd mentioned the newspaper company had paid for him to stay there. He said that Mr. Harlow had commented on how nice the rooms were…"

"Vavinto's…" I say, mostly to myself. Griffin and Elizabeth both nod. "Good to know…"

• • •

The damp grass beneath me almost acts like a soft cushioning, so it's even harder to stay awake. My eyes keep wanting to close, and my pounding headache just won't go away. If only I could let go of my consciousness and drift away. Away and gone forever, softly wiping off all my troubles and worries like a whiteboard.

But I can't. I can't afford to fall asleep just yet. I can't put Griffin and Elizabeth in danger by staying. I need to be sure they're asleep before I can sneak off.

But my plan isn't to go far, far away, into the forest to fade into oblivion. To die, and become a cancer. I want to do something meaningful with the remainder of my conscious hours. As much as I would love to see my family one last time, I can't, as traveling all the way back to the lab is just unrealistic, especially in my state. My heart yearns for it, but truth is truth, and there's no changing it. Like the wind trying to move a mountain. Some things just stay the same, no matter what.

Instead, I have a different plan in mind. Something slightly more achievable, at least in my head, which frankly is too preoccupied to make any rash decisions anyway. I just need to keep a couple things straight.

The phone Elizabeth has, which I think is in the sweatshirt pocket she'd been lent by the people in the barn. I need that. I need the phone. Vavinto's. I need to remember- remember something about-

I need to-

I need to-

I think both Elizabeth and Griffin are finally asleep. Their Labored, conscious breaths have been replaced with deep, relaxed ones.

The cold bites my skin as I stand, brush off my clothes, and scan the two forms. As I had suspected, they are both fast asleep. A pang of mixed emotions shoots through me like a bullet. Guilt. Sadness. The strong, warm feeling of friendship. Am I really about to leave it all behind?

I crouch down and pull the phone out of Elizabeth's sweatshirt pocket.

I rub my numb hands together, my breath making fog in the air. It seems like the nice warm day the universe had given us had turned out to be a slap in the face. A jeer.

'Are you used to this nice weather and comfort? Ha! Here comes the coldest night yet!'

The tall trees around me seem to leer down at me, swaying in the slight breeze. The cold does feel nice to my head, though, so I guess it's not all bad. It cools my temperature, helping with the sickening waves of heat and nausea moving up my body. What worries me is why the cancers haven't shown up.

I look down at Elizabeth and Griffin one more time. It feels wrong to just leave, but what other choice do I have? They won't understand that I have nothing to lose. They wouldn't let me try on my own.

"Goodbye." I whisper, my words carried away by the wind. After a moment of consideration, I stoop down and drape the blanket I had been using over them. I won't need it anyways, and it's freezing out here.

Turning away, I power on the phone. It shines blindingly into my face, so I turn the brightness all the way down. This time, I don't need to preserve the battery life, I just need to see how to get to El Arnica. I punch it into the maps and it comes up with the directions I need. Get back to the road, follow it. Just a few turns and I'm there. There's a red bar on the bottom of the screen notifying me that I am offline, but Griffin must have the entire island saved on maps.

I shut the phone off while it's still at 2% and think. Vavinto's Vavinto's Vavinto's. I can't forget. My mind is already fuzzy, but I need to remember what I'm doing. I need to remember the resturan- I mean Hotel's name. God, I'm losing it fast.

I shake my head as if to rid it of the pain, which actually makes it worse, and walk towards the direction of the highway, which, as it turns out, is only a minute's walk away. When I step out onto the open road, I take in how exposed I am. How truly alone I feel.

My foot is asleep. That can't be a good sign.

I follow the eerily silent road. The night sounds, such as the breeze and chirping crickets, seem to have all died, leaving me in utter, deafening quiet. It's unnerving, really. As I take each step, I hear it hit the ground much too loudly. What am I alerting with my heavy tread?

I catch movement out of the corner of my eye. I spin around to face whatever it is, but nothing is to be seen. The cool air and starry sky, for some reason, only add to the growing anxiety inside my chest. What am I doing? What am I doing?

I take a right at the fork in the road, far too aware that every step I take in the right direction is a step towards what could possibly be my end, and a minute less of my already shortened life.

Because I don't plan on living. I plan on finding Elizabeth's father, if he's still alive, and bringing him back to her. Or maybe, I'll just have to point in the right direction, because at the rate things are going, I won't be able to muster the strength to walk in an hour or two. Tops.

Another left.

A right turn, winding down a road with a particularly large group of cars smashed into each other. Some have as little as a dent, others are flipped over.

I wonder what the rest of the world is doing right now. Are they unaware that any of this is happening? Are they goggling at us, either unable or unwilling to help, watching to see what will come next? And what about my father? Every time I think about him, I feel a terrible, almost physical pain in my chest, but I can't just ignore it. What is he doing right now, as I walk down this cold and empty road that ultimately leads to my death, one way or another. Is he frantically searching for a way to get to the island? Has he already tried, and met the same unfortunate end as the sheriff? Or is he sleeping, unaware that anything has gone amiss. After all, why would it? Nothing ever goes down on Eastrock Island, much less Bluehill.

And he's not even supposed to come home for days. We'll all be dead by then, almost guaranteed.

No. *No.* We aren't going to just end this way. We can't just die, we won't. For better or for worse, life always trumps death. Everyone eventually dies, but everyone who dies has lived. Out of those who have lived, most have produced more life. More living, breathing beings striving to go on, unsatisfied with anything but. We, as human beings, can pretend we're above it all. We can fool ourselves that we're too sophisticated, or smart, or rich, but we all have an animal instinct buried deep inside to survive. To move on. After all, progress is what we always strive for. Survival. That is at the center of what motivates us as people.

Or, in my case, the survival of Mr. Harlow. The survival of Griffin and Elizabeth. The survival of their families, and mine. I operate under the hope that they can continue. Continue on, until their proper time has come. That is what I wish for, in my heart.

Yep. I'm going delusional aren't I...

And now, as I walk to the edge of the road, I can see the civilization spread out far below me, in complete and utter ruins. Long, inhuman, haunting shrieks echo from the town, across the hilltops, and reach me, resonating deep in my chest like a snake burrowing in the ground.

I walk down the winding road, going back and forth along the steep hillside, heading for El Arnica. The large town, which probably would have been lit up and glowing in the dark by this time, is dark, eerie, and silent. It's not long before I am standing right at the outskirts of the place itself. Though it is dark, I can see slightly, due to the moonlight and stars shining down from above. The long street is lined with buildings taller and closer together than the ones on Main Street back in Bluehill Ridge. The swinging shop signs between posts squeal slightly as the wind pushes them back and forth. Every little sound is audible. Even so, I feel blind. Blind to the fact that somewhere, likely near me, there is an immediate danger waiting to pounce on any worthy victims.

I take a deep breath, and step into the normally cheery tourist town. The joyful colors and architecture of the town has been thrown into depressingly dull colors, their shadows framed by the even darker sky spotted with distant stars illuminating galaxies and everything beyond.

The howling of the wind rushes through the buildings and their shattered display windows. Still, though, it doesn't get bad until I turn the corner to face the main shopping street. The one lined with too many buildings to count, and even more cars. Cars crashed into each other. Into stoplights. Into buildings. Cars are in ruins everywhere, their windshields shattered and crushed.

I've rarely been to El Arnica, because we at Bluehill sort of compete with them for tourists, but apparently I've underestimated its size. Tall hotels line the coast, which I can't see, but I can hear to my right-hand side. Their streets and shops are so much larger and grander than ours, I don't know why anybody would prefer Bluehill to here. At least, pre-cancer.

A delightful little dark green trolly is slammed into a stop-light pole, its front dented so badly, you can tell it's beyond repair. I dare to peek inside. The back of the tram-like vehicle is empty of bodies, only backpacks and purses strewn across the floor. In the front seat, though, the driver still sits, leaning against the steering wheel, her face out of sight.

I can see the scenario now. All the panicked people fleeing the trolly, meanwhile the driver is stuck in her seat, unable to join the mob of people running for their own lives. Something, maybe a cancer, had stopped her before she could exit the trolly. I can see a large red stain across her shirt. Maybe she was injured too badly and flat out died. I don't want to get a closer look and find out.

I move on to the rest of the town, occasionally peeking inside cars, and looking at all the once cheerful buildings for the one hotel named Vavinto's. It's disturbing, the lack of bodies, though I am selfishly grateful for their absence. I'll pay for it though, for surely the lack of bodies is due to an increasing cancer population.

Never, not once in my life, have I felt this alone. Every crashed car or wayward shadow makes me want to crawl under a bed and hide. Every shard of glass and fallen brick is screaming for me to run. But I can't. Think I'm joking? My entire left leg has fallen asleep, sending prickly fuzzy feelings up my calf and thigh. It's almost impossible to put any weight on that foot without wincing. At first, it had begun as discomfort, but it is now morphing into pain.

* * *

"Mom," I had asked long ago in my high-pitched kindergartener voice, on the way to my old elementary school. "Why do my feet feel fuzzy?

"Because they're falling asleep baby." She says, adjusting the rear-view mirror so that she can see me in the back. It's an odd detail to remember, but it's something that stuck in my memory; her rose pink nails. Not long, witch nails. Not too bright, begging for attention. A soft, muted light pink, with a little picture of a daisy every other nail. I remember this because she *never* paints her nails.

"Asleep?" I ask, cocking my head, adjusting the seatbelt on my booster seat.

"That's what people call it when your feet feel all fuzzy." She says, and makes a funny face in the mirror that makes me laugh delightedly.

"What makes my feet want to fall asleep?" I ask curiously, staring at my feet that can't even touch the floor of the car, wondering why they would be tired but not me.

"It's just what they call it sweetheart." My mom says, eyes on the road, "It happens when not enough blood is getting to one of your feet."

I am silent, trying to figure it out.

"Or your arms." She says, puffing up her cheeks and bulging her eyes for my amusement, "Or your legs or hands or your-" She sticks out her tongue, "face..."

* * *

207

And that's when I notice it. As I walk along the dark, cold, wind-strewn town, I notice a slightly weird feeling in my face. It is almost as if the thought itself had triggered it. The painful fuzzy sensation running up the sides of my nose. Across my scraped cheekbones. Through my cracked, split lips.

"It happens when not enough blood is getting to your feet." She had said. Or anywhere, really. I worry. The leg could just be a side effect, but the face... It's slight right now, but could my body be blocking the blood from getting to my face so it can perform the first, most complex part of the transformation? Aren't I supposed to be asleep? Why aren't I asleep?

I limp down the road, similar to the way Griffin jogs when he's nervous. This time, instead of peeking inside cars and buildings, I keep my eyes forward, only diverging from my path when a vehicle or the occasional body sits directly in my way.

There's a figure in the dark, standing on two legs, staring straight at me. I stop dead in my tracks, freezing as if in ice. The figure just stands there, down the road, looking at me. It's not a cancer, I can tell because it's not blending in well with the dark, though it's not exactly easy to see either. My hands clench together, despite the way it intensely stings the red slits that cover my grimy palms.

Though its figure looks like a human's, there's something about the way it stands as it peers at me through the dark that makes me wonder otherwise. Maybe the way it's hunched over, or maybe the way the hands seem at an odd angle. Maybe it's the way its neck is twisted unnaturally far to watch me as I am frozen in the street, or the way it's much taller than any average adult I know.

Still, though, I'm convinced it's not a cancer. The coloring is off, and there's something less… human, if that's even possible. It sends shivers down my spine as I think about it more and more. Something is wrong. Something is very, very wrong with this figure standing at the end of the road.

As if sensing I've come to this conclusion, it begins moving away and around a corner. For some reason, I begin jogging faster, trying to reach the corner it had just rounded. Am I following it? I don't know, but something has grasped the inside of my chest, and I don't know whether that's curiosity or a death wish, but something is very wrong.

I turn the corner, but there's nothing in sight… except *wait- There!* I see something round the next corner. An arm, or leg maybe. I walk towards the shape until I realize that the thing hadn't rounded a corner, it had entered a building. When I stop for a moment to take the building in, I can hear things being moved around, scraping on the floor from a window far above. As if someone is moving furniture.

I cautiously walk up to the building and gaze up at the window I think the noise is coming out of, but I still can't see any movement. I look down and peer into the glass doors of the tall building, straining my eyes to see where the shape had gone off to. Instead, my eyes set upon a small, square sign held up by a shiny pole.

WELCOME TO VAVINTO'S
HOTEL AND RESORT

I stand, trying to process the sign's meaning. My brain is noticeably slower, most likely because it's being deprived of the blood it needs to run. I try to steady myself but the world feels like it's literally being turned upside down.

This is the building I need to go in. This is where Mr. Harlow was last. Is he still in here though? Maybe I really am alone in this abandoned town, my only company the cold bodies on the street. And that figure… Maybe I will die alone, not by the side of Mr. Harlow, or any other human being. Would it have been better to stay back at the barn, and at least spent my last hours with people I know? Trust? Call friends?

Too late for that now. I push open the doors and slowly walk into the resort, trying to ignore the fact that I am following in the tracks of that... thing I had seen on the road. Every time I pass a chair or large flower vase, I jump, thinking that it's just standing there, against the wall.

The floor, though a polished wood, creaks under my footsteps, which does not help with my nerves. I'm halfway down the hallway when my disease-ridden brain comes to the thought that should have been first. I have no idea what room he is in. Where would he be? I consider going back to the main desk and checking the list, but remember that it's probably on the computer, and the internet's out. Even if it is offline, by the looks of it the power is out too, or at least unreliable. All the fancy lightbulbs on the windows are cold and dark, gathering dust.

So then where would he be? And then it hits me. Someone, or something, had to be making those noises far up in that window both the figure and I had heard. If there is even a slight chance it could be Mr. Harlow, I need to take it. I can't afford to think of anything but this last favor I'm doing for Elizabeth. If it's a cancer up in that room making that noise, at least I will have known I died trying to do something good. It's better than turning into a cancer and killing my friends along with everyone in that barn.

Still, a part of me, the selfish part, yearns to be back beside that barn. To not care about the consequences, to fade away in peace. Or at least, as peacefully as possible. I want to be anywhere but here, so much so that tears threaten to spill forth. My eyesight becomes blurry, so I have to wipe the moisture away.

● ● ●

I find the stairs and make my way up to the fourth floor, which is the level that noise had been coming from. I'm pretty sure? I think back to outside, trying to grasp an image of all the walls and balconies.

I can barely see a thing, due to the lack of windows, but I think I'm in a long hallway. If I'm not mistaken, the doors to my left are the ones that lead to the rooms facing the street. It had been coming from the middle of the building, so I feel both ends of the wall with my hands to know which direction to go, and prepare to head forward.

It's only when I see the white smudge at the very end of the hall that my heart stops completely. Through the overwhelming dark, the figure is almost inconsequential, a figment of imagination. But I am dead sure I'm not imagining the seven-foot tall, long armed and legged figure at what I judge to be the very end of the inky black hallway.

211

As I examine the shape as much as my limited eyesight will let me, I'm about to back away when I see the smile. Not a smile, really, but there's no mistaking the two rows of teeth, bottom and top. I strain my eyes and I think the teeth go up on the sides of the head, giving it the unnerving appearance of a grin. Whatever this thing is, it has the mouth of a cancer, its face able to swing open on its head.

Except right now, its mouth is barely open, and begins to make chattering sounds that echo quietly through the dark halls of the empty hotel. My blood runs cold.

Can it see me? I'm sure. Though it presumably has no eyes like a cancer, it must have some way of seeing. I have the disquieting sense of being watched.

Back on the bridge, in the car, when the cancer couldn't see through the glass, it wasn't like it could see, but rather know where and what things are. My theory is they're using echolocation.

As I think about it more, the more it makes sense. That noise in the back of their throat must be producing the sound waves they put out, and maybe its blank face is covered in receptors, hence its keen 'eyesight'? Better than eyesight, because they don't need light to see.

As my theory comes together, it even worsens my dread, because now I know that, whether I can or not, it sees me. It sees me now, as it makes those horrible chattering noises with its mouth.

I want to cry. At the unfairness. At why this has to happen to me.

But I can't. I won't. I won't allow my last few moments to go to waste, because I can already feel prickles of pain in my face as the disease begins the transformation. I will spend them doing something good. Something right, in the face of all this horror and fear.

Against my better judgment, I take a step forward.

PART THREE:
THE MONSTER

The smudge at the end of the hall does nothing but continue to smile at me. I keep my eyes on it, which is hard to do because I can barely see anything around me, let alone this foreboding figure. It's odd that I can see this creature at all though, because normally the cancer would be black and I would be blind to it in this darkness. For some reason, this creature is different. A defect maybe?

Its teeth chatter still, the bone chilling sounds bouncing around in the intense, palpable darkness. It smiles still, as I take my next couple of steps. It still stands there, doing nothing but watching me. I think I can even hear the sounds in its throat. It's hard to know for sure though, with all the adrenaline rushing through my ears. How can it be so loud, yet so disturbingly silent at the same time.

When I judge myself to be in the middle, I risk raising my hand in the air to knock, keeping my eyes on the smudge at the end of the hall for a reaction. The chattering of the teeth stops for a moment, leaving me in dead silence, but then picks up again, the creature not even moving.

Not sure how to feel about the reaction the thing gave, I knock on the door. The smiling humanoid figure at the end of the corridor begins a low-pitched screech, similar to what the cancers make. It's different though. More gurgled. When no one answers the door, I step forward in the darkness and try the next one. Still no answer, and the rising volume of the creature's screeches and chattering teeth make me hesitant to knock on the third door.

I raise my fist and slowly knock on the third wooden door three times. I'm about to move to the next one, sure I'm all but teasing the thing at the end of the hallway, when another knock comes from the other side of the door. This knock is no simple knock, though. It has a pattern.

Knock. Knock-knock knock. Knock.

There must be a reason for this pattern. I struggle to form one in my slowing brain. The person on the other side wants me to knock back. To confirm I am still human.

Barely. I think bitterly.

Knock. Knock-knock knock. Knock. I mimic the pattern.

I hear a hushed voice through the thick wood. A man's voice, maybe around his late thirties or early forties if I had to guess.

"Is anybody there." The man on the other side whispers.

"Yes." I mutter, clearing my throat and watching the white smudge grinning in the dark. It's still focusing on me fully.

"Are you alone?" The man says through the door, his speech muffled.

"No. There's something here, watching me, at the end of the hall." I say, my voice cracking a bit as I shake uncontrollably.

I hear the man silently curse behind the door. "Okay listen. I will open the door on the count of three. If you are not inside this room in less than two seconds, I am closing the door, do you understand?"

"Yes," I say, grateful that the man is even letting me in at all, "Okay. Go ahead. It's still watching."

"One." The man says slowly, "Two..."

The thing at the end of the hall must sense the rising tension because I see the teeth widen apart as the figure lurches forward, extending its long hands.

"Three."

The door swings wide open as it races forward towards me. I dart inside as fast as I can and the man behind the door attempts to shut the entrance as quickly as possible, but something from the outside pushes against it. I see a slimy white appendage sliding in through the few inches of still open space between the doorway and the actual door, struggling to be shut.

I charge back at the door, slamming all my weight into the wooden passageway. It tries to violently shut against the gnarled, clawed hand, and the creature on the other side of the door screeches in agony and outrage. It quickly withdraws its hand, but then attempts to stick its head inside. The pale, slimy head can be seen, even from my low vantage point, as it tries to push its way through the opening. When the mouth opens, it's similar to the cancer's, but as it widens, the teeth push outwards even more, angling away from the mouth.

Though horrifying as its face is, the rest of the body remains a mystery, as both the man and I push our full weight against the door, and it loudly slams shut, forcing the creature outside. The man quickly turns the lock on the door, then slides the secondary lock into place, and hauls a couch in front of the entrance, leaving little concern of the thing getting in that way.

Then, both of us slide to the floor, panting.

"Thank you." I gasp, attempting to catch my breath.

The man just nods as he pants, letting his head fall back against the couch he leans on. After a moment, he gets up with much effort, and staggers over to the small kitchen where he proceeds to get water from the sink. The hotel room is small, two beds beside the mini kitchen and a TV, curtains drawn in front of the windows along with furniture reinforcing the thing. The area is lit with a battery-operated lantern sitting on the counter.

"What was that?" I ask, pushing myself to my feet. I wipe the condensation off of my forehead as I stand lopsided due to my foot being completely asleep. Now, I can feel parts of my face twitching. My eyelids and upper lip. My guess is that I'm spending energy that's supposed to be saved for the mutation of my body. That's resulting in the twitching I'm experiencing. I'm prolonging the transformation the more I use energy. At some point though, I'll just collapse, and it'll get to work nice and quick.

"I don't know." The man says, setting the glass down before filling another and gesturing for me to proceed to the kitchen. "it's... it's been here since it all started."

"All started-" I say, trying to shake myself awake. My eyelids are spasming, and I'm exhausted. "You mean you've seen it before?"

"Okay, okay," The man says, holding his hands up, "I think introductions are in order? Who are you?"

"Oh," I say, setting down the glass on the counter, making a *clink* sound. "Yes. Sorry. I assume you are Mr. Harlow?"

The man nods.

"I'm Luke, a friend of your daughter's." I say, "She and another boy traveled here with me to search for you."

"Is my wife here? Or your parents?" The man asks.

"No sir, just us three." I say.

"You mean to tell me that Elizabeth's mother, and your parents, just let you come all the way here all by yourself?"

"No." I say, looking down, "We didn't exactly get permission."

The man chuckles slightly, "That does sound like Elizabeth."

I examine the man, really getting a good look at him for the first time. I can see the similarities between him and Elizabeth. The vivid green eyes. The small splash of freckles across his face. I can't help but notice the difference too. Mr. Harlow has light brown hair, a far cry from Elizabeth's bright ginger. And, despite his actions in the last few moments, Mr. Harlow has the general appearance of a stereotypical nerdy person. Rounded square glasses. A mustache.

Then Mr. Harlow seems to think of something, his eyes widening. "Where is she? Where is Elizabeth and the other boy? Are they out there still? Are they- You don't mean to say they're..."

"No, they're okay." I say, and I can see the man's shoulders relax. "They're just up the hill south from here, at a barn with some other survivors."

"Why aren't they here, with you? How did you know where I am? How did you get through the city without being scratched or killed? How do you know my daughter?" The man says, then realizes that his list of questions is becoming extensive. "Okay. Luke. What's your last name?"

"Anderson." I say.

"Anderson." Muses Mr. Harlow, nodding slightly, "Elizabeth's mentioned you. Your little sister comes over to our house sometimes, right? To play with Maddie?"

"Yes." I say, surprised that the Harlows even knew I existed before this week.

"Is my wife alright? And Maddie?" He asks, anxiety growing in his eyes.

"Both fine." I say, "As far as I know, anyway."

Mr. Harlow sighs in relief. "You have brought me the best news in my life, boy. Thank you. So, why aren't they here with you? Elizabeth and... this other boy."

"Griffin," I say.

"Oh! Griffin! Okay, that makes sense. She and Griffin have been quite good friends for a long time." Mr. Harlow says, then looks at me apologetically, "Sorry, I interrupted. Continue?"

"They're both back at the barn, like I said." I say, "They didn't exactly know I was coming for you. I-" My headache kicks up a notch and I try to form words, "I came here to find you without telling them. Our plan was to come here tomorrow."

"So why did you then? Come without them?"

"Because I won't be with them tomorrow." I say, "I got scratched."

The man looks at me cautiously, examining my face. "Why aren't you asleep? There are strong chemicals that-"

"I know." I say rather rudely, fighting off the dizziness that's trying to sway my body back and forth. It's disorienting. "Sorry. I know. We went to the lab and read the files. I assume you know about that? The lab, I mean."

Mr. Harlow nods, "How'd you know that?"

"Tobias, the man you interviewed, he's up at the barn with Elizabeth, Griffin, and the rest of the survivors." I say, pressing my palm to my temple, trying to eradicate the headache pounding in my skull. "You go south, up the road, and then follow a path of stick arrows. That's the best I can do for you. I really need to get on my way now, before I turn into one of them."

Mr. Harlow looks around, as if deciding something, before beginning to quickly whisper as if sharing a valuable secret, despite us being alone. "I might have a solution. Might. I have a theory. After talking with Tobias, I had squeezed every bit of information out of him that I could, and tried fitting some information together. He told me that the disease spreads through your bloodstream, degenerating, infecting, and mutating your red and white blood cells, first ridding them of DNA. Now, I'm no scientist, and there's a lot of complicated stuff that goes into this that I couldn't hope to fully understand, but my theory is that if you have enough of your blood infected with the cancerous disease, you can do the exact opposite of what the cancer did."

"What?" I ask, completely confused.

"You inject yourself with blood, either your own or someone else's with a compatible type, and do the same thing the disease did to your body, just opposite. Reintroducing those white blood cells just might fight back against the disease. There's a whole bunch of more complex stuff about how the cells will reproduce due to the abundance of the new disease, more prepared for it because the pre-existing white blood cells already knew how to kill the disease but are too infected to do so, but they can teach the new ones which will reproduce, essentially making a better equipped-"

"I have no idea what you're saying." I groan. I could probably better understand it if my head weren't pounding so painfully, but right now I couldn't tell you the difference between an elephant and steam engine.

"Okay," he sighs, putting his hands up, "What blood type are you?"

"I have no idea." I say truthfully.

"And I assume you don't just have a bag of your own blood lying around. I'm type AB so I can't safely donate blood to you..." He thinks for a moment, "But I do know someone who's a type O, which is the universal donor, and she happens to be right where we want to go."

"But wh-" I begin, but Mr. Harlow cuts me off.

"Elizabeth." He says, already beginning to gather his things "Elizabeth is type O. She's who you need."

The preparation is quick and hasty. I barely do anything, feeling too sick to contribute much. Mr. Harlow runs around the hotel room, grabbing documents and all sorts of things, most likely the data he used to figure out this possible cure he has in mind. I don't even know if it will work or not. Maybe it would just be easier to curl up here and-

"Luke," Mr. Harlow says, gesturing for me to come forward to him, "I don't know if it will help, but I get seasick. I wear this bracelet that presses against a nerve or something. It's supposed to help. Tobias said intense dizziness was a symptom, so…"

"Thank you," I say, staggering over and slipping the bracelet on. I take this as a sign of some sort of bond. No, more of a symbol of trust. I look down at the bracelet. It is made of a fabric that stretches easily, but is tight around my wrist. Sure enough, there is a plastic bump against the part that goes against the underside of my wrist, most likely because there is a nerve there, like Mr. Harlow said. I'm not sure if it's supposed to help right away, or over time, but I don't feel much of a difference at all.

Mr. Harlow finishes sliding a couple of notebooks into his computer bag, packing so much in it that it bulges like a balloon about to burst. He sees that my eyes have fallen to the stuffed pockets.

"Don't worry, they're all important. The ones I don't need are in my suitcase." He says, patting the stuffed laptop bag. I look over to his bed and see that there is an entire small suitcase filled just with papers, notebooks, and other journaling things. Only a small portion is set aside for clothes.

"I've been documenting as much as I can. My laptop died days ago, so it's all right there on paper."

"Okay." I say. Maybe the bracelet is working, because my mind seems a bit clearer now, but that may be due to the adrenaline pumping through my veins once again. "So, we just leave? That's it?"

"Unless you have a better idea." He says, clutching the computer bag tightly to his chest.

"Have you been out there since the initial attack?" I ask, hoping for a yes.

"Only downstairs to the cafeteria. Twice." He says, and I sigh in disappointment. If he hasn't even left the building, we're basically going out there blind. I'm sure that if I could hear Mr. Harlow moving around furniture from the street, the ruckus we made with that... thing, will not have gone un-noticed.

"And you're sure this cure is going to work?" I ask, stalling for time, which unfortunately I am running short on. Would it be better to go out there and get it over with? Or would I be content just staying here, in this room, waiting for my body's doomsday timer to go off.

"Not at all." He says, then re-words it to sound brighter, furrowing his eyebrows "But I believe that there's a chance it could."

Way to put a cheerful spin on things, I think privately. *I'm not sure if you'll die, but I hope not!'* Well, it's better than just letting it happen. Mr. Harlow needs to get to the barn anyways.

"You think it's out there?" I ask slowly, "That- other thing?"

"Probably. I'd bet it's not alone either." Mr. Harlow mutters darkly. "They let you walk in. Hopefully they'll let you walk out."

We cautiously open the door, which squeaks a bit too much for comfort. I immediately look down the hall, but see no smudge in the darkness, nor a disturbing toothy "smile" glistening in the little light available.

When I say little light available, I mean none, because when we step out into the hallway, everything is pitch-black. The little moonlight that had shone through Mr. Harlow's window shades is gone. We have the lantern, but it's so dim we can barely see a few feet in front of us. At most.

Out of the hotel we go, and onto the once cheerful, now abandoned streets. Windows smashed, cars open, lamp-posts flickering on and off every now and then, electronic wires exposed and torn. Through the town with the moon gazing down on us, our footsteps echoing loudly in the shop-fronts. Multiple times, I swear I see a dark shape through a window, or crouching out of sight in the back of a store. Are they people? Or are they something else? A couple times, I swear I hear the low pulses they make in the back of their throat, but whenever I stop to listen it's all silent. Maybe it was just my slowing heartbeat. By the time we leave Main Street, I'm almost completely leaning on Mr. Harlow.

I feel relieved, to be out of the town, out of the hotspot. It's like leaving a crowded room of sick people, like I can finally breathe clean air. I can see this effect tenfold on Mr. Harlow's face as he examines the trees blowing slightly in the breeze, the mist creeping along the forest floor. I'll admit, I'd be more rejuvenated if it weren't for the pounding headache and reality-bending dizziness.

We travel up the gravel road, and I notice my headache and dizziness is just getting worse. My face has almost completely fallen asleep, and it hurts to even move it. I can barely move my lips to form words without wincing.

I point out the patch of forest I'd come through, and walk in a straight line the best we can. This should lead us back to the others.

Is it just me or are my hands sort of going grayish? Hopefully it's just the moonlight.

We continue following the arrows, and I can see the sky above turning orange. Sunrise. Finally. It feels like we've been walking for hours. Light is just breaking through the dark sky when I see it. The back of the barn. We must have gone off track at some point, because we should've emerged facing the front, but we've gotten here anyway!

I can't put into words how glad I am to have finally reached the rotting old structure.

Sure enough, I see Griffin and Elizabeth standing, pacing around where we'd slept, looking very agitated. I see them talking back and forth, both of their mouths moving rapidly as they tell the other whatever they're saying.

"Elizabeth…" Mr. Harlow whispers, then shouts jubilantly "Elizabeth!"

He runs forward, waving his hand in the air. "Elizabeth!"

I see Elizabeth stop pacing and look up. First, her face is a mask of confusion. Then recognition. Then joy, her features lighting up, her eyebrows raising, the corners of her mouth upturning in a shocked, disbelieving smile. She runs towards him too and they collide in a tight embrace. They keep talking to each other as they hug, squeezing each other tightly, but I can't tell what it is they're saying because they're talking at the same time.

Finally, they loosen their grips on one another and step back a bit to take in the other.

"-And your friend," Mr. Harlow says, smiling and turning back towards me, pointing with his thumb, "He found me and brought me here."

Elizabeth looks over to where he's pointing, apparently noticing me for the first time. I see Griffin in the background raise his eyebrows too, but say nothing.

Elizabeth stares at me for a moment, before heading my way. Her strides are wide and she's moving fast.

I don't know what I was expecting. A hug? A handshake maybe? At least some kind of thanks?

She extends her arms, and I think she's going for the hug option so I extend my arms too… but then she presses her palms against my chest and shoves me backwards. Unexpecting, and already dizzy, I painfully stumble backwards and almost fall to the ground.

"What were you thinking." She says harshly. I can see Mr. Harlow give an appalled look behind her, but he is too far away to do anything.

She pushes me again.

"You said you wouldn't go. You promised."

I am on the ground, trying to scramble to my feet. When I do, I expect Elizabeth to shove me again, but instead, I find tears welling up in her eyes. She launches herself at me, and this time, it really is a hug.

She squeezes me so tight I can't breathe, but for some reason, I don't care. I squeeze her back, and realize for the first time how truly scared I've been. I feel my back muscles release their tension and my nervousness drain away as we are wrapped in this warm embrace.

"I'm sorry I pushed you." Elizabeth says, still not letting go.

"It's okay." I say, "I deserved it."

Elizabeth sniffles and laughs into my shoulder, "Yes you did."

She releases me, and I feel, if possible, even clumsier than before. I've missed them. Both of them. I look to Griffin, who stands awkwardly back at the sleeping area. I stagger towards him (Probably looking drunk), not knowing what I'm actually planning on doing. A hug maybe? My head is too foggy for any complex thoughts to form.

When I reach him, instead of hugging him, I stick my hand out. "I'm sorry I left. It's good to see you again."

I am surprised by how steady my voice sounds, considering how much or a wreck I feel like. Griffin, still awkward, shakes my hand and nods, looking at my face worriedly.

"Thanks for coming back."

I'm about to nod, when I collapse in a heap on the ground, the overwhelming headache, body pains, dizziness, and lack of circulation is finally becoming too much. I don't know how much longer I can actually hold out.

Startled, Griffin backs away. Mr. Harlow rushes to my aid, checking my pulse. Hurriedly, he sprints over to Elizabeth after confirming that I am in fact still alive.

"I don't have time to explain. He needs you. We need you to donate some blood."

And that's when my body starts involuntarily convulsing in pain, and everything finally blacks out.

The first thing I notice when I wake is the stinging in my arm. At first, dizzy and confused, I think it's a bee stinging me. I swat at my arm, only to find there is a cloth rag wrapped around my bicep. Confused even further, I try removing the cloth but it won't budge. I try undoing whatever knot is keeping it in place, but my hands are slippery with sweat.

With a start, I realize my entire body is covered in sweat, liked I'd been bathed in the hot sticky stuff. The new shirt I am wearing clings to my body because I am drenched. I wipe my slick forehead.

"He's awake." I hear someone whisper hoarsely, then clear their throat and say it louder, "He's awake! Luke's awake!"

I hear shuffling, but I don't try and sit up. I just lie still on the soft grass and soil, eyes on the misty sky. In a matter of seconds, people are staring down at me as I stare blankly up at them. I don't say anything, just take them in, squinting a bit.

"You alright?" Griffin asks. Pushing his brown hair out of his face as he stares down at me. I manage to nod, which takes a lot more energy than it should have.

"You've had a rough night." Mr. Harlow says as he straightens his glasses.

"Night?" I croak, "It was morning when we got here. Wha- what time is it?"

"Ten in the morning. You've been asleep for over twenty-four hours" Elizabeth says, "I donated my blood to you yesterday, and you started squirming around in your sleep, screaming and such. It was really scary."

"I-" I stammer, "I did that?"

They all nod gravely, as if it hadn't been much fun for them either.

"How- how did you transfer the blood?" I ask.

"Back in town, when I first figured out the cure," Mr. Harlow says, "I stole the syringes from the local pharmacy the day everything went crazy. You know, just in case I needed to use it for myself. Anyways, when we got back here, I figured your blood was contaminated enough to try giving you some fresh blood to fight with. By the looks of it, it did the trick."

"How do you know?" I ask suddenly, looking at my sweaty, paper white, wreck of a body, "What if it didn't work?"

"Then you'd be dead by now." Says a new voice. I look around to find a man in a torn coat staring down at me, his brown hair in tight curls atop his head. He has a dark, umber-like complexion, and his eyes look me over, analyzing. "or worse"

"This is Tobias," Elizabeth says, gesturing at the man, "Luke, Tobias, Tobias, Luke. He oversaw your healing."

"Hi." I say weakly, "Thank you."

Tobias nods, "Of course. You're very lucky to be alive. Dean here," He gestures at Mr. Harlow, "was very smart about the cure."

I nod.

"Do you feel well enough to sit up?" Elizabeth asks, brushing her grimy, wavy ginger hair over her shoulder. She looks concerned.

"You pushed me." I croak.

"It just so happens I did." She says, smiling and wiping her eyes a bit. "Like I said. You deserved it."

I look to Griffin. "And you? Are you okay?"

"Never better." He says, crossing his arms and leaning against a tree, the sides of his mouth upturned a little. "Glad that you're okay."

Tobias sighs and rubs his forehead, "It's good that you are finally awake, but I am exhausted. I'm going to bed." He yawns widely, "Wake me if you need anything."

"Bed?" I say looking up at the man in confusion, "I thought you said it's morning. It's been a day since I got back, right?"

"They all stayed up to, you know, watch you- and stuff." Elizabeth tells me. "We wanted to help too, but they said we couldn't do anything and to just get some sleep."

"They?" I ask, looking around.

"Mr. Tobias and my dad." Elizabeth says, gesturing.

"Oh," I stutter, "I'm so sorry, I-"

"It is not your fault." Mr. Harlow says simply, "By the looks of it, you have had a worse night than any of us. I had assumed you'd have needed more, less violent, rest."

I look down at my body, which is slick with sweat and covered in grime and dirt. My skin is a horrible paper white color, and as I raise my hands to examine them, I find there is tons of gunk wedged under the nails. I can't see my face, but it feels like when the blood began running through it again, it had burnt. There is still a residual warmth there that is in stark contrast to the cold surroundings.

"Hey," I say, noticing where I am for the first time, "We're in the barn."

"Yeah," Griffin says and both Mr. Harlow and Tobias walk away to try and take a nap, "we brought you in here last night."

"Why is there so much hay around us?" I ask, for we are tightly boxed in by bails of hay that had, if my memory is correct, been previously piled near the door.

Griffin winces. "Last night, when you were outside the barn... Well, you were screaming and thrashing around so much they brought you in here and tried to muffle the sound. I- I expect most will sleep in today, because I don't think anybody got much rest."

I look around. Even Elizabeth, who acts like she's fine, is a shade greener. Is she feeling sick because she got no rest last night? If so, that's my fault.

I feel bad about keeping everybody up, but I really don't have the energy to express it right now so I don't. Instead, I lie back down and exhale. Maybe Mr. Harlow was right. Maybe I do need some more rest. I'm exhausted, despite just now waking up. In fact, I do think that a nice peaceful, undisturbed rest would be in order.

"I'm just gonna-" I say, closing my eyes, but I never get to finish my sentence because the minute my head rests on the ground, my muscles all relax and I'm instantly asleep.

I had expected nightmares. I had expected to be tormented in my sleep about all the horrible things in El Arnica. The smashed cars. The trolly driver. This new... creature that I still don't know anything about.

Instead, a memory is sparked from deep within...

● ● ●

My fingers type away on a keyboard.

"-therefore – rising – the – blood – pressure – of – the - organism." I mutter as I write. "There, finished."

Ginny, a brown-haired girl, swoops down into the seat next to me.

"Thank you." She gasps, resting her elbows on the desk and propping up her face to look at me, "You're a life saver, truly."

"Don't mention it." I say, downloading the file to email to her. "You'll have to make it a different format in order to turn it in, but that shouldn't be too hard."

"Mhmm," She mumbles, looking across the room. "Hey, do you think you could do Roman's too? He and I are going out tonight, and he won't really have much time to do it so..."

Roman. Another one of my friends, and Ginny's boyfriend. Well, for the moment at least, who they're dating tends to change every few days.

"I think." I say, "Which one?"

"Same thing as you just did for me. The essay, or whatever." Ginny says, leaning in next to me and watching my computer screen.

I nod, creating a new document. "No problem. So, where are you guys going? For the date, I mean."

Ginny's response is to side hug me, before heading across the room to latch onto Roman's arm.

Now the memory goes blurry for a bit. Nothing really interesting happens. I work on my laptop some more, presumably on Roman's essay. Next thing I know, the study hall is finished and we're being dismissed from the class. I shut down my electronics, close the textbooks, and stuff it all in my backpack. Roman comes over across the room, Ginny in tow. "Thanks man, I really owe you one."

"Yeah, no problem." I sling my backpack over my shoulder and head for the door.

"I'll need that one by tonight please," He says from behind me, "I also have another one, if you don't mind taking a look at it."

I flash him a thumbs up before the classroom door shuts behind me.

The hallway is now beginning to filter kids through, everyone heading to their next scheduled class. Mine is biology, so I make a left and head for the stairs. I always forget that the biology lab is on the second floor, as this is my first year taking it.

As I approach the bottom of the stairs, the hallway begins to grow crowded, everyone leaving the classroom.

I'm about to make another step, heading up the staircase, when I catch movement out of the corner of my eye. I turn just in time to watch some kid face-plant in the middle of the hallway, his cheekbone hitting the tile with painful force.

I wince, but do nothing. Most snicker, though one red-haired girl glares around the room at people as she crouches down to see if he's okay. Once that's confirmed, she grasps his hand and helps him up.

"What was that for?!" She spits out at the others standing around, the ones who had let out poorly restrained laughter. One girl (I realize with a start that it's Ginny) responds.

"It's his fault he's so clumsy. Nobody tripped him, he did that on his own."

The redheaded girl snorts and begins walking towards Ginny in a determined manner. "I saw you stick your foot out, you stupid lying-"

The boy who had tripped reaches out and grabs her arm, "No, it was me. Don't Eliza-"

"What's going on?" A teacher says loudly, pushing her way through the crowd of kids who had gathered to watch. "Don't you all have classes to get to?"

Everyone, disappointed, slowly begins to disperse and head for their classrooms. The redheaded girl, who remains by the boy's side, flips Ginny a certain finger as she walks away. The boy's nose is now beginning to bleed.

"Ma'am, Ginny-" The girl begins, but is cut off by the teacher.

"Please go to the office. Now."

"But-"

"I said now, Elizabeth."

The girl glances at the boy, before giving stink-eye to the teacher and heading towards the office. She passes right by me, because I haven't moved. I'm frozen at the bottom of the stairs, watching the whole thing play out.

"What are you looking at." The girl says as she passes, "Ginny's your friend, isn't she? Why don't you go catch up with her."

The way she says Ginny's name, you'd think she was referring to a particularly smelly bag of dog poop.

"Elizabeth." The teacher says sternly. She reluctantly moves on, glaring at me until she's out of sight.

"As for you," The teacher says to the boy, "go take care of that bloody nose. The nurse can get you ice if you need it."

"Thanks." He mumbles.

The teacher walks away, leaving the hallway empty except for the boy and I. He picks up his backpack, which had fallen to the floor, and tries to sling it over his shoulder. Unfortunately, it's unzipped, and the books go flying out. They slap against the tile, sliding everywhere.

The boy curses and stoops down to retrieve them, when he glances up and sees that I'm still here. Instantly, I realize that I should have left ages ago. I consider helping him with his books, but then what would Roman, Ginny, and all the others think? Would my fragile social status be shattered? No, I can't risk it.

He locks eyes with me for a split second, before I turn away and climb the stairs, leaving the whole incident behind.

●　　●　　●

My eyes crack open and I'm slowly brought back into the real world, the dream fading into oblivion. I hear whispering from the hay bales around me and see that Griffin and Elizabeth are still by my side, talking. I smile a bit. Had they stayed by my side this whole time? I think so, they're still in the same spots, though adjusted to be more comfortable. It is this moment that I have a weird sentimental feeling in my chest at the thought of them. Maybe this summer hasn't been a complete nightmare.

"-spread all over the island," Elizabeth is saying, "If we could get the news about the cure back to Bluehill Ridge... It worked on Luke, even though we didn't know his blood type."

"So," I sniff, taking a deep breath and trying to sit up to look at her, "I assume anyone could use your blood then? Being type O and all?"

A huge yawn escapes me.

"Look who's awake," She says, smiling and showing me a bandage wrapped around her arm just like mine. "About that. My father pulled me aside and told me not to mention my blood type to everyone else. He said to tell everyone you and I had compatible blood types, because if everyone knows I'm a universal donor, they'll want to keep me here. We already asked. Nobody else here is an O, or knows if they are. Since my blood is a cure for everyone, it may be unwise."

"They wouldn't keep you here," I say, "The people here can't be that selfish, right? I mean they're letting us stay here."

Someone pushes aside the hay bale that serves as the entrance, and enters into the already cramped space. I don't recognize this woman, who has pale skin, dark raven hair, and wears a bandana over her face, covering her mouth but not her brown eyes, which look at me in a slightly repelled manner. Of course she does, she probably had to put up with my screams or whatever all last night.

"Tobias wanted me to tells you." The woman says in a very thick accent. French maybe? I'm not surprised because El Arnica, which I assume is where she came from, is a super touristy destination. This woman must have just been caught up in it all. Lucky her.

"He says west of here. In the forest. There is a- uhh- pond you can wash in." She struggles to say the words right, and then a small child rushes into the hay area and grabs onto his mother's leg.

"Pourquoi parles-tu au garçon qui crie?" says the boy, reaching up to his mother and jumping up and down.

"Parce que c'est un garçon puant" The mother says, scrunching up her nose and crossing her eyes, making the little boy squeal and laugh. The mother picks up her child and walks away, glancing back at me before turning the corner and out of sight.

"What do you think they were saying?' Elizabeth asks once they're out of earshot.

"Probably commenting on how good looking I am." I say, striking a pose. In my sick state, I probably look ridiculous, but who cares. Despite my appearance, I feel absolutely alive. Alive and awake and well. I realize that apart from my back, I really didn't have any severe injuries. Now that the sickness has been finally been killed and passed through my body (I don't even want to think about how I had to pass waste while asleep), I feel like a million bucks. My back is even regaining feeling, which I take to be a good thing despite the pain.

"Whatever helps you sleep at night." Griffin says, chuckling, though I still see an underlying worry in his eyes. I must have really sounded bad last night for him to be looking at me this way now. He passes it off easily enough though, evidently relieved at my seemingly speedy recovery in progress. "You really should go use that pond and wash off. You're a mess."

"I second that." Elizabeth puts in, *sniffing* me and then miming throwing up.

I laugh, which is a good sign because just hours ago I didn't feel well enough to even speak properly. I'm so sore though, that it hurts.

"C'mon." Elizabeth says hopping to her feet and making her way towards the hay bale entrance, "Griffin and I will walk you there. Then we'll leave, don't worry."

"You know, it almost seems like you're trying to get rid of me." I snort.

Elizabeth wrinkles her nose, "You stink. C'mon."

All three of us exit the barn, and I can't help take in how everything looks the same as it did when we first arrived. Like nothing has changed, but everything has. I haven't gotten a chance to discuss the thing back in town, the creature, but I know it is going to throw a wrench in things somehow.

The sky seems like it can't decide if it wants to be misty or clear today, so I guess it settled on something in-between. I can see bits blue sky between the clouds, which I guess is good. Nothing special. Nothing noticeable. Just a normal day.

Except it's anything but.

"My dad says that we're heading back as soon as he finishes his nap." Elizabeth says, "He says he needs the energy, and then we'll head straight back to the lab, which is hopefully where they are. If not- well, he says we'll cross that bridge when we get there."

I walk, no particular emotions playing on my dirty, grimy face.

"What do you think we'd be doing if everything were normal?" I ask. I can tell I've caught both Griffin and Elizabeth off guard because they both look at me in a confused way, "What would we be doing? Us three. Right now."

"All three of us? Together?" Elizabeth asks, looking back at the woods and continuing to walk, checking the compass on her father's phone, which he'd lent her.

"Yeah." I say.

"If this weren't happening?" Griffin asks, biting on his nail as he asks the question.

"Yeah." I say, then realize I'm speaking much too loudly given the circumstances, then realizing that I don't really care. We've been through worse. If they're here, I don't care. "What would we be doing if all three of us were friends back when it was normal. Today. Right now."

"I guess we could be headed to get some lunch or something. It's about that time" Griffin says, quieter than I had been.

"We could be going to your mom's café." Elizabeth says, thinking, "Maybe we could eat out on the porch, overlooking the ocean. It's a nice day, not too cold."

"I'd have had to get money from dad, since my wallet's been lost since Sunday." Griffin mutters. Elizabeth and I are silent, awkward, and Griffin realizes he's dampened the conversation. "I'd order the biggest hamburger your mom's place has to offer. With a large shake."

"And a heaping plate of French fries for the three of us to share." Elizabeth says, trying to move on like nothing happened. After a moment, the lightness of the mood is recovered. After all, we deserve just a little bit of time without all the stresses and pressures and grief that's been weighing us down like chains. All of us are eager for a bit of normalcy, even if that bit of normalcy is made up.

All three of us are silent as we bring the thought forward in our minds. A giant plate with piles of hot, salty, oily french fries. Chomping down on the stuff.

Just the thought of it makes my mouth flood with saliva. I'll be the first to admit it; we are hungry.

"Do they have food back at the barn?" I ask.

"They found a small stash, but everyone back there is just as hungry as us." Elizabeth says, "They say they're planning a trip back to El Arnica for food supplies tomorrow, since most of the people in there are starving."

"And water?" I ask, because you can't last long at all without water.

"Same pond you're going to bathe in." She says, and when she sees my face she adds, "Obviously they purify it first. They normally don't let people use it for cleaning themselves, but you're kind of a special case, so they allowed it I guess."

"Thanks." I say.

"I mean, she's got a point." Griffin says un-helpfully, "You smell like-"

"Okay, okay, I get it." I say, flopping my hands into the air.

"Just don't pee in that water." Griffin says, which childishly brings a round of laughter from all of us. I don't know why it's funny, but it is. My nerves are so frayed I don't even know what's considered funny anymore.

"So," Elizabeth says in an obvious tone of changing subjects, "They think it's safe for us to just come out here? I'm surprised they didn't make an adult go with us."

I clear my throat. "Yeah, I was wondering the same thing."

"Well," Griffin says, "My guess is that they know all of the cancers are in civilized areas, so they're pretty sure we're safe on this part of the island. And, I'm also assuming they know we've been through a lot, so they probably deem us responsible enough. And I bet Elizabeth's father doesn't even know, because he would have never allowed it."

"Yeah." I say, "That's probably true. Still though, I would have liked a gun or something."

"Do you even know how to use a gun?" Elizabeth asks condescendingly.

"I do." Griffin says, "My dad taught me a while back.

"Oh, cool." I say, thinking it would be a really handy skill right about now. "I don't, but I wish I do. I could use a bit of protection."

"Here we are." Elizabeth says, coming to a stop.

A silent, stagnant pond is spread out in front of us. It's not a lake, but plenty big enough for me to be able to go for a swim in. Lush tall grass grows on the sides of the greenish murky water. In some places, little swarms of gnats flutter around, watching the Lilli pads float still on the undisturbed surface.

"It's pretty," I say, looking at the silty pond "But I'm not sure I want to get in it."

"Well, you're gonna, otherwise neither of us are going to travel with you. You smell like a dead pig." Elizabeth helpfully informs me, and Griffin nods seriously.

"I don't have any extra clothes." I say.

"Well, they didn't give us any." Griffin says, "When you get back, we can ask if they've got any spares. For now, just wear those again."

"Or nothing," Elizabeth snorts, "You'd give us all a show."

I roll my eyes, "Okay. I'll be back in a bit. Wait for me at the barn."

They give me a thumbs up and leave back into the forest, I watch them until I can no longer see their forms or hear their footsteps before turning back to the pond. It's really beautiful and peaceful with its glass-like surface and thick plants growing at its edges, but still not something I would want to get in. I can't even see the bottom past *half a foot*, and I don't know how deep it is. With how wide it is, I expect it could be pretty deep in the middle.

My own smell is the only thing that drives me to undress and get into the water, setting my clothes on a stone beside the bank.

The murky water is cold on my exposed skin, but I force myself to get in all the way to my neck. I sit still for a moment, trying to get used to the temperature. When I finally do, I have no idea how to get washed, since I don't have a sponge or anything.

I dunk my head beneath the surface and run my hands through my floating hair, scrubbing it and brushing off all the grime and dirt that has been embedded in it for much too long. All the muck that's been building up for days.

The water refreshes and energizes me. I try to scrub the rest of my body off in the water, and I can't help thinking how nice it feels to finally be clean again. Once I'm done cleaning myself, I overcome my fear of going out into the middle of the pond and do a couple of laps, just sliding through the water.

I can feel the squishy mud on my feet up until a certain point, and then it drops down to who knows how deep. I stay near the surface, still a bit creeped out by what I'm not be able to see way down below the surface.

In fact, I nearly jump out of my skin whenever my foot touches a submerged log under the water. It is after touching two or three of these that I decide it's time to head back.

Of course, that is when I spot it. The cancer. At the very edge of the pond. Its featureless face is towards me, and it's frozen as it takes me in. It makes those sounds in the back of its throat that must mean it's looking at me. One hand is in mid-air, above the pond surface, as if it's just as surprised by me as I am by it.

I stare at it for a moment, and it appears to stare back as I try and process what to do. Get out of the pond? Run? Can it even swim?

When it begins stepping into the water, something finally clicks. The way they got the sheriff. In his boat out at sea. They can swim. The sheriff leaves, but a cancer hops up onto his boat. It scratches him and he falls unconscious. Maybe he drowns or maybe he makes it to shore alive, but he got to where Griffin and I had found him so many days ago.

I don't know how I didn't put this together sooner. This changes everything- but surely mainland is much too far for them to swim, right? They need air? Rest? Surely the mainland is safe.

Or is everyone there going through what we are, just on a larger scale?

My mind is pulled from its thoughts as the cancer silently slips into the glass-like water, barely making any disturbance. First its front appendages, then its head, followed silently by the rest of its body, disappearing in the murky dark water, shadowed by the unknown, yet as present as the eerie submerged logs that reach for my exposed feet from the depths of the pond. The last thing I see is the row of thin curvy spines, swishing back and forth as it swims deeper and deeper, fading out of sight.

As panic grips my chest, my first impulse is to thrash as fast as I can to get back to land. Will this disturbance provoke the monster? Surely, its echolocation works underwater (as whale's and dolphin's do), which is much better than even a pair of eyes. It can see without fault in any conditions. The murky water that blocks my view of it has no effect on the cancer.

I take a deep breath. I can't just tread water in the middle of the pond, exposed. I can't just wait for it to jut out of the depths like those arms of the logs and grass reaching up for me. To try and pull me down.

Movement. There. Nearer to me, I can see a dark shape beneath the surface as it continues gliding towards me, sinking even farther underwater. For all I know, it's underneath me now.

Or maybe it's taking its time, knowing that I have no chance of escape.

I slowly begin to swish my legs back and forth under the silty water, propelling myself towards shore. It's terrifying, not knowing what's right under you, yet fully aware something is in the water, actively trying to kill you. I feel like I'm in a pond full of alligators, blending with the logs and silty pond bottom, watching me from below. Waiting for the right time to strike.

I reach the shore (*Oh my God I reached the shore*) and slowly put my feet down, expecting to feel the form of the creature right beneath me. Much to my short-lived relief, I feel only squishy mud. I slowly crawl up onto the shore, shivering from the combination of cold and fear.

My first instinct is to bolt. Into the forest, fleeing for the barn, but then I'd rather not storm in buck naked, running through the camp like a psycho. You can say I've got my priorities wrong, but I'd rather be killed right here and now than do that.

Grimacing at the mere thought, I creep over to my pile of clothes on the rock and slowly pick up my first undergarments. I keep my eyes on the pond the entire time, watching for any stray ripples or bubbles rising from the deep. Instead, I can make out a very vague form swimming in the pond, so shrouded in silt and floating mud I can only see its outline. It moves like a snake as it slithers back and forth in the water, searching. I guess it hasn't realized I'm out of the water yet. Maybe all the mud and particles floating around *does* affect its echolocation? At least somewhat?

I finish slipping on my underwear and begin my pants. Once I have the pants on, I fumble around with the belt, which jingles slightly as my hands shake.

Is the belt really worth it? I decide it is, because these are someone else's pants and they are much too loose for me. If they fall down, it won't be as comical as it looks, because it will affect my running if I end up needing to make a quick escape.

I finish with the belt and see the smooth, tar black head rising from the pond. It has discovered I've escaped the water, and come to find me above the surface.

I grab the shirt and begin backing away. The moment I think I might just pull off getting away without being noticed, a branch breaks beneath my foot and the cancer's head jerks towards me. By those noises in its throat, I know it sees me.

I wait a moment, before spinning around and breaking into a run. It takes a moment for the cancer to respond, but then its leaping through the forest on all fours like a dog. Sprinting, I struggle to put my shirt on over my head and accidentally jam my shoulder into the side of a tree. I slip the shirt on and curse, continuing to run for my life. I can hear the panting of the animal behind me, and I'm sure it will catch up to me in a matter of seconds. I'm sure it can.

Yet it doesn't. Its speed seems restrained.

Unfortunately, I don't put two and two together, and before I know it I'm back at the barn, yelling my head off for everyone to stay inside and to shut off the barn from the outside. When I get to the door, I see everyone is frozen, shocked.

"They're here!" I yell at them, "One's here!"

I look back to the cancer, which is at the edge of the very close, rounded tree line. Instead of pursuing, it raises up onto its hind legs and points its face/mouth to the sky. It makes the sounds it uses for echolocation, but ten times as loud. The sound echoes through the forest, and I can already hear other cancers closing in. They were already here. Already close.

"It's an ambush!" I scream at everyone, "They know we're here! They're coming! Close everything up!"

"We can't keep them out!" Tobias yells back at me from the other side of the barn, "This will become a slaughter house if we lock ourselves in!"

This was the exact worse thing to say in this situation. Everyone panics and runs at the door. Someone grasps my arm and I try to shake it off before I realize it's Elizabeth and Griffin.

"We need to get back to Bluehill Ridge." She says, panicky, "It's bound to be safer there now. Or the lab."

"Hear that everyone?" One man yells to the crowd, "Get to the road! Go to Bluehill! They say it's safer there!"

This, unfortunately, creates a stampede. Everyone sprinting, stumbling over one another. A chaos-fueled frenzy.

Mr. Harlow materializes out of nowhere, his bag over his shoulder. "Go. Go, we need to go now." he shoves us three out the barn door just as the forest comes alive. Cancers in trees and emerging from tall grass pop out of everywhere.

"GO!" Mr. Harlow screams at us, "Get to the bridge!"

"What about you?" Yells Elizabeth, struggling against the flow of people.

"I'll meet you there! At the bridge! Don't take the road!" And then he disappears, into the crowd. I realize he must be getting weapons, something very important out here. We've been careless with our security, and this is how we pay for it.

"Go! Go!" Griffin says, looking around frantically and moving us forward. He subconsciously moves with the crowd, towards the road.

"No," I say, "Through the forest. Liz's dad has a point. It's less of a target."

We swerve to the left and begin sprinting fast and hard, passing the cancers heading for the crowd. Apparently the crowd gets it too because they all split up, diverging into the woods, for the road, and some even backtrack to get away from the cancer horde.

We race through the thick woods, knowing we are headed for Pirate's Avenue, but not knowing how far or how long it will take. A cramp forms in my side, but I try to ignore it as the adrenaline pumps through my veins. I am still wet and cold as I run due to my bath, but this does nothing to help with the sweat forming all over my body. Angry red rashes begin appearing across my skin as the clothes chafe against my soaked body.

My almost healed burns and countless cuts, including the gash on my back, sting and begin to bleed again as I exert myself. I'm really starting to hate this "living in a constant state of fear" thing. Always injured, running, or a mix of the two.

We weave between the wide tree trunks around us. If I look to either side, I can see others stumbling through the forest too, hastily clambering over large roots and rocks that stand in their way. Every now and then, someone violently tumbles to the ground, before the cancer that had taken them down sprints forward, the spines on their back twitching and rattling around. People keep falling, attacked by the creatures hunting us through these woods, but the survivors always keep running. We hadn't been that far from the bridge, right? It shouldn't take long now that we're running full speed. Sure enough, people begin veering to the right, towards the bridge.

We run and run and run until finally, through the trees, I see the large river-looking body of water ahead. I race to the shore and look behind us. We wait for a minute, knowing we've gotten here before the rest.

"Do we go up to the bridge?" I splutter. The fast-moving water ahead of me is dark blue, and gracefully slides over the submerged rocky shore by my feet.

At that very moment, a group of people burst out from the forest and onto the elevated passageway, which is about two or three hundred feet down Pirate's Avenue to our right. At first it seems like it's just them, but then a wave of black bodies, bony limbs flying everywhere, bursts from the trees and leaps onto the concrete structure as well.

Mr. Harlow runs out of the tree line maybe twenty feet away from us and we all run to meet him.

"We need to swim." He pants, "There are too many on the bridge, and they're coming here too. We have no choice," He says, hefting up the large gun he's holding.

"Here," I say, reaching for the weapon, "I can carry it. It'll be hard enough for you with that bag."

I stare back at the bridge. There are large concrete supports going down into the water to help keep the bridge up.

"We can go under it," I say, "Try and latch onto the supports if we need to."

The screams from up on the bridge cut through the air as we run to get under the long structure. I notice the body of the cancer is gone. Griffin realizes it's gone too. "Huh, so it didn't die. That fall should have killed it." He grunts.

"Okay," I say and exhale stiffly, wading into dangerous waters for the second time today, "hurry. The water is fast, but it's either this or the bridge."

We all wade into the water, shivering at the freezing bite it gives, but motivated by the sounds coming from above us, on the bridge.

I frantically swim for the nearest concrete support, trying to slide through the water as I had in the pond. This, unfortunately, is much harder. Pirate's Avenue, though not a river, has a relatively strong current pulling out to sea. The heavy gun strapped around my shoulder weighs me down, and I nearly sink beneath the surface as it pulls against me, tugging me downwards. When I finally get to the support, I reach for it, clawing at it with my already numb hands. They rake across the slick surface, only tearing off bits of algae. Finally, right as I think I'm going to be swept right by, I find a small grippy area and hold tight.

The rest of the group has the same amount of trouble I did, and Griffin ends up having to grab hold of my foot before he is swept away. It's when we begin swimming towards the next pillar that people begin falling. Jumping off the bridge, accepting that they'd rather face the impact of the water than what awaits them above.

Or rather, some of them don't even seem to be jumping, but falling. Pushed off. Some hit the water gracefully enough, feet first in a pencil position. Others flail as they hit the water, making a loud slapping sound against the surface.

Slap! Slap! Slap!

It's a nightmarish cacophony singing out from all around me.

When we get to the next support, it seems to be raining people, as they fall from either side of the bridge and into the water. The ones that can keep consciousness after the fall seem to have the same idea we did, and cling to the little handholds or occasional mussel on the supports.

Ones who don't have something to grasp onto, grab other people and stay at the support with them, or more often, dragging them back into the current of the salty water.

We reach the third pillar after a strenuous swim, and I want more than anything to stay clinging to it, but there are two more concrete supports left. I am more motivated to move quickly when the black forms of cancers begin falling into the water with the people, sliding beneath the surface and out of sight.

"Not again," I mutter.

Elizabeth curses, "They can swim! Go!"

People behind us begin inexplicably jutting beneath the surface, as if something grabbed ahold of their feet and pulled them under. I'm kicking as hard as I can, needing to get out of the water. One could be right next to me. Right under me.

Griffin seems to be having a particularly difficult time swimming, his kicks straggled and unsynchronized. I try to call out to him and help, but he can't hear me over everything else going on. Is it just me or did I just see a shape dart beneath the water? Is it a fish? Or something else?

I see Tobias the scientist plummet from the bridge above and land in the water. He begins paddling frantically for a pillar, but something below the surface jerks him down and out of sight. Will he escape? I guess I might never know, because I continue to swim the hardest that I ever have in my life.

It's not enough.

As I cut through the water, occasionally inhaling mouthfuls of the stuff, something catches my attention. If I had been thinking straight, I'd have dropped the gun weighing me down and beelined it out of there. Instead, disoriented by the terrible shrieks coming from all around, I continue to struggle on, ignoring the *swish* I had just felt brush against my feet.

Then, something catches the ankle of my pants. There's a tight tug, before I am violently swept beneath the water. I am caught completely off guard. *What is going on? I can't breathe...* Water juts up my nose, causing a terrible burning sensation. I try to scream, but my voice is silenced by the water pressing against me.

My pants keep tugging at my hip. I begin to panic, thrashing around. *I can't breathe.*

Still, my pants pull downward. I look down, and see a blurry shape in the water. The swishing of something moving back and forth. The tail?

I gather my thoughts enough to begin clawing at my belt. I try and try, but my fingers are so numb because of the cold water that the attempt is futile.

Deeper and deeper I go. I feel my ears begin to pop. *I can't breathe.*

And now, I really do begin to panic. *I can't breathe, I can't breathe. Oh my God, I can't breathe.* I feel the water pressing in on all sides, suffocating me-

"Help!" I try to scream for my life, but once again the water steals my voice, reducing my cry to a stream of bubbles.

That's when I'm reminded of the thing strapped around my back. The rifle. The gun.

I struggle to reach over and pull the strap across my shoulder. After failing once, I succeed in pulling it into my hands. By this time my lungs feel like they're going to explode.

I raise the rifle above my head, and jam the butt of the thing into the dark shape dragging me down. I feel the pressure loosen on my pants, so I do it again. This time, I hear an audible crack. The thing lets go completely, and juts into the dark gray water.

I'm about to begin frantically swimming upward, when I see the shape again, coming from the side this time. I see the tail swishing back and forth, the spines on its back like the fin of a shark. It swims up to me, but stops to float there about five feet away. It learned from its mistake, staying out of reach. *It learned.*

Well, it hasn't learned enough.

I raise the rifle up to the shooting position, the deadly end of the barrel pointing directly at its head. Mr. Harlow had prepped the gun and everything, all I have to do is pull the trigger. Do rifles work underwater? I'm about to find out.

I set my finger on the trigger, aim, and squeeze.

Instead of the loud bang I had expected, there is silence. The trigger doesn't even move. By now, I'm sure I'll black out any second. My lungs feel like someone has lit a campfire inside them, burning the flesh.

And then it comes to me. I slide my hands down the gun, and feel it. The safety. I press my thumb against it, and click it off.

At the sound, the creature swings its mouth open wide and begins to shriek. The sound is muted by the water, but somehow is even more blood curdling than above the surface.

I clutch the thing tight, position my finger on the trigger. *Ready. Aim. Fire.*

I shoot the thing *point-blank*, right where I think the gaping mouth is. It's instantly silenced, and a dark cloud begins to billow away from the shape.

I can't take it any longer. I drop the gun, letting it sink into the darkness, and try desperately to reach the surface.

I won't make it. I'm going to drown.

The corners of my vision begin to darken, the strength sapping from my limbs-

I reach the surface! I partially throw up, ridding my body of the salt water I'd taken in, and take the biggest gulp of fresh air I've ever had in my life. I can't rest yet. Not now. I keep swimming.

We reach the fifth and final pillar, only 40 or so feet away from the shore. Safety is just in reach...

And we're on land, sprinting into the woods, crashing through the thick undergrowth and foliage and weeds and bushes, soaking but alive, and best of all, unscathed. We dart left and right to avoid trees, headed down south through the island. We run and run and run until finally I'm about to collapse.

"Can we-" Griffin says, panting, "stop now?"

The moment Mr. Harlow nods we all collapse in a heap, exhausted and soggy.

We all just... lie there for a while. I don't feel like going anywhere, or exerting any energy on anything. Though I am soaked through and through, I no longer have the clean feel the bath had promised. Now, I am a soggy mess, rashes breaking out everywhere on my body.

I feel waterlogged.

We wait. And wait. And wait, until finally Elizabeth says something.

"I assume nobody has a working phone? How will we know where we're going?"

"My phone isn't waterproof. I assume it's broken," Mr. Harlow says, "But I have a compass in my bag."

Mr. Harlow unzips his computer bag and sighs when he sees the inside. All the papers have been turned into a white mush. Ink is bleeding off of the pages that still resemble a rectangle, but all of them are soaked and are an unusable paste.

Mr. Harlow picked out his laptop, which pours water from all openings as he tips it, and reaches deep into the bag. He pulls out a rounded compass, gold and shining in the filtered light reaching down through the thick tree branches above.

"I always keep one on me just in case. I also have flint and steel if we need it. If we want to get to the others though, we head south," Mr. Harlow says, "Where are they?"

"In the research lab down the middle of the island. Right after all the hills and little mountains sort of end. The road leads straight to it I think, but it might be too risky to travel that way."

"We're east of the road right now," Mr. Harlow says, "So let's head west and travel parallel to the path. That way we can escape if something walks down it, but not be totally lost as to where we're going."

So that is what we do. We travel west until we come to the road, then continue walking south. We aren't that close to it, so I keep my eyes glued on the road. I know it's stupid, since we have the compass, but it somehow makes me feel more anchored as to where we are going so, I try not to lose sight of the worn asphalt path.

Maybe it's just to distract myself from everything else going on.

We stop a couple of times to gather some inner bark off of the trees around us using Griffin's knife, and as I slowly cut and peel away the stuff, I tell myself I'll just have to pretend they're french fries. This, unfortunately, proves impossible because when I stick the first one in my mouth, I gag. I do down it though, because food is food, and when you're hungry enough it doesn't matter what it is. I'm thirsty, but it's not terrible because they'd given us water back at the barn.

I assume it's around three or four in the afternoon when we finally catch our first glimpse of the lab. Way down the hill we are on the top of, I can see the square, concrete roof of the plain structure. We are so high up on the island, I can see the forest stretch out for a far distance, though the ocean and town must be shrouded in fog because I can't see them.

We take another look at the compass and make our way down the hill. When we finally reach the lab, I stand, frozen, staring at the concrete walls in disbelief. I can't believe we've gotten here already. Last time, when we were headed to El Arnica, it had seemed to take so much longer. We had left late at night, and camped out on the southern half of the island until morning hit. Then we had come across the trouble on the bridge after facing crippling effects of dehydration. Everything seemed to have taken so much longer.

Yet here we are. I find myself smiling at the wall.

"Luke, you coming?" Elizabeth says, her hand on the knob of the same door we had used to leave the lab two- no- three nights ago? I can't keep track, but it feels like it's been much shorter than it has. Like yesterday. Elizabeth tries the knob, but it just rattles and doesn't turn. Of course, they wouldn't just leave it unlocked. That's a given.

I bang my fist against the door three times. No answer. Elizabeth does the same thing, to no avail. Griffin actually throws his weight against the door, but it doesn't budge, and no one answers it.

"You think they're even in there anymore?" He whispers. "Or did they never get in in the first place…"

"Maybe they just don't know it's us. How could they?" I say, and take a big breath to shout at the door, but Griffin's hand suddenly clamps over my mouth.

"They're still looking for us." He says in a low whisper, "We've been loud enough already, better not call them all here. They can still hear us, remember? Hopefully they're too, uh, preoccupied back near Pirate's Avenue."

I bang my fist on the door again, over and over, until finally, a knock comes from the other side.

"Hey!" Elizabeth says loudly, pressing her face against the crack where the door opens and ignoring Griffin's advice to stay silent. "We're here! It's us! Let us in!"

Then she falls silent. For some reason, she looks sick. What's that about? Her face is a tinge greener, and she looks as if the call had made her unsteady.

But then my thoughts are pulled back to the door, to the lab, because I hear something.

A muffled, canny voice comes from the other side of the door. It's a man's voice and I'm confused until I remember all the other scientists with them; "Who are you?" He says gruffly.

"We were here a couple of days ago." I say into the door, "Our parents are here. This is Luke. Griffin and Elizabeth are here too. We have Mr. Harlow."

I hear the man step away from the door for a few moments, evidently discussing something with someone else on his end. After 15 seconds or so, the door clicks and cracks open, an eye peeking through the opening. When it sees us, it widens and the door is thrown open. It's my mother, and she throws herself at me, squeezing me so tight I can barely breathe.

"Oh, Luke," She says, embracing me, "I thought- well I- Oh, I'm so glad you're okay!" She steps aside and lets Mrs. Harlow step out and embrace Elizabeth, before taking in Mr. Harlow in disbelief. They move in for their own embrace, but the scientist quickly ushers us into the lab. It's pitch-black, and once door is shut, I can hear multiple clicks that are presumably the locks.

"Lukie!" I hear a small voice sound out from the darkness. Something wraps around my legs and as the lights turn on I see my little sister Calla squeezing her arms around me and jumping up and down. I crouch down and give her a tight hug.

"Where did you go?" Calla squeaks excitedly, crossing her arms in her usual way. Gosh I've missed her so much. I'm so glad to see her alive and well, in my arms.

"I'd like to know the same thing." My mother says sternly, gesturing for me to get up. Well, sternly isn't the right way to put it. She's trying to be mad, but I can see the only emotion she's feeling at the moment is relief at our return.

When I stand, she takes my face into her hands and examines all of the scratches and cuts that I sport there. She rubs her thumb over one and I grimace. She looks concernedly at me before taking in the rest of my body.

"Your clothes are wet." She says, and my clothes have indeed not fully dried quite yet, I'm sure leaving nasty rashes all over my skin.

"Long story." I say.

She puts her hand on my back to feel how damp my clothes actually are, and that's when I yelp. The gash there, though healing slightly now, has regained feeling once again, and unfortunately that includes intense pain whenever it comes in contact with something.

My mother frowns and lifts up the back of my shirt. She gasps and clamps her hand to her mouth when she sees the gnarly gash tearing through my shredded flesh. Tight, inflamed skin. Oozing pus. The works. She gingerly touches it and my entire body clenches up in intense pain.

"What happened?" She whispers, "This should be bandaged! How did you get it?"

And we tell them everything. Griffin, Elizabeth and I all spout out everything that had happened from our putting things together in the lab to the escape. From our intense dehydration and starvation to our swim across Pirate's Avenue.

"-And I did have a bandage," I say after explaining what had happened in El Arnica, in which Griffin and Elizabeth had both been silent, listening intently as I haven't told *them* about my venture either. There just hadn't been enough time, "But when I had washed off in the pond I took it off. There was no time to re-apply it when we'd gotten back to the barn."

"Well," Mrs. Harlow says as she helps my mother bandage the wound on my back, which has apparently begun to bleed again, "we don't have any extra clothes here, and those wet clothes can't be comfortable. Especially after that long walk back."

The mothers seem to be postponing our punishments for running away, too preoccupied with the state we're in. After we had explained the entire story, Griffin has been pretty quiet and it is only now that I realize why. He has neither a mother nor a father to care for him anymore, while the rest of us are fussed over by our parents. I scoot closer to him, and apparently the parents have recognized this too because they have begun to give him more comfort, even after his cuts and scratches have been cleaned up. It turns out he did have a relatively deep bloody wound on his arm, but he'd had it wrapped up tightly the entire walk so none of us even noticed it.

When my mother and Mrs. Harlow ask if he has any wounds on his legs, he shakes his head a little too quickly, telling them no, but thanking them for asking. It's a little suspicious to me, and I wonder if it has to do with his constant limp.

Everybody talks over everything that has happened, and Mr. Harlow explains the cure to the group. How it works, though, he admits most of it is a mystery to him too.

Finally, after about an hour of discussing what to do, all of us have a plan, and even the scientists have agreed to it, desperate as they are.

We leave. Now. As soon as possible. We all go home, gather what we need, get changed into dry clothes for those of us who need them, and meet at the docks where we'd found the sheriff's boat. We'll take any guns we have at home, any potential weapons. The rifle would be nice right about now, but since I dropped it in Pirate's Avenue it's not much help to us anymore. Now is the time, when the tragedy at the bridge is still fresh. We can't just wait around for another mass killing. Now, while they are distracted and far away, now is the time to make our move.

We know the things can be injured, though whether they can be killed is still a mystery. The cancer we pushed off of the bridge had lived. Then again, how would it live with a bullet through its skull.

I'm startled by the explicit thought. Crazy how just a few days can change the way you think entirely. A thought like that back when everything was normal and I'd have been worried for my sanity. Now, it feels insane not to want to kill those things. Not to want to obliterate them. Finish them off before any more people get hurt.

The hope is that maybe, between all twelve of us, including the scientists, we could fight off the cancers preventing us from leaving the island. Maybe we could keep our boat safe and get to the mainland without being scratched or killed. Tell everyone of what is happening here on Eastrock Island. Feel the pressing weight of death lifted from my shoulders.

It's almost like a dream... Yet we are planning the whole thing right before my eyes.

And it's not long before we poke our head through the back door and sneak out to the parking lot of the lab. Our car has shattered windows, slashed tires, and dents in every square inch. It's not a problem though, because we had planned on walking anyways. We all cautiously sneak down the forested road until the time comes for us to go our separate ways.

My family goes to the Harlow's house along with the Harlows themselves. Griffin and Mr. Wilkins (the scientist we'd first met at the lab) go to his house on Main Street to fetch his clothes and other necessities. The rest of the scientists go to the docks.

As we walk along the road, we are alert, clenching our fists and wiping sweat from our brows as we anticipate an attack. When one doesn't present itself, it's more unsettling than comforting. I don't know what it is about it, but something isn't right. We should be running for our lives, right? It feels like this temporary moment of peace is more like the fuse of a bomb slowly burning out, before the explosion rocks the earth.

I turn my thoughts to the possibility of escape. From this terrible nightmare we seem to be living in. This island has quickly gone from the only home I've ever known, to a cage I am desperate to escape. Saying it has been the worst past week in my life would be an understatement. I am thoroughly certain that I will never go through something as horrible as this ever again.

Something about today speaks of finality. Maybe it's the possibility of escape from the imminent threat of death, but one way or another we'll never be the same. I'm already different, really. I wonder what the Luke of a week ago would think of me.

Would he approve of the way I'm responding to everything that's happening, as if he was watching a movie? Or would I be the character walking straight into his death, the audience calling for him to stop. To be smart about whatever choice he's making. Of course, that character always dies anyways.

Before I know it, we're standing at the front door. We waste no time, and I quickly slip on some of Mr. Harlow's old, small clothes. They fit surprisingly well on me and he even managed to get me a t-shirt, not some stiff button-up or polo. I hate those things. They're too hard to move in and feel like they'll choke you to death.

I slip into a light blue pair of jeans that still have the tags because Mr. Harlow never wore them. They even lend me a warm, well-fitting sweatshirt. The blessing of dry clothes against my miserable, wet, rash-covered skin makes me sigh in relief.

When we all meet by the door, it's only been about five minutes in the house. I notice Mr. Harlow and Elizabeth are both in dry clothes as well, and they hold a couple personal belongings too. Elizabeth holds a small Ziplock of printed pictures. Of her family. Of Griffin and some other friends from school, smiling up through the bag, holding up ice cream cones and laughing.

Maddie is crying, and when I ask Elizabeth why as we step out of the house, she shakes her head sadly. "Maddie wants to bring our cat. I do too, for that matter. We can't though, the thing won't let us pick it up. Plus, we can't afford to haul him around everywhere we go."

"I'm sorry," I say quietly.

"It's fine. It's always been annoying anyway." She mutters, but then sniffles, which kind of defeats the nonchalant remark.

We exit the house, leaving the door wide open for that cat, and head back towards Main Street. When we arrive there, we follow the road parallel to the beach, which goes over the sea cliff and around a hill, and finally arrive at the docks. Griffin and the four (including Mr. Wilkins) scientists stand there, waiting. When we join them, I can't help looking down the shore and seeing the tip of a white boat. The sheriff's boat, I think, though it could be the boat we'd been on when we found it.

Other boats are tied up on the docks again. There are three narrow platforms on either side of a much larger, taller, and wider dock for ferries and larger boats. The water laps against the shore, not angrily but not exactly calm either. I wonder how much trouble the turbulence will be.

"Hey!" Griffin calls as he spots us, running over. His hands are filled with personal items, which he sets on a barrel near the shore, "Help us, we're finding a boat big enough for all twelve of us. Did you get weapons?"

Mr. Harlow sets the handgun on a plastic table, which still holds piles of life jackets from the first evac. attempt.

"Perfect." Griffin nods, "Come on, we're checking the gas of each boat too we- What's she doing?"

He points at something behind us and I whirl around, my heart pounding in my chest. Why does everything need to be constant fear? Why does everything always need to happen one thing after the other. Can't I just get a bit of-

Calla is standing at the edge of the forest, looking up into the trees. She sees something that is hidden above her amongst the branches... And now I'm running. Running for Calla and running for the trees. But it gets to her before I can. The black shape swoops down from the branches it had been perched on, and launches itself at Calla. At my little sister, which is when I fall apart.

CHAPTER SIXTEEN

The gunshot rings out behind me and the cancer collapses to the damp earth before I can even reach it. The creature twitches on the ground as I turn around to see my mother holding the gun, her hands shaking slightly, her face shocked at her own dauntlessness.

I run to Calla, but I can already see it's too late. I violently kick the cancer away as it finishes dying with the bullet hole through its chest, and pull Calla into my arms just as her eyes flicker shut. She's already begun the coma that supports the- the-

I am so sick at the thought that I actually puke up the little bile my stomach has left in a bush, then wipe my mouth before hoisting Calla up and examining the cut in her arm. Not as deep or large as the one on my back, but just as effective. More so, because she is so small it won't take long for her blood system to lose the fight against the disease before the transformation begins.

I almost begin to sob when I remember. I remember how I'd gotten well. Elizabeth. She's type O. She can save Calla. And maybe we can make our escape and-

I carry Calla back over to the group, and my mother gasps as she sees the cut, covering her mouth in horror. I look to Elizabeth. She and she alone can save Calla. She can cure her; she has to be able to. If she couldn't, I don't know what I'd do.

"Elizabeth," I say, my voice having a definite tone of desperation, "Elizabeth, you can save her, right? Right?"

Elizabeth nods, but Mr. Harlow intervenes, asking the scientists a question, "She donated blood to Luke here yesterday, is it safe for her to donate again?"

"It's very unhealthy," The scientist says, "But you can do it in a case like this. As long as her blood isn't contaminated."

"Contaminated?" Mr. Harlow asks.

"Oh, you'd know if it's contaminated." Another scientist says gravely, "She'd be getting chills and immune system problems. She'd get dizzy at random, and feel extremely sick, but that's only if she's had a blood transfusion *from* another person with the wrong blood type in the past week or so."

I get a sinking feeling in my gut. The time she looked nauseous back at the barn. The time she'd looked a tad green and unsteady at the door of the lab.

Elizabeth and Mr. Harlow look at each other, "She's been having chills and fever for the last couple of days, especially that first day we'd returned and Luke was asleep, but it's nothing serious. I can't imagine what could have caused it. She was *giving* blood."

"When she donated blood to him," The blonde scientist asks, eyeing the both of us, "How many times did you have to inject her blood?"

"Four times." Mr. Harlow says, "It didn't take much, but It's a small syringe." He pulls out the thing from his bag.

"And you only had that one syringe for all four transfusions?" The scientist furrows his eyebrows.

"Yes."

"It's possible that *his* blood infected *her* blood through the syringe. An ounce of incorrect blood infusion can be fatal, and even a little can severely complicate future blood transfusions. It'd only take a slight misstep. I wouldn't suggest Elizabeth here donate to anybody for a long time." The scientist gestures to Calla, "She's much smaller, and I have no idea how badly it could affect her."

"But this is life and death," I say, "It doesn't take much blood. It's either this or she dies. It's- how can it not even be an option?"

What if I lose Calla? I can't let her turn into one of those things, or die because she's too small. Like that lab pig. What if I let that happen to her? I can't. If she does, it would be like I'd have nothing to live for. This seems more like the end of the world than when I myself had been scratched and infected, waiting for death. I'd trade places with her without hesitation. Barely held back sobs struggle their way up into my throat, trying to choke me. All I can think about is this death sentence my little sister has just been served.

"Well," The scientist says slowly, "If it's that serious, and she can't wait until we reach mainland- I suppose it'll have to be worth a shot. I wish I had a microscope to see how badly Calla's blood is infected, because you said you need to be infected enough to be treated right?" He nods to Mr. Harlow, "most of your blood needs to be the disease before you re-introduce the blood?"

Mr. Harlow says something about not knowing for sure, but it seemed to work, but I don't listen. I stopped listening at the mention of the microscope, because it has sparked a memory in my mind. Back at the Harlow's, after the fire. Calla said she'd brought the microscope- *and some samples.* Is it possible that one of those samples could be that blood we'd collected from her leg so many days ago? If Mr. Harlow is right, and we only need to *reintroduce* the blood cells to her system once the disease runs through her veins instead of blood, would the tiny vial be enough?

It would have to be.

"Wait." I say, "I know where some of her blood is. We took a sample from her scrape and I think it's in her backpack back at the Harlows." My mother's face lights up, because surely she remembers the day where she'd come home to find Calla and I playing with the microscope.

Mr. Wilkins is the first to pose a question. "How long will it take for you to get the blood?"

"Twenty minutes if we hurry." I say, "Elizabeth, Griffin, and I will all go get it."

Immediately there are protests, but Elizabeth silences them by yelling above the noise; "We have the most experience with the cancers! Luke knows where the blood is, and Griffin and I are going with him. That's final. The two moms need to look after Maddie and especially Calla, two of you scientists need to search the boats for some type of medical kit with rubbing alcohol, use strong drinking alcohol to sterilize the needle if it really comes down to that, there's bound to be a cooler. I know you can't re-use needles, but we don't really have a choice here.

My dad and Mr. Wilkins need to find a boat, make sure it runs, and load it with gasoline."

The adults stutter for a minute, stunned, trying to come up with a reason why the whole thing is a bad idea.

"Please." I say, grabbing my mother's hands, "The more adults here, the faster we can get on the water. We won't be long, plus us three really do have the most experience with them. You have to trust us. Do you trust us?"

My mother is silent for a moment, before speaking in a level, though slightly shaky voice. "Yes. Yes, I suppose it makes sense. You're nearly an adult, you're responsible enough. I trust you Luke. I trust you. Just be careful, please, and be quick."

She presses her phone into my hands; "I know the cell towers are down, but you can use it as a compass, or a map, maybe. I have the whole island saved on there. It still has half its battery."

I look to Mr. and Mrs. Harlow, and they nod after a full five seconds. They hug Elizabeth; "Stay safe. We love you. Get back as soon as you can."

Mr. Harlow presses the handgun into Griffin's hands, because he's the only one out of the three of us that knows how to use it.

"Keep them safe for me, okay?" Mr. Harlow says to Griffin

"I will." Griffin says, he and Mr. Harlow exchanging a firm handshake.

And then we're setting off, walking down the parking lot and away from the group of parents and scientists. We approach one of the many cars with the keys still in the ignition. My guess is that when the cancer attack happened back in Main Street, some people tried escaping by means of the boats here. Did it work?

I step into the driver's seat and both Griffin and Elizabeth get in the backseat.

"Go."

The engine roars to life and I slam my foot on the pedal, causing the car to bolt forward. In no time, we've turned the corner and the parents are gone from sight. Here we go again, one last time.

We race through the forested road, bolting past stopped cars and wrecks, and the sky above turns to a dark pink, going on purple. It won't be long before the sky is completely dark, and the intensity of the situation thickens like mud. I have a feeling the cancers like it dark.

We choose speed over stealth, which is mostly a good choice, but when we slam head-on into a deer, it delays us about five to ten minutes as we have to drag the body from the car and tear the entire bumper off. It had twisted in a way that interfered with the wheel. As we pull away from the animal's body, its blank glassy eyes stare at me until we pass it, leaving the creature behind. I don't believe in omens, but if I did, I'd consider that a bad one.

When we finally do arrive at the Harlow's house, the sky is black, the clouds blocking any trace of the twinkling stars above. For a moment, once the engine is off, we just sit in the silent car, staring at the empty house alone in the dark.

"So, we just go in?" Griffin asks. I nod. My fingers cold against the door handle, I slowly pull the latch and get out of the car. Night sounds instantly fill my ears. Crickets chirping, owls hooting. My shoes land softly on the pavement, and I close the door of the car so quietly, I barely hear it click shut. No turning back now. I couldn't anyway, not with what's on the line.

Griffin and Elizabeth stand beside me before long, and we creep towards the structure, which looks much more menacing now that the sun has fallen below the horizon and night has begun. The path leading up to the door glows in the little available moonlight, though the yard lights are dead.

"I never thought my own home could be this... frightening." Elizabeth mutters as we step through the front door and into the house, which creaks eerily as we swing it open wide enough for us to slide through, making the least sound possible.

The inside of the house has such an empty feel I can almost taste it.

"I don't like this." Griffin whispers, "Where's the blood. Let's grab it and get out of here."

Where to look first.... I know Calla had mentioned having her backpack at the Harlows somewhere, but where exactly is a mystery to me. The earliest I remember of the Harlow's household is waking up in the kitchen. Before then I'd been dead to the world.

The kitchen...

"Liz, you know where her backpack is?" I ask Elizabeth in the dark. She shakes her head and shivers.

"Why not start in the kitchen." I suggest, "I know she was there, so why not?"

Neither Elizabeth nor Griffin protest, so I creep down the hallway that leads to the large living room and kitchen. We pass family portraits and kids drawings hanging on the wall, most of which look somewhat haunting in the limited light, peering down at us as we quietly pass.

The cold air bites my exposed skin, and even manages to reach me through the sweatshirt I'm wearing. When the first rumbling crack of thunder roars from outside, the temperature seems to drop another ten degrees. Is a storm coming on? Of all times, why now? Surely, it will mess with our escape one way or another.

'*Focus*' I chide myself, because Calla is my main concern now. Besides, all storms here are very temperamental. They tend to last ten minutes before shutting off. Either that, or they're heavy and drawn out. Hopeful thoughts, right?

Hopeful thoughts are hard to form in this dank, silent hallway.

"Here," Elizabeth whispers, gesturing at an open doorway. "That's the kitchen."

I approach it carefully, and take a peek inside. The counter. The oven. The pantry. All seems just as I remember it the day after my house had burnt down. I am quiet for a moment, looking around for any threats, but when nothing catches my eye, I slowly straighten up and enter the kitchen. Following my lead, Elizabeth and Griffin do the same.

I don't talk, but gesture for them to search the counter and pantry while I move onto the kitchen, which is just on the other side of the cold, marble counter. They nod, and I keep heading forward. I never thought of the Harlows as a rich family, but their house is definitely on the higher end of the neighborhood. The crystal chandelier, shiny but not boastful, hangs above the smooth oak table just beyond the counter. The counter is a rectangle shape, with open space on either side, so I guess it's more of an island.

I'm about to make the turn to go around the corner when something on the other side *stands up*.

The humanoid figure rises from out of sight, scaring me out of my skin. I drop down to the tile floor so fast, I practically smack my face on the hard surface, and stifle a curse. Curling up into a ball under the edge of the counter, I hear the monster on the other side breathe heavily, like an animal. It had been turned away, facing the dining table, so it hadn't seen me. I worry if it had heard anything, but it seems not to have taken notice of me yet.

The cold tile floor presses against my bare skin and thunder rumbles outside again. This time, the bolt of lightning shines through the dining room window, casting a shadow of the standing, humanoid figure on the wall behind it. Its arms are too long, and by the looks of it, the thing is over seven feet tall. Of course, it's a cancer.

On my arms and knees, as low to the ground as possible, I crawl away from the counter and towards the pantry, where Griffin and Elizabeth still remain silent. On my way over, when I am in the middle of the open floor, I can't help but look back at the standing creature. I only catch it for a moment though, as it lowers back down onto all fours, sinking out of sight behind the countertop.

"Hey," I whisper.

Elizabeth and Griffin hold a cloth bag, filling it with food, presumably for the long boat ride we're about to embark on.

"Drop it." I say, quietly, "we have bigger problems."

Elizabeth looks and me and slowly puts the bag down onto the tile floor, where the metal cans on the bottom of it clink mutedly. I gesture for both of them to get down on their hands and knees like me. They look at me worriedly, but do so.

"There's one here," I whisper so quietly it's hardly speech, "There's one in the room with us."

Elizabeth's face goes pale and Griffin looks like he's ready to bolt out as fast as he can, but they both restrain themselves. I gesture out into the kitchen and Elizabeth pokes her head out, though Griffin stays back. When she looks back at me, she mouths "All clear."

She slowly begins to crawl out into the open, Griffin and I in tow. Right when I think we'll sneak away without a problem, the creature starts moving. I hear claws against the tile. We all scuttle away, terrified, and press up against the wooden bottom of the counter. We wait there, until another noise sends us scurrying to the other end of the countertop.

I press my back to the wood. Kneeling and trying not to let my stomach escape through my mouth. I shiver and when I hear its first step back into the kitchen, it's like someone has poured ice-cold water down my spine.

In the muted moonlight, I can see Elizabeth's bottom lip tremble as she presses her back to the counter she's been using for years, her eyes swiveling around to take in the nightmare that used to be her home. With the next round of lightning, I can see the heavy downpour of rain from the sky. Crazy, really, how quickly weather can turn on an island like this. No warning whatsoever.

I hear the creature's claws scrape across the cold tile floor on which we all crouch, hidden from view. It begins to round the corner and we all scramble around the opposite side as soundlessly as possible. Griffin looks petrified, his movement slightly uncoordinated. No, uncoordinated isn't the right word. More like some of his limbs won't cooperate the way his body is telling it to. Namely, his leg.

The low, haunting screeching coming from the creature now rips through the air, making an unnatural, bone-chilling sound. And the chattering of the teeth begins as we continue to round the counter in an attempt to stay out of sight. The hard floor is unforgiving on my knees and freezing to the touch. I can now hear the heavy rain pattering against the roof of the house. More thunder. More lightning.

We're on the dining table side, and this time, a slimy goo substance lathers the floor. It's a sickening green-red-white color mixture, like a nightmarish Christmas combination.

"Don't touch it," I say, "It probably can infect you just like being scratched."

They both frown but carefully ensure only the rubber parts of their shoes touch the stuff. When we round the corner once again, I realize something. The continuous teeth chattering and low screeching have ceased, leaving only the sound of heavy rain on the roof of the house, and the occasional rumble of thunder.

"Did it go somewhere?" I whisper to Griffin, who shrugs, timidly looking back around the corner.

"I don't see it." He says.

Warmness. That is what I feel against my scalp, which confuses me until I reach up to my hair, and my fingers come back down covered in warm goo. Dreading what I already know, I slowly look up. It's on the counter, looking down at me, its mouth cracked open in a smile as unnatural saliva drips down from its white, lipless muzzle.

It's the one from El Arnica. The different one.

Elizabeth screams so loud my eardrums feel like they might explode, and the creature begins roaring too, which is so eardrum-shredding I actually wince in pain. We all try to scramble to our feet, but we only manage to hastily scoot away on the floor, fueled by adrenaline and terror.

It roars at us for a moment, before leaping off of the counter and straight towards us. Its goo-covered claw misses Elizabeth by half a foot, before it slips on the tile floor and slams its skull into the unyielding table surface, giving us just enough time to jump to our feet and bolt down the hallway. Despite the sickening *crack* the thing had made, it's already beginning to rise to its feet.

"In here!" Elizebeth shouts, pointing at the second nearest door. We all sprint for it, but the creature has recovered too fast and is hurling itself down the hallway, its maw fully open, exposing its massive array of needle teeth. It violently knocks the framed photos off of the wall in its haste to reach us, which shatter loudly against the hard floor.

I slip into the room and yell; "SHUT IT!"

Griffin launches himself at the door, slamming it shut with his weight. Elizabeth flips the lock of the door and gestures for some help dragging her bookshelf in front of the entrance. I get up to help her move it, but it doesn't budge, and I hear the creature outside scratching at the wood. The door groaning against its force, I get on one side of the bookshelf and have Griffin help me tip it instead of slide it in front of the door. It falls with a deafening crash, all of the books flying out onto the floor, but it survived the impact and now effectively blocks the entrance.

I slide to the floor against the wall. "This is familiar."

"What?" Griffin asks, panting.

"Nothing." I say, pressing my hand to my forehead and wiping off the sweat there, "We need to go."

"What about the backpack?" Elizabeth asks, "Calla, she needs it. They're counting on us. *She's* counting on you. Luke, you can't just-"

"Elizabeth, I know." I say.

"But, Luke. We can't just-" she falls silent, apparently overwhelmed by the hurricane of emotions. We all are.

I scoot over to her and make the boldest decision I've ever made. Here and now, despite it all, I wrap my arms around her and squeeze her tightly. She buries her face in my shoulder and sobs. I'm holding my own burning tears back too. I can't fall apart now. I want nothing more than to collapse on the ground and cry it out, but I can't. Griffin and Elizabeth need me. *Calla* needs me.

And now, I do choke out a sob. Calla... I couldn't find her backpack, and it's unlikely I will. She's going to die and it's my fault.

"My- my house. I can't believe- why..." She says, her speech muffled by my sweatshirt.

"It probably knew you'd just left here." Griffin says, staring at me with a look in his eyes I can't quite place, but for some reason, he doesn't look as if I have crossed a line. He doesn't look jealous. Sad, maybe? Possibly a sort of sore happiness? "My guess is that it came here right after you guys left. You know, when you got clothes and such. But Elizabeth is right, what is that thing? It's not a cancer, right?"

He's talking about the creature still trying to get into the room at this very moment. The one I'd seen in El Arnica. The white one, smiling at me from the end of that hallway, back in the pitch-black hotel when I'd found Mr. Harlow.

"Mr. Harlow mentioned it to me," I say, "I meant to follow up on it more. Anyways, he says it's sort of like... the original infector. The first."

"Ground-Zero." Griffin mutters quietly.

"What?" I say.

"Back at the barn, Tobias told us about a cancer that's different than all the others. He called it Ground-Zero. The term is generally used referring an explosion of some sort. He described Ground-Zero as the epicenter of the whole ordeal. The one they had been studying in the lab. He explained it like the original cancer cell."

I think it over, but then I notice the lack of noise coming from the door. Ground-Zero has left, gone to go do who knows what. Find other people to get at, probably. I selfishly hope it heads north, though for all we know it's still in the house, looking for another way in.

"So," I say, "We know it's smart. Smart enough to know we were here, even after we'd left. What else can it do?"

I think back to the green veins that can be seen through its nearly translucent skin. The haunting call. It's intelligence. Well, if it's really that smart-

"I know how the cancers found the barn. They followed Mr. Harlow and I back, knowing we'd lead them to more people. They let us pass, they let us get back to you guys and waited to attack until they were certain more people weren't coming. They're smarter than we think, especially, uh, Ground-Zero."

"If it's really that smart-" Elizabeth says, pulling her face back into view and looking around her dark bedroom, "What's to stop it from finding a way in here."

I stop for a moment. She's right. The room has multiple windows, and not enough things to block them with. It even has a large AC vent on the ceiling if the thing gets desperate enough. This is when I realize how trapped, not safe, we actually are.

"We need to get out of here." I choke out, "Elizabeth, we'll just have to take a chance with your blood. It's better than, well..."

Lightning cracks through the sky outside the thin glass window and the loudest, most bone-rattling round of thunder yet follows, echoing through the rainy sky beyond. What has it all come to. Constant fear, running. We haven't even made any plan of attack. To fight back.

"Griffin." I say, "Do you still have that gun?"

His face lights up and he pats his pockets, but then it slowly morphs into a mask of despair. "I left it in the pantry when we were getting all of the canned foods. We needed both hands, so I set it down... *I set it down on the shelf next to the cereal...*"

His voice quavers a bit on the last sentence.

I choke a little. "It's- it's fine." We now have no means of defending ourselves. "We'll just have to escape then. Maybe we can go through the window or something."

"Speaking of," Elizabeth says, pointing at the window, "What's that?"

At the rate things are going, I expect to see the form of Ground-Zero staring through the glass, its inhuman grin illuminated by the next round of lightning, but instead, I see something in the sky. A small little shiny dot zooming through the clouds. At first, I think it's a shooting star, but when I get a closer look at it, I see spinning blades on top of the thing. It's a helicopter, though it's hard to make out any closer details than that.

"Is that a helicopter?" Griffin gasps, looking out the window.

"Yeah," I say, transfixed, "I wonder what it's doing."

Thump. Thump. Thump.

I am silent, as I listen to the rain patter on the top of the house. Another round of footsteps come from above. Something is on the roof.

"Okay, listen," I say to Elizabeth and Griffin, "We can't move the bookshelf without making too much noise. We'll get out through the window if we can."

"No," Elizabeth says. "there's another way."

"What." I ask her, looking around for what she could mean. She squeezes my hand before shakily standing up and walking over to another set of doors I had written off as the closet. I can't help but think in the back of my mind that every second we're not running, that... thing, Ground-Zero, is that much closer to finding us.

Elizabeth opens the doors, and it turns out it *is* a closet, her sweatshirts and jackets hanging from a raised bar. She pushes the sweatshirts aside and shows another row of clothes on the other side, though this time they're much smaller, and very pink.

Those aren't Elizabeth's clothes. She'd never be caught dead in something like that.

She waves for us to follow. We do. "My and Maddie's room used to be connected. We added a closet in the doorway so we could both have our own space." She says as we push the clothes aside and enter Elizabeth's little sister's room. There is a purple bed with a large dollhouse by its side, the door swung wide open and small dolls strewn across the floor. Another round of lightning illuminates their smiling, unmoving faces.

Elizabeth sees me looking at the mess. "She and Calla had been playing in here before you recovered."

But I have stopped listening. I've frozen in my tracks. As thunder roars, and lightning strikes while Ground-Zero stalks us from above, I freeze as I see the only other thing that can concern me more. A small, pink, glittery backpack lies on Maddie's unmade bed, zipped closed.

Do my eyes deceive me?

As if in a daze, I slowly walk towards it and pick the thing up. A small wave of pink glitter falls onto the comforter below it, dusting the purple fabric. As I examine it in the dark, I can still see the mud stains on the sides from that day when Calla had come home, wearing this exact backpack.

I slowly unzip the thing and peer into its dark depths, too shadowed to really see what's there. I grasp around, and find that my large microscope is jammed in there, the lenses being scratched by the plastic toys that surround it. I pull it out and examine it. The thing looks the same as when Calla and I had used it the day she'd fallen and scraped her knee. The only difference is the small specks of glitter that sparkle slightly with every strike of lightning.

I reach into the pack and pull out a handful of small plastic minifigures, which I gingerly set on the comforter. When

I reach in for a third time, I hear the *clink clink clink* of glass. In disbelief, I pull out a crystal vial. No, this one is too big. This must be the planter water. The second vial I pull out, however, is miniscule and filled all the way to the top with dark liquid.

I hastily pull out my mom's phone, and use the light of the screen to illuminate the vial's contents. Dark red. My hands shake slightly and I tighten my grip on the vial. It feels like it's going to slip from my frozen fingertips and shatter on the floor, yet it's here, in my grasp, my little sister's life.

I squeeze my fist around the thing and smile.

I rip off a part of the bedding sheet and wrap the glass vial in it, before slipping the thing down my pocket. When I turn around to face Elizabeth and Griffin, they look at me expectantly. I grin and pat the side of my jeans. They grin too, and everything seems to have a hopeful touch to it now.

And I see something behind them in the window. A figure, standing in the rain, looking through the glass without eyes, chattering its teeth.

"We need to go." I whisper, dropping my smile and walking towards Griffin and Elizabeth. I wrap my hands around their shoulders before they can turn around and see the window, and guide them out of the room. When I turn around to close the room, the creature is no longer there.

"The garage." I say.

"Our car isn't there," Elizabeth tells me, "It's-"

"I know." I interrupt her, "You have a garden in your backyard, right?"

"Yeah, but why the garage?" Elizabeth asks.

"Where do you keep your gardening tools?"

Elizabeth looks at me. "You really think that'll work? That we can do this?"

"I do."

* * *

The dark house is cold and empty as we sprint down the halls, Elizabeth directing us to the door that leads into the garage. We stop in the kitchen for a moment, and Griffin grabs the handgun out of the pantry before resuming to run through the house. Once there, we slam the door open and I use the flashlight on the phone to search around, picking out what we need from the array of tools.

I explain what I plan to do.

A large pitchfork in hand, I tell Griffin to stand next to the garage door, making sure that the gun is ready to fire at a moment's notice, the safety clicked off. Elizabeth has a large metal baseball bat similar to the one Griffin had had when we'd found him after the Main Street attack. She holds it in a defensive position, ready to slam the heavy club into anything that comes near her. Though her eyes are still slightly red, she has her emotions under control once again, and looks braver and even more determined than Griffin and I combined.

I look at her. Then to Griffin, who looks like he's scared out of his wits but still determined.

"Do it." I say.

Elizabeth begins banging the club on the concrete floor as hard as she can, making a *CLANG CLANG CLANG* sound over and over again. She's screaming her head off, yelling at the creature to come find us. To get us if it can, calling it all sorts of obscenities.

"COME GET US! COME GET US!"

Griffin takes a deep breath and raises the gun above his head. He closes his eyes and pulls the trigger, launching the bullet up into the ceiling and making such an ear-piercing bang it'd be impossible for Ground-Zero not to notice.

Sure enough, within the minute, the Garage door starts rattling and loud screeches reach us from outside. I grip my pitchfork tight and pat the pocket that contains the vial of Calla's blood.

"I'm coming." I whisper.

Elizabeth stops banging the bat against the floor and looks at me, a fire in her eyes so intense it actually unsettles me. I turn to Griffin. His face is set in stone, his eyebrows turned down, his knuckles white around the gun. He slowly nods.

"NOW!" I shout over the raging shrieks and roars of the creature outside.

Griffin jams his fingers under the garage door, and with a strength I've never seen in him before, shoves the garage door upwards and open. Ground-Zero, which is on the other side, takes its opening and charges into the garage, soaking wet from the downpour of rain outside.

Griffin sprints outside of the garage, before spinning around on his heel and facing the monster again, fiercely pointing the deadly end of the barrel at the thing. The creature with its sickly white skin. It's long claws and needle teeth. It's mouth, opened to its full extent, releasing a roar the likes of which I've never heard anything in my life.

And more than ever before, I want it dead.

BANG! BANG! BANG!

The gun in Griffin's hands kicks back, followed by the agonized shriek of the creature. It turns around to face Griffin, bringing the three nasty bullet holes in its back into view. Torn flesh, with pitch-black liquid streaming from the wounds. It outstretches its claws and lunges at Griffin, but Elizabeth is at its side out of nowhere and slams the metal baseball bat into the side of its chest. There is a wet crack, and the creature moans in pain and anger, curling its claws and getting down onto all fours, screeching.

Elizabeth darts back to my side, and Ground-Zero slowly turns its head to face us. It opens its mouth wide and shrieks, raising its claws and charging again.

BANG! BANG! BANG!

The bullets make impact, but the creature only staggers, temporarily slowed before it struggles towards us again, back on its feet. There's now puddles of the inhuman blood smeared across the concrete floor.

BANG! BANG! BANG!

Goes Griffin's gun, followed by a click, but the creature keeps coming, painfully and determinedly stumbling towards Elizabeth and I in the darkness of the garage. It's large array of teeth exposed, coming for us. It's going to launch itself off of the ground and on top of us, I can see its hind legs getting ready for the move.

I push Elizabeth away and launch myself forward first. I raise my weapon.

This is for Griffin. This is for Elizabeth. This is for Calla, and my mother, and every other living soul on this godforsaken island who had the misfortune to be here when all of this started.

I plunge the sharp tips of the pitchfork into Ground-Zero's chest, sinking them in *deep*.

As I watch it die on the ground, spending the remainder of its life twitching and making agonized screeching sounds, I feel no pity. This creature never was human. This creature never had emotions, or a home, or a family. All the dying thing before me has done is kill. Kill, and spread, and cause every terrible thing that has happened on this island I used to call home.

No, all I feel is satisfaction, and an intense need to get on the move. Because Calla is waiting, and every second we spent on killing this thing, if Calla doesn't make it, that's a second less of her life.

Tick, Tock. Our time is running out.

CHAPTER SEVENTEEN

I hop into the front seat of the car, and Elizabeth and Griffin are once again in the back. My hair is dripping and clothes are soaked from our run from the garage to the car.

"*That,*" Elizabeth pants exuberantly, "was amazing."

I flip the keys and the engine roars to life, adding to the sound of heavy rain pattering on the metallic car top. I shiver and can see my breath mist a bit in the dim light of the electronic screen as it comes to life. I flip the heater up all the way and back out, make a two-point turn, and race onto the road.

"We're out of ammo." Griffin says, holding up the gun.

"It's fine," I say, "Elizabeth has her bat, hopefully that's enough."

We speed down the road, heater blasting, windshield wipers at full speed, and pedal to the metal. I know we're going at dangerous speeds but I need to get to the docks. I need to get to Calla. It is in my haste that I almost don't see the helicopter above. The green and red lights blinking on the body of the aircraft as the bright spotlight shines down on the trees, illuminating the heavy rain falling from the sky.

"Guys, there's another helicopter above us." I point out to Griffin and Elizabeth, slowing slightly so I don't wreck the car against a tree.

The helicopter flies slightly to the left of us at about the same speed. I watch it for a while, but then it takes a sharp turn to the right and flies out of sight.

"You think they're here to save us?" Griffin asks, leaning up into the front seat area so he can see my face.

As if in response, the phone in my pocket begins making an alarm. Not like a timer or phone call, but more like a tornado or tsunami alarm, with a buzzer effect. The sound seems to be specifically designed to inspire fear, because it gives me the chills.

At the speed I'm driving, plus the rain, I don't feel safe pulling my phone from my pocket so I have Griffin do it for me. He holds the screen up so that I can see, and Elizabeth leans up from the back seat. The screen features a large, triangular ALERT sign. Below it, the letters WEA in all caps stands out in a bold font. Below *that*, in smaller print, it says; *Wireless Emergency Alert*.

"What is it?" I ask.

"Don't know," Griffin says, leaning back into his seat and buckling again, "It has an option for more information. Should I click it?"

"Yeah," Elizabeth says, "I think it's something like an Amber alert."

"Amber alert?" I ask, confused, because I have no idea what she means.

"I've gotten one before, back on mainland." She says, "Everyone within a certain distance of a cell tower can get it. It's basically a warning or alert, for when a kid goes missing and stuff. If I remember right, blue alert is for dangerous persons, and- well you get the point"

"What does a WEA mean?" I ask.

"It said," Griffin tells me, "Wireless Emergency Alert. You read that, right? It means they got the cell tower working somehow. They're trying to tell us something. Here, I'll read it."

"I bet it's the people working with that helicopter," Elizabeth mutters, "There have to be more of them"

"EVAC. Information." Griffin reads, "Head to bridge over Pirate's Avenue, connecting northern and southern Eastrock Island for evacuation. All EVAC. aircraft, vehicles, and boats will be leaving by tomorrow morning. For directions, use your mobile device. Service is now available."

Griffin stops.

"What." I say, "That's it?"

"No, there's more." Griffin groans. "It says, 'DO NOT CONTACT ANYONE USING CELLULAR DATA, OR YOUR EVACUATION WILL BE DENIED.' All caps."

"What?" Elizabeth gasps in disbelief, grabbing for the phone, "Let me see."

When she apparently sees that what Griffin says is true, she huffs in confusion, "Why wouldn't they want us to contact anybody? Are they trying to not cause panic back on the mainland? And who even are these people?"

"I don't know," I mutter, "something doesn't add up. But that doesn't matter for us. If evacuation is possible for them, it's possible for us. I say, if we have enough fuel, we wait the storm out and go. Getting to the bridge would just complicate things."

"Agreed." Griffin says, and so we zoom on, heading for the docks which are surely being attacked by the angry ocean. Everyone back there is probably taking shelter in one of the boats or cars. After thinking about it, I'd guess the latter is more likely.

The trees that pass by are illuminated by the bright headlights, making visible the big drops of water falling from the dark heavens. It isn't long before we pull into the parking lot of the docks, screeching to a stop and hopping out of the car.

I am instantly soaked by the rain, and a strike of lightning streaks across the sky, lighting everything up like it's day. Then, it falls back to darkness, followed by a low powerful rumble of thunder. As I walk towards the docks, my shoes splash in the puddles that have formed on the pavement. How long had we even been gone for? We'd left before sunset and it has to be at least ten at night.

It really didn't feel like it had been that long.

Everything is abandoned. The cars still and devoid of light, there's no sign of life on the docks, which seems to be getting bashed up by the boats hastily tied there. I'm pretty much sure none of them are in those boats.

Everything is empty.

Officially concerned, I run around the parking lot and check every car, actually climbing inside the ones that are unlocked, looking for everybody else. Seeing me, Griffin and Elizabeth do the same. It's not long before each and every vehicle has been searched to no avail. Where could they be?

"You don't think they could have gone to the bridge for the evacuation!?" Griffin yells over the storm, his last words obscured by another crack and rumble of lightning and thunder. He's right. They probably got the WEA and went to the bridge.

"Car!" I yell to both of them over the rain, and we all head back to the silver minivan we'd taken. Once inside, I slam the door tightly, grateful for the warmth and dryness. The heater is still blasting out the blessing of hot air.

"You're probably right." I say, "As much as I hate it, you're probably right. They might have thought that's where we'd go after the WEA, so headed there."

"So much for 'stay put and wait'." Elizabeth jokes, but then is silent.

"Okay then," I sigh, revving the engine to life, *again*. "We'll go to the bridge." I pull out of the parking lot, the tires screeching in complaint against the slick pavement. We drive through a couple of puddles, which sprays dirty water all over the vehicle, before exiting the parking lot and pulling onto the road at full speed.

The drive to the bridge really won't take that long, since we were able to walk back to the lab in half a day. It had taken much longer the first time around, but that was because of dehydration and the fact that we'd left at midnight. Memories aside though, the speed of the car is exhilarating and in no time, we're nearing the bridge.

Before we reach it though, we stop and park on the side of the road, because there's something suspicious about the whole "no contacting" thing. Especially at the expense of our escape.

Instead of taking the road, we turn the car off, (and sadly the heater too) before stepping back out into the harsh rain. When we enter the heavily forested area just off of the road though, the rain lessens a bit, most of the impact taken by the trees.

I shiver and extend my hands in front of me so I don't run into the shadowed trees, or walk into the spindly twigs that seem like bony hands reaching for me, dripping from the heavy rain and illuminated every time lightning spikes through the sky.

What really scares me is what is lurking *in* the dark because, unlike Ground-Zero, cancers are practically invisible in this kind of darkness. With the rain messing with the visibility, I wouldn't be able to make one out in this thick forest until it was actually on me.

I consider using the phone as a flashlight, but decide against it, tucking the device under my sweatshirt so that hopefully it won't get wet. Because everything is wet. The usually damp forest is now so soaked, large muddy puddles have turned to little streams that run into my shoes, dampening my socks.

I run into a tree trunk and curse under my breath, when Elizabeth calls over to me through the forest.

"Hey, Luke," She doesn't quite have to yell because the rain is slightly muted by the trees above. "I see the bridge. You might want to take a look at this."

I walk over to her, limping a little, and squint at where she's pointing. Down on the bridge, everything is so transformed I can barely even recognize it. Tall, blindingly bright spotlights are standing tall and shining down onto the bridge, powered by a large generator.

White E-Z ups are scattered across the road, in which people try to huddle under to get out of the rain and into more comfortable conditions. Two helicopters are on the road, people in camo suits walk back and forth between the helicopters and stand at plastic tables, talking to other people who are lining up. Some people accept white packages the people in green give them, some don't receive packages at all.

People in green.

They must be the military. *Our* military. My doubts are washed away as I see the people with those large guns strapped around their necks, and all I can see that bridge as is safety. All the crates scattered across that bridge. The helicopters, and promise of other aircraft and boats. All of it has now transformed from suspicious, to comforting.

What else could this be, but a legitimate evacuation. If our families and those scientists really are here, maybe we truly are about to escape. Escape in a way that doesn't involve risk.

"Let's go find them then." Griffin says. I couldn't agree more, and we all make our way down the hill.

● ● ●

The tall spotlights looming above us are blinding. I squint around, peering through the thick groups of people as they mill around in the rain, struggling to fit under the limited dry areas on the bridge. I begin to walk over to the crowd, but a large muscular man in uniform stops me.

"You have to register first, please." He says gruffly, gesturing at the plastic tables under the easy-ups with more military personnel working there, talking with the growing line of people and writing things down on clipboards.

"I guess we have to get in line." Elizabeth says exasperatedly, walking to the line and waiting. It actually moves

295

faster than it looks and in no time, we're standing in front of a woman in uniform. She looks at us funny.

"Just you three?" The woman asks, raising an eyebrow.

"No, actually, we were wondering if you have our parents registered here." I ask.

"Maybe. I'll need you to answer a couple of questions first though." The woman says, and we nod, "Are any of you seriously wounded?"

Elizabeth rolls her eyes, "Obviously not, otherwise we wouldn't be standing here, now would we?"

The woman scowls at us. "Full name and age for all of you please?"

"Luke Anderson, Elizabeth Harlow, and Griffin Remington." Elizabeth says, pointing at each of us respectively. "I'm sixteen. Luke is too, I think, and Griffin just turned seventeen a week ago."

"Thank you." The woman says, tossing her black hair over her shoulder and taking some notes on her clipboard. "Now who did you want to know about?"

"Anyone under the name Harlow, H-A-R-L-O-W, or Anderson, A-N-D-E-R-S-O-N." Elizabeth answers, "They were also traveling with a small group of other people but I can't really remember their names."

"Harlow..." The woman mutters, "Harlow, Harlow, Harlow... Ah, yes, here it is. Yes, they're here. Both names." The woman stops for a moment as something is being said into her earpiece. She listens, before tapping it and saying, "Okay, will do."

She then looks back at us. "Here, I'll go get your parents, I'll be right back, okay?"

We nod, "Thank you."

The woman walks through the crowd and out into the rain. The thunderstorm feels so powerful it seems to rattle the bridge with its intensity. With every lightning strike, the entire visible stretch of Pirate's Avenue is lit up for everyone to see. I can make out the violently swaying forest and the rushing water below covered in tiny ripples, a result of the heavy rain bombarding it.

My mom's phone suddenly rings, vibrating in my pocket. It's not the fear-inducing alarm from before, it's a phone call. I pull the device out of my pocket and look at the others. It has an unknown caller ID. After a moment of consideration, I click the green "ANSWER" button and press the phone to my ear.

"Hello?" I ask, looking around at the crowded bridge. Under the bright lights that highlight the pouring rain, I examine a particularly nasty argument between a large burly man and a father with his child as they push each other around, trying to stay in the dry spot of the easy-up, "Anybody there?"

"Hey Luke, it's mom."

"Oh! Hey mom!" I say, and Elizabeth and Griffin nod in understanding.

"The phones are working," She informs me, pointing out the obvious, "Somebody must have fixed the cell tower. Did you get that alert?"

"On the phone? Yeah, we did." I say, and I notice the rest of the workers at the tables are also leaving the stand and disappearing into the crowd, leaving the table unmanned with a long line of people still waiting. Probably off to go and find someone just like the lady who helped us did.

"So," My mother continues, "Did you get the vial? Calla is getting pretty sick. Her fever is off the charts and she's thrashing around everywhere."

"Oh no,'" I say, my fear going up, "Is she still, you know... How's her face look?"

"Not too bad yet, but I do think there's a little bit of swelling." She says through the phone. Despite this terrifying information though, my attention is elsewhere. I see all of the army personnel running through the crowd, and can hear the helicopter blades begin to turn. The *swoop swoop swoop* of the aircraft seems to cause all the confused, crowded people to stir. They are starting to surge forward, raising their fists and pushing ahead.

"Oh no," I mutter, "That's not good."

"No." My mother agrees, "Are you almost back?"

"What?' I ask distractedly, and the people begin to seem angry, some even resorting to throwing things over the rest of the crowd's heads, but my view is blocked and I can't see what they're looking at.

"Are you almost back?" She gasps exasperatedly, "To the docks. The wind and rain is crazy out here, but we found a dry spot under the pier and we're going to wait for the storm to die out before we get going."

"But-" I stammer, and I see the first helicopter rise into the sky. Nobody but military forces can be seen inside the passenger area. They're not evacuating anybody. They're leaving. "But the lady said- Wait, mom, the lady said you guys are here."

The second helicopter lifts off the ground, over the crowd's heads, and both aircraft flip on their spotlights before turning to fly away from the bridge, out of reach for even the blinding lights here on the road. That's when I realize there are no military personnel left on the bridge. It's just us.

"Honey," My mother asks through the phone, an audible note of worry causing her voice to waver. "Where... Where are you?"

Something is wrong. Something is definitely wrong and my gut screams at me to run. To ignore all the angry people surging towards the helicopters, yelling obscenities at it, and run off the bridge. To get as far away as possible, because what just happened is not something people trying to save you do.

"I gotta go," I say into the phone, and hang up. I look at Elizabeth and Griffin, "Let's go. Right now. Quickly."

We run along the bridge, pushing people out of the way, shoving aside anything that stands in our path. Griffin trips over his feet and nearly falls, but regains his balance just as the first ones are coming. Down over the side of the bridge, in the water, I see black shapes sliding through the dark liquid. When the next round of lightning strikes, I can see hundreds of tar-colored, inhuman bodies swimming through the dark, angry water and towards the supports of the bridge.

Thunder rumbles as we run on, Elizabeth and I helping Griffin along because his foot doesn't seem to want to cooperate.

The pebbles that litter the road grind under our shoes as we tread on them, running for the end of the bridge. I can see it. I can see the road; all we have to do is get to the minivan. To the docks. Our parents are not here. Why would the woman have lied to us? Why would they leave?

As we near the very edge of the bridge, something in the trees stops me. I put my arms out and stop both Griffin and

Elizabeth, who pant as the rain slides down their foreheads, their breath fogging as it leaves their mouths.

Something is in the trees. At first, I had thought it was the shadow of a branch, but now, I see a long, skeletal, black appendage reach out from the shadows and into the light of the bridge.

I back up, pushing Griffin and Elizabeth back too. Back onto the bridge. It's when the black surge of monstrous bodies bursts from the trees that I break out into an absolute run for my life.

At the nearest car, I grab hold of the handle to the door and swing it wide open, making Griffin and Elizabeth cram in before myself. I close the door tight, and lock it.

The black wave of swarming cancers rush right passed our car, their focus set on the bigger target. Those people in the middle of the bridge. As they leap onto and over our car, the suspension bounces up and down and the metal frame of the vehicle scrapes against the pavement below. Before these cancers can even get there though, the cancer horde we'd seen in the water climbs over the side railing of the bridge and begin their free for all attack.

Once the last of the cancer wave passes the car, I slam the door open and all three of us get out, running for the road once again, soggy and sweaty, the cold air and rain definitely not helping our speed.

It's when we reach the very end of the bridge that the *ear-drum shredding explosion* tears through the air behind us. A violent wave of hot air hits me from behind, and I whirl around to see the massive explosion of flame and debris shooting into the air.

And when the shockwave reaches us, it's already loaded with bits of concrete and creature, blowing us backwards and showering us with chunks of all sorts of stuff. A particularly large and heavy piece of wood hits me in the chest, knocking the air out of my lungs.

I try to regain my breath, but for a scary moment, everything around me is so searing hot I can't breathe. There is no oxygen for my lungs to take in.

And then it's over, and I'm lying on the ground in a cold muddy puddle, gasping like a fish out of water. The rain seems to resume and my skin that had less than a moment ago seemed to be cracking under the heat, is now once again plunged into the freezing cold rainwater.

I groggily sit up, and look around. Flaming bits of- *things* lie everywhere. On the shore. In the trees. Not on the bridge though, because the bridge is completely, and utterly gone. All that is left in its place, is empty air and the ghosts of those who had stood there not a moment ago.

How many people survived? By mere chance, as we had.

"Hey." Says a small voice, "Hey,"

I ignore it, transfixed by the display of fire before me. All of that destruction... for what?

"Hey!"

And the shining water below.

"HEY!" Says Griffin, who's in front of me, "Hey! We need to go!" Some survived! Do you hear me? Some survived!"

I am snapped back to reality and put back on alert. Who survived? At first, I think he means some people, and my hopes rise somewhat, but then I realize what he's saying. If one of those cancers could survive a fall from the bridge, as the one that

Griffin had attacked had done, then surely there will be a survivor. A straggler left behind, even if the only reason it survived is because it was in the water.

I understand what Griffin is saying and I'm up on my feet, heading towards Elizabeth. It seems she has kept her head on better than I have, and is up in a matter of seconds.

"We need to get to the van," I say, and we start limping up the road, already regretting parking so far away. Although, it turns out, it really wasn't that far up the road, and it just felt like it as we had bushwhacked through the forest, for it only takes us a minute to reach the silver minivan.

We hastily get in and make a U-turn, roaring down the road faster than I've ever seen a minivan go in my life.

"We should have gotten a better car." Elizabeth croaks, "That whole parking lot and you chose the minivan"

We race down the road, even faster than we went to get to the bridge. Calla is running out of time, and surely those stragglers Griffin had mentioned will be after us soon. Surely they will have realized there are still more people. The ones either unable or smart enough not to be on the bridge.

We near the docks at record speed, but I stop the car before we turn the last corner. I slow, and listen, and no, my ears had not deceived me. Elizabeth and Griffin are silent, at first confused, but when I pull to the side of the road and turn the engine off, they hear it too.

A loud engine can be heard, even through the glass windshield. The rumbling of the engine is only disturbed by the loud, powerful rumble of thunder as it echoes through the dark sky. Or, maybe not so dark sky, because it is beginning to glow a bit, as if the sun is rising over the sea, and the rain is gradually getting less and less heavy.

The steady engine gets closer and closer, and it sounds like a tractor or semi-truck, because the engine is so low and loud. And then it turns the corner, a huge dark green truck with its headlights blazing. It ignores us, a dark and still car on the side of the road, and continues on. The front of the truck is wide and boxy, and the back has a canopy strung over it. When it has passed, we can see more soldiers sitting in the back, large black guns glinting in their arms as they adjust them.

"We'd better walk from here." I say, "These are the same people from the bridge."

Elizabeth nods, "But why would they blow up the bridge? That *was* them, right?"

"I have no idea." I admit, opening the door and stepping out into the rain, which has become less of a downpour, but is still heavy enough to douse me in ice-cold water. I shiver slightly, and my breath billows from my mouth as a cloud of fog. I try to breathe on my bare hands, warming them up.

We stumble clumsily along the road, drenched and cold. When we turn the corner, we face what may be the biggest surprise yet. A huge boat is stationed at the edge of the middle large dock, a ramp leading down from its rear. Two smaller boats accompany it, carrying two more of the trucks we'd just seen drive by.

We crouch behind a bush.

"What now?" Elizabeth sighs exasperatedly, "First the storm, then the house, then the bridge, then this. I'm starting to think this island really doesn't want us escaping"

People mill around, unloading crates (like the ones on the bridge) from the large boat and taking inventory of anything useful. No sign of our parents. Are they hiding? Did they run when the ship had arrived?

"There," Says Griffin, sticking his hand out of the bush and pointing. Multiple figures can be seen struggling against some of the military people up the boat ramp and in the cargo bay. I make out the scientists and the parents as they fight to release the soldiers' firm grasps. I can hear muted yelling coming from both sides.

I also notice Calla's lifeless form lying on a bench inside of the boat, and Maddie on the floor, crying as she watches the quarrel go down.

Elizabeth stands up and starts marching towards the parking lot.

"Elizabeth!" I whisper loudly, but she just shakes her head and keeps determinedly marching on. "Elizabeth!"

I stand too, and Griffin follows as we try to catch up to Elizabeth.

"*What are you thinking*" I whisper harshly.

"These people," She says angrily, "Government or not. They have no right. They- they- the bridge. How could they be on our side after that? These are the same people!"

"Yes, but-" I begin to protest, but the deep bellowing horn of the ship begins to ring through the air. Steam or smoke begins to pour from one of the exhaust funnels and I can hear the enormous engine deep in the boat slowly coming to life."

Elizabeth curses under her breath, "It's leaving."

I don't register what this means for a moment, transfixed by the chugging of the boat's engine, the rain that has become a light drizzle, and the dazzling sun rising over the ocean, turning the water to a reflection of liquid gold.

"Luke! Griffin!" Elizabeth suddenly starts to panic, "It's going to leave!"

I shake my head, clearing my thoughts, and begin sprinting. Elizabeth catches up no problem, but Griffin falls behind. I can still see the adults in the boat struggling against the soldiers, but it's getting more tiresome as they realize how hopeless their situation really is.

Why are they leaving? I can still see other gear and vehicles inside the bowels of the boat, waiting to be unloaded. Why are they suddenly pulling away, with at least ten of their own people still on the dock, taking account of unloaded supplies. For some reason, my brain is still holding onto the slim hope that they're here *for* us. Why are they leaving? Again?

"Griffin!" I yell back, "C'mon! Go!"

Griffin stumbles and falls, which is his big mistake because in the golden light of the rising sun, I see a black shape slide out of the forest and leap forward, towards the parking lot and towards us. The spines twitch back and forth as it sets its sights on Griffin.

The straggler.

This is why they're leaving. This is why they need to get away. They know how well those things can climb; it doesn't matter if the ship is closed up. There are windows to be broken. If they don't get away from the island now, it could get inside the boat. It only takes one to become hundreds. One must have followed us all the way from the bridge, another sign of its intelligence which we have been underestimating for much too long. It knew we were heading for more people. It must have sensed it.

I stop and run back to help Griffin. Elizabeth stops too, but I tell her to keep running. To tell them to stop the boat. She pauses for a second, before nodding, and continuing to run.

Griffin stands shakily.

"C'mon Griffin, you can do this." I tell him as we continue to run, though nowhere near fast enough to escape the cancer, which is already a mere fifty feet away. "Run, Griffin! What's wrong, are you hurt?"

He shakes his head and makes his way forward, uncoordinated and using my shoulder for stability at times. The cancer is closing in, thirty feet.

"C'mon Griffin!" I yell, "You can do this, we're almost there!"

I can see Elizabeth nearing the docks, waving her hands up at the boat to stop, to wait for us, but they must see the cancer too, or maybe don't want to have to deal with us, because the engine just keeps chugging on. I can now see the ramp of the boat sliding away from us, slowly but surely. The boat is beginning to move.

Twenty feet. Ten feet. The cancer behind us leaps into the air, and reaches out for us but misses by a foot and falls behind. Unfortunately, at the slow rate we're going, it regains its bearings quickly and is on our tail again in a matter of seconds. This time, I can see it keep its head locked on target, aiming more carefully before it leaps into the air a second time.

Its face swung up revealing the large mouth inside its head, it flies down on us and catches its claw in Griffin's rain jacket. The claw punctures the garment, tearing the fabric as it falls behind again, but this time it manages to regain its hold by sinking its needle teeth deep into Griffin's leg.

He shrieks a blood-curdling shriek, and is dragged behind by the creature. I spin around to see Griffin struggling to gain traction against the pavement of the parking lot.

I leap forward and manage to grab his hand before he is dragged out of reach. He grasps my hand firmly and holds tight as the cancer pulls at his leg, trying to tear him away from me. Griffin's eyes are filled of fear and panic, but I am surprised to see them relatively lacking in the pain department. Is he in shock? Is the pain of his leg so bad he can barely even feel it? Has the numbing of the cancer's venom already begun its work?

It is as if we play a nauseating game of tug of war with Griffin's body for a moment, but then Griffin looks me dead in the eyes. I see fear there, but I also see a fire of bravery. What is going on in that head of his.

"Let go." He whispers to me, but I take one look at that cancer tearing at his leg and I tighten my grasp.

"No." I whimper, "Please- don't"

"Let me go." He says again, this time his face red in some emotion that I can't quite place.

"Elizabeth..." My voice quavers violently, "What about..."

"Luke." He says firmly, "Let go."

And before I even know what's happening, his grip lets go of mine, loosening my fingers, and he's being dragged across the pavement away from me. He's trying to reach for the cancer, most likely in a futile attempt to try and loosen its jaw, but he's struggling and can't even reach past his calf, he's gripping his jeans for traction-

And then his leg comes clean off.

I shriek Griffin's name, rushing forwards, expecting to see him lying on the ground, suffering and bleeding *everywhere*. Instead, he is scrambling to his feet (or I should say, foot), limping towards me *without his leg*.

I am absolutely horrified, but then he reaches me and grasps my shoulder, gasping, "Run. Run!"

Absolutely confused, I look down at where his leg used to be, but there is now only open space and the shredded remains of the end of his pants leg.

The cancer has something in its mouth, tearing it apart with its needle-sharp teeth. I catch a glimpse of a long white sock and a black and red shoe that matches the one Griffin is wearing on his *one remaining leg*.

"What- that's your-"

"Go!" Griffin yells, and in complete confusion, I support him by wrapping his arm around my shoulder and leaning all his weight on myself. We run the best we can, though it isn't fast considering that one of Griffins legs is in the maw of the creature behind us.

But it still doesn't add up. No blood. No screams of pain. Griffin seems to be fine, physically anyways. We stagger towards the boat as fast as we can, and I dare to glance back. The monster is finished with the leg, and it is strewn to the side, except it's not a leg. The shoe has come off, and the sock had been torn so bad its hardly there anymore. Now, all that remains is white plastic and metal covered in teeth marks. I look back at Griffin. He ignores me.

"Wait!" He shouts at the boat, trying his best to run as fast as we had earlier, but it's hopeless. The cancer has regained its footing and now is coming at us again, pulling pieces of plastic and Griffin's sock out of its teeth.

Our feet hit the beginning of the wooden dock, and Elizabeth is gesturing for us to hurry, as the ramp of the boat is about to fall off of the dock. Would they leave us here on the island to be killed, or scrape out an existence that might leave us thinking dead would be better?

The wood creaks and groans in complaint as we stumble towards Elizabeth, who seems to make a decision and runs to help. She takes Griffin's arm, slings it over her shoulder, and between the three of us, we actually make good time.

The edge of the ramp falls from the docks and I see the wire pulley system begin to pull it up, to seal us off and trap us on the island.

"You let our children on this boat right now!" Mr. Harlow screams, shoving a soldier to the ground and sprinting towards the ramp controls. He reaches them, and slams his fist into the big button, keeping the large doorway wide open. But the boat keeps going, and Mr. Harlow is shoved to the ground, where he hits his head on the corner of a crate. A soldier scurries over to him, pulling his unconscious body away.

"Dad!" Elizabeth shrieks, frantic tears welling up in her eyes "No! No, you get your hands off of him! You get your hands off!"

Another one of the soldiers hurries to the ramp door controls, but my mother, who had just slipped from the grip of her captor, swings a wooden board into his forehead, knocking him aside and onto the ground. A gash appears, causing blood to pour down into the man's eyes as he tries to regain his bearings. My mom then turns to us and yells something, but I can't hear the words over the loud chugging of the engine.

I get the general idea though.

Hurry.

We keep running forward at top speed, almost to the tip of the dock, almost away from the cancer, almost in reach of safety. One of the men finally resigns to pulling his gun out and pointing it around, telling everyone to settle down.

"Oh no you don't." Elizabeth mutters, because we're almost there. We're so close to the edge of the docks and we can't stop because the cancer is mere feet behind us. She pulls the gun from Griffin's hip and points it at the man with the weapon.

"DON'T FIRE OR I'LL SHOOT!" She screams at him, "I'LL DO IT!"

She knows full well that there's no ammo left in the thing, but the man doesn't.

And we reach the end of the pier, but the end of the ramp is already four or five feet out. We have no choice but to launch ourselves into the air, Elizabeth and I carrying Griffin's weight with us...

For a moment, everything is frozen in time as we are above neither boat nor dock, just wide-open water out beneath us, but then our feet hit the tip of the ramp! I try to gain traction, but I feel my shoes slipping. I shove Griffin up and onto the boat, and Elizabeth does the same, but the tip of my shoe slides out from under me and I painfully slam my chest into the edge of the ramp.

I swear I hear some sort of *crunch* in my ribs. Pain wrenches my body, spiking up and down through every inch of my being. My foot catches the water behind and I begin to slip off all the way. My hands grasp at the wet metal, but there is no grip for my fingers to take hold of. My nails slide on the cold wet surface to no avail, and I'm slipping. I can see Elizabeth facing the same problem, grasping up for a handhold that isn't there.

But then Griffin manages to spin himself around and reach his hand out for Elizabeth. She stretches and just manages to grab hold of it before being dragged into the fast-moving water behind us, because we're beginning to move much quicker now.

Elizabeth, unable to turn around, swings her leg so that I can grab onto her foot. Griffin, with his one leg, scoots us up on the ramp enough for us to regain our own traction and lie in a heaping mess, panting. Resting my head on the floor of the ramp, I watch Eastrock Island grow farther and farther away, putting well-deserved distance between us and what used to be our home.

The boat ride back is more than I ever could have imagined. Sure, for the first half we're locked up in a room while everyone on the boat tries to figure out what to do with us. All they do is examine my ribs, and tell me to suck it up because they're just bruised. I'm tossed an ice pack, before they leave to "discuss". Once they finally come to the conclusion that we could be helpful, they give us new clothes and a full meal before even beginning the questions.

But the second I swallow the last gulp of my steaming stew, they ask away, posing every imaginable question, squeezing all the information out of us that they can. And why wouldn't we tell them? How could it hurt? But just because I cooperate with them (for now) does not mean I agree with them. I've tried asking multiple times why they'd blown up the bridge. Why they'd forced our parents onto the boat once they'd found them at the docks. Why they wanted to leave us behind.

They always say that; "When we feel the time is right, we'll tell you." which bugs the heck out of me but what am I supposed to do? Run to our government? This *is* our government. Still, the silencing of my questions does not stop them from crowding up my brain like a water balloon attached to a faucet.

Where did the cancers come from?

Why were they on *our* island?

Why was it kept a secret?

The list goes on and on and on. Fortunately though, I'm able to ask all the questions I want to our parents, the scientists, and even Griffin and Elizabeth, who have a lot of explaining to do. And Calla, who is still making her recovery in the fancy first aid area on the ship.

First, I ask the parents why they hadn't been at the docks when we'd arrived the first time. They say that the cancer my mother had shot hadn't been dead and that they had to hide under the docks to stay away from it. The storm must have muted our calls and engine. Then, they say, the ship comes out of nowhere and docks. A bunch of trucks and jeeps unload, and they kill the cancer for real, taking its body back into the ship to study it.

"Wait," I had burst out, an edge to my voice, "It's in here?"

"Trust me." My mother had said, placing her hand on my shoulder, "It was dead. Let's just say it wasn't all in one piece when they were through with it."

I had scrunched my nose up in disgust.

Now, I explain in full detail what had happened on the bridge, and Mrs. Harlow says quietly; "It must have been the crates. I saw what was inside the ones they have here. Explosives."

"But why would they want to kill us?" I ask no one in particular, "We're the citizens. The ones they're supposed to protect."

"Yes, but you have to take into account all the cancers the group of people drew in," Mr. Harlow says darkly, "You were the bait. Plus, if you think about it, the more people killed the less cancers there can be."

Now that's a happy thought.

Next, I move on to Griffin and Elizabeth. I point at where Griffin's leg used to be. "Talk."

And they do talk. Griffin explains how he'd been born without a leg. How, back when he'd used to live in the city, they'd given him a prosthetic as he'd grown up. He says how much practice it took to master walking relatively normally, which was still easier than most because the amputation had been just below the knee, making it easier to control.

He tells of how he'd met Elizabeth, who had also lived back in the city. How they'd become friends, and she was the only one who didn't tease him. Because the "teasing" was more than just teasing. Elizabeth tells me of how people would take advantage of his disability, being all sorts of cruel I didn't know kids were capable of. He'd moved to Eastrock Island for a fresh start, and Elizabeth's family had moved too, saying Elizabeth needed her friend, and there was a big job opportunity for her father there anyways.

And so, he'd managed to keep his leg a secret all of this time, from all but Elizabeth. He'd even managed to keep me from finding out, through everything.

He tells Elizabeth and I how his limp got worse as we'd travelled to El Arnica and back, saying that the water and grime and dirt was messing with the artificial joints.

All of this, of course, comes to me as a shock. How could it not. Though I have a million questions, I only pose one. It's not even a question, really.

"You could have told me, you know." I say quietly, patting Griffin on the shoulder, "I'd never have, you know... have teased you about it or anything."

"I know." Griffin says, looking at his foot, "It's just... You're so brave. So brave and perfect and popular. I thought maybe you'd look down on me even more if I told you."

"Look down on you more?" I say exasperatedly, "Griffin, I never looked down on you. I'd viewed you as an actual friend from day one- and as for me being perfect and brave and all? Forget it. I've been practically peeing myself these past few days. All those friends I had back in school... they weren't real. They never viewed me as an equal, and I guess I just wanted to fit in. I liked being liked, you know? I didn't have the courage to step away and say I don't care. I admire that in you. Your bravery. You're brave, Griffin."

He is silent. I would be too, that got really cheesy. Oh well, it's the truth.

"C'mon." I say, reaching for his hand to help him get up. He looks up at me, his eyes asking a question. "Just follow me."

He stands on his one foot and slings his arm over my shoulder. I gesture for Elizabeth to come too, and she supports him on the other side. Together, we limp away from our small corner and out a double door, which swings on its squeaky hinges behind us.

We are now outside, on the side of the ship. There is a railing, and we all walk to it, lean against the metal, and stare out onto the golden horizon. We've been on the slow-moving ship for almost the entire day, being questioned and such, and now, I can see the faint outline of land way in the distance. The graceful golden sun sinks low in the sky, lighting up the sea to the golden glow it had taken on this morning.

This time, though, everything really does seem to be made of gold. My mom is safe. My sister is safe. My friends are safe. This alone fills me with a warm, comforting feeling.

And as I stand next to the two people I'd gone through it all with, all I can think is:

If I had to go through it *all over again*, just to end up friends with these two, I would.

The mirror above the dresser is chipped on the top corner. Everything around this place is either broken, or too expensive to touch. I suppose I should be thankful to even have a place to stay, and I am. Over the past couple of weeks though, I've learned that I am *not* a city person.

Still, the place is free and provided by some operation, which has promised to pay for a more suitable home in no time. They say they just need time to get things "Back to normal".

What does back to normal mean? It means bribing the few survivors of "The Eastrock Event", (which is what they're calling it now), into silence, and threatening those who push back. Still, however much money they give us, and whatever shiny new house they provide, they can't take back what happened on Eastrock.

They say it's not their fault, but the farther they push us away from answers, the more I want to know. For the public, however, they're saying that a dangerous virus was released from the lab on the island, killing all but a specific few. Still horrible, but contained, not directly affecting everyday people, and most importantly; not traceable back to the government, who I'm now sure had a hand to play in it all. I know it makes me sound crazy, but something just isn't right about the cover up.

I do think I'm going to get answers now, though. I've been offered an "Internship" at some lab in the city we're living in to help study the "Eastrock Event". At first I was hesitant, but when they offered money, I had an idea. I said I'd do it for free if, number one Elizabeth and Griffin get to intern as well, and number two, they pay me with answers rather than cash.

I got a personal guarantee from the manager of the operation, that I could have access to any and all information I needed if I helped with the efforts. My first meeting with them will be on Tuesday. I'm hoping that maybe, somehow, I'll be able to put some of the puzzle pieces together and figure out what really went down on Eastrock.

I finish getting dressed and open the creaky apartment door, stepping out onto the shaggy carpet and into the kitchen. Mom stands at the counter, stir fry sizzling on the stove.

"Hey Luke," She says, stirring the cooking food, "where's Griffin?"

Griffin, who had been left as an orphan after everything that happened back on the island, now stays with us. The higher-ups even did all the paperwork for us, and Griffin is now officially my adopted brother. Never has there been a time that I have been so close to a friend than I am to Griffin now. Calla especially likes him, always amused by his jokes. Yes, it turns out that when he's not being chased by bloodthirsty monsters, he has quite the knack for humor. Even if it *is* in his own, quieter way.

Calla had received official treatment first thing when we'd gotten back to the mainland, and the doctors say she's supposed to make a full recovery. She would've died on the way here without that vial of blood we'd gotten, so I'm proud to say I contributed to her survival (along with Griffin and Elizabeth). Her case, though not as far along as mine had been, was worse because she's so small. She has a couple spots on her arm that have shriveled, old-looking skin. The doctors say that should clear up too.

"Uh, I think he's on the balcony reading." I say, poking my head into the living room and seeing him through the sliding glass doors that look out onto the grand city beyond. "Yup, he's there."

"Great," She says, "Can you go tell him that dinner's almost ready?"

I nod, and she yells to Calla, who is in the living room watching TV on the small screen hanging from the brick wall. "Calla! Can you go tell daddy it's time to eat?"

Dad. How amazing it had been to see him once again. He'd brought something back into my life that I'd been missing back on Eastrock Island. Apparently, he hadn't even been aware anything was amiss. He'd been so busy with meetings and such, that when the few times he was able to call failed, he assumed we were just unavailable.

We'd had our reunion in the office building. He hadn't even known we were coming, or that anything bad on Eastrock Island had even happened. We just barged into the conference room in the middle of a meeting. He stepped out to ask what was wrong? Why were we here? Were we okay? That's when I finally fell apart and practically sobbed it all out. I'll never forget the shocked face he'd made when my mother had nodded, confirming everything I was saying.

He was the only person we were permitted to talk to about what had really happened.

I walk out onto the deck, which looks way down upon the streets far below, buzzing with activity. Griffin has a large book in his hands, his eyes moving back and forth. His new prosthetic leg, which is white and plastic, is exposed since he's wearing shorts. It's still weird to me, his lack of a leg. Not in a bad way, it's just that my brain is still accepting it to be the truth. That it's not just my mind playing tricks on me, like it does so often nowadays. PTSD, or whatever. I'm no expert, but the doctors and whatnot are still treating me like a glass vase, ready to shatter at any moment. Honestly, that's not too far from the truth.

I walk up behind him, but I don't think he's even noticed me yet.

I tap the cover. "Good book."

"No way you've read it." He says, looking up at me

"Of course I've read it!" I insist, chuckling "How could I have not?"

Griffin scowls at me.

"Fine, fine, I haven't. I've read one by the same author though. Good books. As you can tell, I suck at small talk. Anyway, mom says it's time for dinner. You ready?"

I can never tell if I should say 'my mom' or just 'mom'.

"Yup." He replies, before seeming to remember something and flashing me a smirk, "So... What are your guys' plans for tonight?"

"Shut up." I say, punching him in the shoulder.

"No, seriously," He persists, but his laughing sort of contradicts the statement. He sets the book down and turns to me, "What do you guys have planned? A romantic walk? Maybe a movie?"

"Something of the sort," I sigh, "hopefully I don't mess it up."

"Oh, you'll mess it up." Griffin says in a matter-of-fact way, "But it's Elizabeth, so she won't care. She'll probably ignore every mistake you make and never tease you about it ever again."

"Is that sarcasm I detect?" I ask, and Griffin snickers, "Seriously though. Are you sure you're okay with, you know, with *us*..."

"Yeah Luke." He says, standing up and sighing. "For the millionth time,"

"Yeah I know but-" I start, but he shushes me and continues.

"We're just friends." He starts, but sees my amused expression, "Yes, I know that's the most cliché phrase out there, but really. I mean, obviously I used to sort of like her, but after everything we went through- I see her more as a sister than anything else."

"Another cliché phrase," I point out helpfully, "but I know it's genuine coming from you, so I'll let it slide."

We look down at the street below, listening to all of the engines and honking horns and chatter of people, oblivious to everything we'd just gone through. So many people doing so many things all at once.

I break the temporary silence.

"So you think I'll mess up? For real?"

"You got this." Griffin grins. "Tell me how it went when you get back."

"Will do." I reply, saluting and walking through the glass door back into the living room. "Oh, and also, mom's making stir fry. Smells really good. I'd get my butt in here if I were you."

He smiles and gives a thumbs up through the glass.

I walk into the kitchen, where mom is setting four dishes on the table. My father leans against the counter, talking to her, and Calla is reaching up into the watermelon bowl, picking out the biggest and juiciest slices. She sees me looking and smirks, withdrawing her little hand and licking off the juice running down her fingers.

"Okay," I say, "I'm heading out. See you later!"

My mom rushes over and gives me a hug, squeezing me tight and telling me to be good and to text her when I'm heading back.

"I will, I will." I assure her, squeezing her back.

She lets me go and looks at my face. "Are you sure you don't want me to pack you two some stir fry? It really won't be any trouble at all."

"Thanks a lot mom," I say, hugging her again, "but I've got plans."

She hands me the picnic basket I'd bought the day before, pressing it into my hands. It's still lightweight as it was yesterday, so I know she hasn't snuck any food into the thing.

"Okay, okay," she says, brushing off her apron and smiling.

"Good luck." My father says, brushing aside his short light-brown hair and smiling at me, the dimples on either side of his mouth crinkling.

"Thanks." I say, then hug Calla goodbye and step out of the apartment, waving until the door shuts and I am left in the empty hallway. I walk down the corridor, following the dark red carpet towards the elevator.

Dark red. Like the blood on the floor in that dark, eerie lab. The sticky stuff caking onto my shoes and clothes- even my hands. The dank walls and flickering lights-

I shake my head to rid myself of the thoughts. My "trauma counsellor" tells me to just try and focus on things around me, in the real world. Of course, I take her advice about as much as I do a fried turtle's, so the thought is merely academic. Nothing I can do will stop the flashbacks I keep experiencing. Nothing anyone can do, because everyone that was on that island gets them.

The elevator dings and I step in, ridding my mind of Eastrock. I focus on what is happening here and now. I press the "LEVEL ONE" button and next thing I know I'm walking through the apartment lobby and out onto the street. I glance at my new phone for directions, before looking back up at the sidewalk and walking on. The sun sets in the sky, turning it a puffy pink.

I take a left, then a right, dodging the large groups of people. Did I mention I hate the city? It stinks. Oh well. Where we're heading, maybe we'll be able to forget.

Soon, I'm at my destination and I walk into the restaurant. I order what I think I remember to be Elizabeth's favorite, before paying, receiving the food, and tucking it into my basket as I walk out the door again. On impulse, I stop by a little hole-in-the-wall place and order a couple coffees (Griffin would be jealous, he practically lives off this stuff), before beginning to walk towards a different apartment.

I'm not sure why they decided we should live in separate apartments, maybe they didn't really think about it before it was paid for and they were moving in. Whatever the reason is, it doesn't matter. I walk into the apartment and take their slightly faster elevator up to the sixth floor.

I knock on their door and Elizabeth opens it, standing there and smiling at me. She says her goodbyes to her family and promises to be back at a decent time. We walk back down the hallway and take the elevator to the lobby.

"You look great." I comment, glancing at the red, spotted blouse and sky-blue jeans she wears. Her ginger hair, ridded of the oil and grime it had taken on during our trek across Eastrock, is now up in a simple ponytail. I can now say these kinds of things without being glared at, which is nice because she truly does look stunning no matter what her outfit is or the state of her hair. Even so, I can only get a few compliments like this in before getting scolded.

"Thanks," Elizabeth grins as we exit the building, "So, where exactly are we going?"

We both look up at the sky, which is slowly turning purple, highlighting the clouds that glide regally through the air.

"It's a mystery." I say, bumping my shoulder against hers and pulling out my phone.

"Ahh, I see you have a picnic basket." She says, nudging the thing.

"No peeking until we get there." I say sternly, "I got an Uber, they should be here any time now."

"Oh, poor Luke." Elizabeth teases, "You're almost seventeen and you don't even have your license yet. You have to call an Uber."

"You don't have one either." I counter, grinning despite myself.

"Who's taking who on the date?" She says.

I raise my hands in the air as a sign of surrender, "Okay. Okay, you got me. Any time now..."

The Uber car pulls up, a blue Honda, and we greet the driver. I tell him that I had already previously entered in the destination. He nods and pulls into the road, heading out of the city. Elizabeth and I make a little small talk, and when she asks why we're leaving the city I just give her a mysterious, "I don't know." And she scowls at me, which makes me laugh.

We arrive at our destination and I tip the driver, thanking him. Elizabeth looks around. The sky is now a dark blue, and the light is fading fast. I grab Elizabeth's hand; "C'mon, I want to get there before it gets completely dark."

She follows me into a little park, and we pass a playground and trees. Finally, I spread my hands, gesturing around at a small open grassy area with no foliage. "Tadaa!"

Elizabeth looks at me and smiles, "So, a nighttime picnic then. I love it."

"Ohh," I say, laughing a little, "No, that's not all. Here, look."

I set the basket down on the soft grass and sit cross-legged beside it, patting the grass next to me. Elizabeth smiles and sits, looking at me through the falling darkness. Normally, the dark still scares me, but when I'm with her, somehow it's not as bad.

I open the picnic basket. Elizabeth peers inside and grins. "Oh, Italian!"

"I heard you liked it. I know it's not exactly a normal picnic food..." I ramble, pulling out the lantern inside and setting it on the grass.

"I'm not exactly a normal person now am I." Elizabeth smirks, before snorting and turning back to the food, "It's perfect. And the drinks too"

"Okay," I begin, "so I know you must be wondering why we had to drive so far just for a picnic."

Elizabeth nods, so I lie down in the soft grass, turn the lamp off, and peer up into the heavens. I gesture for Elizabeth to do the same. She does and gasps.

"It's beautiful." She sighs.

"I figured since you used to live in the city, and there was so much fog back on Eastrock..." I say, examining the twinkling array of brilliantly shining stars above, "that you probably hadn't seen many stars."

"You guessed right then." She tells me, "The city is so bright you could never see them."

We lie on the soft grass, gazing up into the infinite galaxy of stars above, and they almost seem like I can reach up and touch them. The picnic basket of the evening's dinner lies full and promising to my left, and she's on my right. We are holding hands as we lie here, star gazing. How weird, yet right it feels to be with her, after everything we've gone through. After everything we did for each other to get to where we are today. The mere thought of her beside me, her hand in mine still gives me butterflies.

Yet it's happening. Here and now. It's like a far-fetched dream come to life in so many beautiful colors.

"So," she says, turning away from the stars and looking into my eyes, "you were falling for me pretty hard on that island, huh? How'd you find the time for that, with everything going on?"

"You know me," I grin, "I'll always find time for you."

"Oh?" Elizabeth replies, and pauses for a moment. "So how's it feel to finally date the *girl of your dreams*?"

Her eyebrows bounce up and down in a way that makes me laugh.

"It feels great." I finally say, "It's amazing. Couldn't ask for anything better."

We watch the sky above for another moment, the shining sea of colorful stars.

"So, how's it feel to date the *man of your dreams*?" I mock-muse, lowering my voice at the end for dramatic effect. I half-laugh, before meeting her eyes again. Absorbed in those vibrant, endless, colorful irises. The windows into the soul.

She's silent, as if thinking for a moment, and before I even know what's going on, before I can even process what to do or say or act, we're kissing under the shining night sky. When we pull away, she's smiling in the moonlight and I'm beaming too. We lie back down in the grass and face the heavens once again.

"It'll do."

END OF BOOK ONE

"Take a seat." The man says.

The room is a brightly lit, white-walled, office. A long rectangular window looks out into the hallway we'd just entered from. I can see myself in the reflective glass surface. My dark blonde-brown hair has been cut, my skin rid of scrapes and scabs. I look like an entirely different person than I had merely four weeks ago.

"Thank you." I say, turning back to the man in front of me. He gestures for me to sit in the old, twisted, wooden chair opposite to him, a desk in between. I pull the chair out and take a seat, resting my hands on the plain surface top in front of me. There's a painful throbbing sensation in my ribs, but I try to ignore it. They still haven't healed completely from my fall on the boat.

The man, Mr. Leviticus according to his name tag, has prominent cheekbones and a strong facial structure. Piercing blue eyes, short brown hair, and is overall intimidating.

"Nice to meet you." He says firmly.

"The pleasure is mine." I say, straightening my hair self-consciously. It suffices to say that I'm nervous.

The man leans forward, "Okay. Let's skip the pleasantries, shall we? Thank you for agreeing to help with our little project."

I nod. "Glad to."

"So, even though I have many questions I need to ask you," He says, intertwining his fingers and resting his hands on the desk. "A deal is a deal. You need answers."

My entire body clenches up. Answers. I'm getting answers, right now, whatever I ask. What do I want to know first?

"What are the cancers." I blurt out, looking Mr. Leviticus in the eye.

"We don't know." He says, and I scowl, "I am being truthful. We are trying to figure out what and where they came from right now."

"Is it an alien?" I ask carefully, remembering Mr. Tobias' and Griffin's theory.

The man smiles and laughs, "No, no, nothing like that. We're fairly sure wherever it came from, it was on earth. Any other questions? Preferably ones I can answer?"

"Why us." I say, lowering my voice a little. "Why our island. Don't you have some higher-level lab here on mainland?"

"Of course we do," He says, "But due to the nature how the creature spreads, it was too dangerous to keep it here. We needed to study it somewhere contained, but already had a pre-existing high-level biology lab. Eastrock Island met both of those requirements."

"So what you're saying," I whisper, "Is that you decided studying this thing was more important that everyone on that island."

"Would you rather have had it escape here on the mainland?" He fidgets with a pen he'd found in a drawer, "It'd be just like that little island of yours, except so much worse. Entire cities, gone. Your father. Gone. We needed to know how these things operate."

I am silent. Not because I am angry, but because I grudgingly understand how it makes sense. What if they had just kept it here on the mainland. What would be left if they had.

"The bridge." I say, a little balloon of fury inflating inside me as I remember those helicopters taking off, the crates exploding.

The man looks down at his hands, and sighs, "That was a necessary move. Lots of hard choices had to be made, like cutting those shipments off so the thing wouldn't escape on the boats. They were having trouble containing it so we didn't take any risks. It's the same thing with the bridge. Draw the fuel in, which draws the consumers in, and then destroy both."

"Those were human beings." I'm starting to get visibly angry now, "There were children, entire families on that bridge. You can't just-"

"We did what had to be done." The man says warningly, putting his hand up to quiet me. I begrudgingly fall silent, and glare at this man in front of me. Who does he think he is? What gives him the right to sit there, all high and mighty, talking about all those people like pieces of a chess game? I watched those people die, violently, and now *he's shushing me?*

He sits there quietly, as if thinking deeply. For some reason, this annoys me and I feel the urge to speak.

"What, finally feeling bad about all those lives you ended? Grown a soul, have you?"

"No," He mutters, unfazed, "and for the record, I didn't want to use explosives. Too messy. At any rate, what's in the past is in the past."

"So what's got you looking like that." I snap, not bothering to elaborate. Apparently, he understands what I meant because the foggy look in his eyes clears and his gaze falls back onto me.

"Just thinking."

"About?"

Mr. Leviticus pauses for a second, scratching the stubble on his chin. Those piercing blue eyes of his seem to stare into my soul.

"It's funny, really..." He mutters, "How quickly we go from predator to prey when hunted by something smarter than we are."

I think back to the island. To all of my encounters with those monsters. The skinny bodies. The tar black skin. The spines, the tail, the mouth, the teeth, everything. Scary enough to give me nightmares, and dangerous enough to kill entire towns, but smart? Intelligent? Sure, they had their moments, but I'd always had the impression that they were dumb... animals.

"I wouldn't say they're smart, sir." I voice my thoughts aloud, "You weren't on that island, they're-"

"Oh I know the cancers were nothing special in the brains department, that much was clear," He waves a hand. "but that Ground-Zero variant... it was different. And there's always the possibility that-"

"Okay, okay." I interject, tired of his droning on. I swear, I'm beginning to hate this man for the smallest of reasons. His voice. The way his hair falls atop his head. And most of all, that self-satisfied look he wears so proudly on that face of his. "I have other questions."

I think. What else do I want to know. This is my chance, and I can tell Mr. Leviticus is running short on patience.

"Why didn't I go into a coma?" I ask, calming myself down.

"Now that," The man says "is an interesting question. Let me ask you this; Had you been scraped by a cancer beforehand and survived?"

"What?" I say, knitting my eyebrows together, "No, no that was the first time. How would I have, we'd only discovered the cure when we found Mr. Harlow."

"It doesn't make sense," The man says, looking at me, "Your body *could* be resistant to coma inducing chemicals, but the odds of that are astronomical. The venom uses so many ways to put you asleep all at the same time, and for you to be immune to all of them? It's hard to believe."

"You think I'm lying?" I ask, perking up, "You think I really did go into a coma?"

"No, we believe you." He says, "But the thing is, once you've survived your first introduction to the venom, your cells are taught *by the venom* how to fight the coma inducing drugs. That's how the cancers aren't affected by their own chemicals. So, once you've been scratched once, and survived, you won't fall asleep."

I look around, suddenly feeling an irrational sense of being cornered, "And you think I'd been scratched before that? Listen, I swear I didn't-"

"Some of the soldiers we have on the island are going through the exact same thing you did at this very moment. Only the ones who had been introduced to the venom previously."

"Listen, whatever you think I did-"

"Enough of that now." The man cuts me off, "We'll need to do some tests on you, but first..."

The man stands up from his desk and pushes the chair aside. He walks over to the metal door and opens it into the hallway beyond. He sticks his hand out and gestures for me to follow.

"I need to show you something."

ABOUT THE AUTHOR

Yoshio Daggett is an author in Placerville, California. He is the author of the Middle-Grade adventure series "Eight Wander", and the Young-Adult Thriller "Faceless: The Eastrock Event". He wrote and published his first book at the age of fifteen, and continues to craft stories to share with the world.

FACELESS will return